AN UNLIKELY DEBUTANTE

Laura Martin

MILLS & BOON

First published in Great Britain 2017
by Mills & Boon, an imprint of HarperCollins*Publishers*
1 London Bridge Street, London, SE1 9GF

Large Print edition 2018

© 2017 Laura Martin

ISBN: 978-0-263-07469-7

MIX
Paper from
responsible sources
FSC
www.fsc.org   FSC® C007454

This book is produced from independently certified
FSC™ paper to ensure responsible forest management. For
more information visit www.harpercollins.co.uk/green.

Printed and bound in Great Britain
by CPI Group (UK) Ltd, Croydon, CR0 4YY

Laura Martin writes historical romances with an adventurous undercurrent. When not writing she spends her time working as a doctor in Cambridgeshire, where she lives with her husband. In her spare moments Laura loves to lose herself in a book, and has been known to read from cover to cover in a single day when the story is particularly gripping. She also loves to travel—especially visiting historical sites and far-flung shores.

Also by Laura Martin

The Pirate Hunter
Secrets Behind Locked Doors
Under a Desert Moon
Governess to the Sheikh
A Ring for the Pregnant Debutante

The Eastway Cousins miniseries

An Earl in Want of a Wife
Heiress on the Run

Discover more at millsandboon.co.uk.

For Luke, for making it all possible.

Chapter One

Lina ducked under her uncle's outstretched arm and darted forward. Normally she was too quick for her lumbering relative, but today Uncle Tom had abstained from the drink that often addled his brain and slowed his body, so he caught her roughly by the arm.

'One week, Lina. I want my money in one week.'

'I'll get you your money.'

She wriggled to get free, but his fingers were gripping her too tightly.

'You'll pay me one way or another, don't you doubt it.'

Her uncle released her, but before Lina could escape to a safe distance his hand caught her wrist and gave one final warning squeeze, tight enough that Lina knew she would have bruises in the morning. Lina felt herself begin to panic as the pain mounted, then just as suddenly as he'd cornered her, Uncle Tom was gone. She had no choice, she would have to find the money she owed from somewhere, but right now she had no idea where.

As Uncle Tom scurried away Lina wondered at the furtive looks he was casting around him. He'd always been unlikeable and secretive, but never before had he threatened her as he had today. Quickly Lina hurried off in the other direction before he could change his mind and return to collect the debt there and then.

Not for the first time she cursed her impulsivity, the flaws in her personality that meant she found it almost impossible to say no when directly challenged. If only she had been a little more circumspect, a little more cautious, then she wouldn't be in such trouble.

'Tom giving you trouble again?' Raul called as she ran past him.

'Nothing I can't handle,' she lied, flashing her brother a dazzling smile and hurrying on. Raul knew nothing about the debt she owed Uncle Tom, nor the foolhardy bet she had made that had got her into this predicament. He'd saved her too many times from her own foolishness, this time she would figure out a solution without her brother having to swoop in and put things right.

Money. She needed money. One week wasn't very long to raise ten pounds. *Ten pounds*—what had she been thinking? It was more money than she'd ever seen in her life and she'd tossed the figure out there as if it was a couple of shillings. She'd been so confident when they had passed the field full of wild horses, so sure that she would be able to coax and mount one of the magnificent animals, all she'd had to do was ride it the length of the field and ten pounds would have been hers.

Lina knew it wasn't only her impulsivity that had driven her to shake Uncle Tom's hand as he eyed up the frisky horses. Ten pounds would give her a new life, fresh opportunities, the chance to actually do something she wanted to do for a change.

'Lend me a hand, Lina,' Sabina called out as Lina wove her way through the crowds.

The whole family were working the Pottersdown Fair. A few of the older men, including Uncle Tom, were busy sharpening their tools and setting out the hand-carved pieces of furniture they were hoping to sell. The older women had set up a rickety table with jars of sweet jams and other tempting treats. Raul and the other young men had started to pluck away at their instruments, providing a lively tune for the villagers to dance to. Sabina, with her wide smile and fluttering eyelashes, was doing a great job of enticing the young men and women of Pottersdown to get a glimpse of the occult and hear exactly what their futures had to hold.

'I was going to start the dancing,' Lina fibbed, knowing Sabina wouldn't let her get away with it.

'Liar. I've got a queue ten people long, just see a couple for me.'

'I'm not as good at this as you.'

'Nonsense, you read people very well.'

It was true. The skill she didn't possess was patience and you needed patience after the tenth twittering young girl had nearly swooned over the idea of being swept away by a tall, dark stranger.

'It pays better than dancing,' Sabina cajoled.

Lina glanced over to where Uncle Tom was now polishing a beautifully carved, small table and summoned up a smile for the customers. Telling fortunes wasn't going to make her ten pounds, but it was a start until she came up with a more lucrative idea.

Sabina led the next young woman behind one of the screens, leaving Lina to greet a woman of about her age, dressed in clothes so fine Lina had to stop herself reaching out and stroking the immaculate silk.

'Care to hear your fortune, miss?'

The young woman laughed, her eyes sparkling with enthusiasm, as she tugged on the sleeve of a gentleman standing a few feet away.

'I know exactly what my future holds,' the young woman said. 'But I would like to hear what my dear brother has to look forward to.'

Lina watched as the gentleman in question turned slowly, looked her up and down and then raised an eyebrow in question to his sister.

'Oh, please, Alex? It's just a little fun.'

'It's nonsense,' he said, starting to turn back to the conversation he had been conducting before his sister interrupted.

'For me, Alex.'

The gentleman sighed, the long-suffering sigh of a put-upon sibling, and grimaced.

'Come on, then, let's get this over with. Impress me with your insight.'

Lina felt herself bristle at his tone and offered her sweetest smile.

'Step this way, sir.'

Guiding her new customer behind one of the screens, Lina watched as he took a heavy coin purse out of his jacket and handed her the fee. For a moment her pulse quickened, hearing the money jangle as he tucked it away again.

Despite the bad reputation gypsies suffered in England, and indeed across Europe, Lina had never once stolen anything. *Just because they say we're thieves doesn't mean we have to actually be thieves,* her mother had told her time and time again. Proficient at pickpocketing, a skill Raul had taught her not long after she'd started to walk, Lina had never put the training to use.

'A little about the present first,' Lina said, looking up at the gentleman from under her long eyelashes. 'Would you tell me your full name?'

'Surely you're meant to be the one with mystic powers.'

'I tell fortunes, I don't divine names,' Lina said shortly, smiling to soften the ice in her voice.

'Lord Whitemore. Alexander Whitemore.'

A titled gentleman. He probably wouldn't even miss the money in that purse, it would be small change to him.

'An influential man, Lord Whitemore,' Lina said, injecting the silky, dreamy quality into her voice the customers seemed to like so much. 'A man of responsibilities. You have an estate to run and a sister to care for.'

'She's good,' Lord Whitemore's sister whispered in his ear.

'Nonsense. Anyone with half a brain knows a titled man will have an estate to run and you shouted out to the whole fair that I was your brother.'

'Shall we see what else my half a brain can determine?' Lina asked.

Lord Whitemore grunted, turning back to her, but allowing his eyes to roam around the rest of the fair.

'I already know you're short-tempered and grumpy,' Lina said, eliciting a laugh from Lord Whitemore's sister. 'But I think that is a front, a facade you put up to keep people at a distance. There's been heartache in your past, a woman.' Lina paused, but knew she couldn't help herself. 'Someone in love with your warm and friendly demeanour?'

'Indeed,' Lord Whitemore murmured, looking at Lina properly for the first time.

'She left you. A wife?' Lina watched carefully for his reaction. The twitch just above his left eye gave her a clue. 'No, a fiancée.'

'I thought you were meant to be telling my fortune.'

'Your future is affected by your past.'

'Just get on with it,' Lord Whitemore grumbled.

'You're bored,' Lina said.

'How could you tell?'

'Not now—with your life. You're stuck in a rut and you don't know how to get out.'

Taking hold of his hand, Lina made a show of tracing the lines although they meant nothing to her. The skill in telling fortunes lay in reading people, in understanding their facial expressions and reactions.

'There will be change soon, a great adventure, a new love. Someone who will challenge you.'

'See, Alex, there is hope.'

The withering look Lord Whitemore directed at his sister wasn't lessened when he turned back to Lina.

'Is that everything?' he asked, standing up.

From the corner of her eye Lina saw the outline of the coin purse inside his jacket and knew soon the opportunity to raise the money to settle her debt would be missed. She hesitated, hating the gnawing pain in her gut, knowing that she would never be the same person again if she did pick this man's pocket.

'Do tell your friends to visit us,' Lina said, stepping forward and pretending to trip over an exposed tree root. She careened into the solid body of Lord Whitemore and slipped her hand into his jacket. Her fingers closed around the soft leather of the purse and for a second she hesitated before withdrawing her hand and patting Lord Whitemore on the chest with her open fingers. 'Sorry, how clumsy of me.'

His eyes met hers and Lina had to look away as she realised he'd known exactly what she had been up to. Only his confusion on finding his purse still full and in the correct place lightened Lina's embarrassment a little.

'Your trouble is you're bored, Whitemore,' Mr Richard Pentworthy, Alex's brother-in-law, said.

Alex took a long mouthful of local cider whilst allowing his eyes to roam over the people at the fair. Pentworthy was right, he was bored. His life was good, easy even, but there was no excitement, no challenge. After inheriting at the tender age of nineteen he could now run his estate with his eyes closed and hands tied behind his back. His only

sister was comfortably married and happily pro-
ducing bouncing, healthy babies and the women
who fluttered and flirted with him during balls
and dances all seemed unimaginably dull. Alex
couldn't bear the thought of having to choose one
of them as his wife.

No, the only thing that got his pulse racing these
days was a visit to the auction house to bid on a
promising new horse, or breaking in a lively young
colt, that battle for power and mutual respect between animal and rider.

'There's more to life than horses and racing.'

'What are you two talking about?' Georgina
asked as she bustled over to the two men. Perpetually nosy, that was how their parents had described Georgina at the age of five, and Alex was
sure she'd only got worse with age.

'I was observing that your brother is bored.'

'And lonely,' Georgina added.

'He needs a wife.'

'Someone who will challenge him.' Georgina
pursed her lips. 'How about Annabelle Mottrem?'

'Too quiet. And her nose is rather large,' Pentworthy said. 'He wants someone at least passably
attractive. What about Caroline Woods?'

Georgina rolled her eyes and swatted her husband on the shoulder. 'The girl is as vicious as a hungry cat.'

'Pretty, though.'

Before Georgina could launch into a long-winded reprimand Alex held up a hand to stop them.

'I don't need a woman. And I most certainly don't need you two matchmaking for me.'

'You haven't done very well these last few years on your own,' Georgina murmured. 'We just want to see you happy. Ever since...'

'Don't,' Alex said sharply. 'Don't say her name.'

Georgina sighed. 'Ever since *she* left you haven't looked at another woman seriously.'

It wasn't true. Alex looked. He smiled and charmed and danced with women. He listened to the empty twittering of the debutantes year after year and wondered if they were trained to talk only of the weather, fashion and—if he was especially lucky—the latest opera they had seen. Maybe it was unreasonable to want more, to want excitement and humour and that spark of attraction, but he'd experienced all of that with Victoria and refused to settle for anything less again. True, his liaison with Victoria had ended in a heartbreak even he wasn't sure he was fully recovered from three years down the line, but at least she'd amused and enthralled him with her quick wit and sharp observations.

'And you do need to produce an heir...' his sister said, dropping her voice.

'But preferably one with at least average intelligence,' Alex murmured.

'You do the young debutantes a disservice,' Georgina reprimanded him. 'From an early age we women are told that men like us meek and obedient, without strong views on politics or other worldly matters. If you would just get to know one or two young ladies properly, I think you'd find surprising depths.'

'I'm not sure I want a wife who believes to please a man she needs to blend into the crowd.'

'I'm not sure you want a wife, Whitemore,' Pentworthy said quietly.

All three fell quiet as they contemplated the truth behind the words. Alex saw his sister open her mouth and knew he had to say anything to stop her getting her next quip in. Sometimes his sister could be too sharp, too observant, and his character flaws had taken enough of a verbal beating today already.

'All I'm saying is I could take any woman here today and turn her into the perfect debutante. All she would need is a few fancy clothes, good manners, some passing knowledge of banal topics of conversation and me as her sponsor, of course.'

Georgina sighed and rolled her eyes. 'Have I ever told you you're arrogant and insufferable?'

'Once or twice.'

Pentworthy held up a hand. 'Wait, wait, wait. I have an idea. A wager.'

Alex eyed his brother-in-law uneasily as he saw the excitement shine in his sister's eyes.

'Whitemore, we give you six weeks to turn one of these country lasses into the perfect debutante. The first ball of the London Season will be around then—that can be the test. If she fits in, has a full dance card and doesn't do anything scandalous, then you will have won the wager.'

'What are the stakes?' Alex asked. He knew he should decline right away, but he'd never been able to resist a challenge.

'If you win, Georgina and I will never mention marriage or try to pair you off again.'

Already Alex felt the smile spreading across his lips. He would be free to accept invitations to dinner without having to worry whether some eligible young miss would be placed next to him, expecting to be wooed.

'And if he loses?' Georgina asked.

'Then he has to seriously look for a wife.'

Alex waved a hand dismissively. Admittedly the stakes were high if he lost, but he wasn't in the habit of losing and didn't plan on starting now. How hard could it be? Most of the young women in attendance at the Pottersdown Fair were the daughters of the country gentry. Even if he were unlucky and a servant or shop girl was selected, six weeks was a long time. He was sure he could teach them the basic etiquette for the ballroom.

'Who chooses the woman?' he asked.

'We'll leave it to chance. Once we've agreed and shaken hands, it'll be the next unmarried woman of an appropriate age to walk past us.'

'And if she doesn't agree?'

'That is part of the wager, my dear fellow. You have to persuade her.'

'And you're not allowed to pay her,' Georgina added quickly.

Alex nodded slowly. There was a small chance the woman or her family might flatly refuse to be part of this, but Alex was charming and eloquent and there weren't many things he couldn't per-suade people to do. Besides, what young woman wouldn't want to be bought beautiful dresses and escorted to sumptuous balls?

'I'm in,' Alex said, holding out his hand and suppressing a smile as his sister squealed in delight. He shook Pentworthy's hand, then slowly all three turned to look to see who would be the next eligible young woman to walk past.

He saw the brightly coloured skirt first and with his heart sinking in his chest he slowly let his eyes travel upwards to confirm his fears. Beside him, Georgina was in hysterics, laughing in a very unladylike manner. Even his brother-in-law was chuckling softly.

'Do you want to give up now?' Pentworthy asked quietly.

Alex shook his head, but even he knew it would be a stretch to transform the pretty gypsy girl into a member of the gentry. Gypsies had a bad reputation, much of it unfounded, but Alex knew the young woman walking towards him would be more at home dancing around an open fire than waltzing through a ballroom.

Chapter Two

Lina eyed the gentleman in front of her suspiciously. 'You want me to do what?'

He sighed, threw a glance back over his shoulder to where his sister and another young man were sitting, barely able to conceal their mirth, before trying to explain again.

'My name is Lord Whitemore,' he began slowly.

'I got that part,' Lina said, adding under her breath, 'I'm confused, not deaf.'

'The woman sitting over there is my sister. The man with her is her husband. They have made it their aim in life to see me settled down with a wife and no doubt multiple children.'

'That's lovely,' Lina said. 'But I hardly see how any of this concerns me.'

'I have made a wager with my sister and brother-in-law that hopefully will stop them meddling in the affairs of my heart for the foreseeable future. You are that wager.'

Ever since Lina had blossomed from a gangly girl into a pretty young woman she had received many indecent proposals both from the men she travelled with and the customers she flirted with at the fairs. She usually found the best way to deal with them was a sweet smile, a swift knee to their nether regions and a quick escape.

She'd just summoned the sweet smile when Lord Whitemore's eyes narrowed and he quickly stepped back.

'Not like that,' he clarified. 'Goodness, what sort of man do you think I am?'

'We have been acquainted for less than five minutes,' Lina said. 'I have no idea what sort of man you are, Lord Whitemore. Now, if you would excuse me, I have work to do.'

She moved quickly, darting away through the crowds without looking back until she was sure she must have lost him. The fair was getting busier as the morning turned into afternoon and it was easy to hide herself amongst the large groups of visitors.

'You're quick on your feet,' a low voice came from close to her ear.

Lina tried to hide how she jumped as Lord Whitemore's words tickled her neck.

'All the better to get away from lecherous men,' Lina said, turning to face the young gentleman.

'I understand your reluctance to consider my proposal, but I'm in a bit of a sticky situation. I cannot lose this wager. My sister would see me settled with some sweet, banal wife before the year was out and my life would be miserable. And I do hate to be miserable.'

Despite her instinct to run as far away from this man as fast as possible, Lina felt a little intrigued. When she'd told his fortune, he'd been dismissive and bored, but even then she'd sensed an energy, a simmering vitality hidden underneath. A few minutes earlier she'd found herself watching him from a distance as he'd laughed and joked with his brother-in-law, wishing she knew exactly what it was that made his eyes sparkle and caused him to fling his head back and let out a raucous laugh. Now he was right here, in front of her, and she knew the safest thing would be to leave and not look back.

'What was the wager?'

'Come share a drink with me and I'll explain everything.'

'What was the wager?' she repeated without moving.

Lina watched as Lord Whitemore appraised her before answering. She got the sense he wasn't a man who people said no to, but she stood her ground, crossing her arms in front of her chest.

'I made a comment about the conversational ability of today's debutantes,' Lord Whitemore said eventually. 'And I said I could turn any young woman into an acceptable debutante within six weeks, no matter her background.'

'And your brother-in-law challenged you to do just that?'

'Exactly.'

'With me?'

Lord Whitemore grimaced. 'It wasn't you specifically. It was the next woman of marriageable age to walk past.'

'And I'm the lucky girl? What happens if I refuse you straight away?'

'I lose the wager.'

'Why should that matter to me?'

Lina watched as Lord Whitemore's eyes narrowed ever so slightly and she saw the flicker of a smile on his lips.

'Right now of course it doesn't, but come and have a drink with me and we can work the details out.'

Glancing over her shoulder as a ruse to buy a few seconds to make a decision, Lina deliberated. Although she knew she should be working, trying to earn the money she owed Uncle Tom, Lina had been performing at village fairs since she could walk and she was bored. She wanted more in her life than travelling with the same people, working the same jobs. She wanted excitement and adventure, and maybe this was her chance.

Lord Whitemore was already walking away towards one of the tents serving the local cider by the time she turned to face him again.

Muttering a string of expletives under her breath, Lina watched him go, wondering when he would realise she wasn't following him. As much as she complained about her gypsy family and way of life, she couldn't stand the arrogance of the upper classes. No one in her family would act so imperiously, especially if they wanted a favour. This Lord Whitemore needed her—he'd admitted as much not two minutes earlier—and now he was expecting her to scamper after him like some obedient puppy.

With one hand lifting her skirts, Lina hopped

over a muddy puddle and wove through the crowds back towards the lively country music. She allowed herself a satisfied smile at the thought of Lord Whitemore arriving at the cider tent on his own, joining the small group of young women hovering by the musicians.

Raul was plucking away at his strings, tapping his foot to keep time for the little group. When he caught sight of Lina he nodded towards the empty space that had been cordoned off for dancing. It was the same at every fair—people would wander about for the first hour or two, enjoying the cider, looking at the different goods to buy and inspecting the livestock, but before long they would gravitate towards the music. Huddles of young women would look longingly at the fresh-faced young men across the open-air dance floor, hoping someone would ask them to dance. Of course no one wanted to be the first to sashay out into the open with everyone watching, and that was where Lina came in.

'Ready?' she asked a young man whom she was probably distantly related to. John was only a few years older than her, with a mass of dark hair and deep brown eyes. He was popular with the village girls wherever they went. He and Lina always took to the dance floor together, performing for the onlookers before splitting up to entice others to dance. It was a well-practised routine and as Raul saw them come together he motioned to the other musicians to up the tempo.

One of Lina's greatest pleasures in life was dancing. As the music washed over her, she didn't even have to think about the steps, just allowed her body to take over and move instinctively to the music. At these times she forgot about the audience gathered watching her and instead danced this first dance as if she was the only person in the entire world.

Round and round they spun, their feet barely touching the ground, and only as the music slowed temporarily did Lina catch sight of Lord Whitemore making his way to the front of the crowd.

'My dance, I think,' Lord Whitemore said as he reached them, catching Lina by the hand. At the same time John winked at a young country girl, beckoning her out to join him, so now there were four on the dance floor.

'Lord Whitemore, I applaud your persistence, but I am working,' Lina said, pulling away.

'Enticing people to dance?'

'Exactly.'

'Then let me help.'

Before Lina could even open her mouth to protest

Lord Whitemore had gripped her firmly around the waist, pulled her in closer so her body was pressed tightly against his and whisked her off across the grassy dance floor.

'I don't need your help.'

'It is nice to help out your fellow human being. Rewarding.' He spun her unexpectedly and flashed a flawless pearly white grin.

Out of the corner of her eye Lina could see her brother looking in their direction. She gave an almost imperceptible shake of her head. The last thing she wanted was for Raul to come hurtling at an influential landowner. One well-placed punch and they would be moved on before the fair was even fully underway.

'Fifteen pounds,' Lina said, as she was twirled backwards and forward. Lord Whitemore was a good dancer and it was taking all her considerable skill to keep up as he guided her this way and that.

'Fifteen pounds?'

'That's my price.'

'That might be a slight problem.'

Lina bristled. 'You don't think I'm worth fifteen pounds?'

'Not at all, my dear, I'm sure you're worth ten

times that figure. But one of the conditions of the wager is that I am not allowed to pay you.'

'Then why would I do it?'

'From the goodness of your heart?'

Lina laughed. 'My heart isn't that good. Six weeks is a long time. If I'm with you, becoming the perfect debutante, I'm not working. I'll lose money.'

As the last note of the dance sounded, Lina felt Lord Whitemore release his grip just a little. He still wasn't letting her go, but seemed content to hold her at arm's length and regard her for a moment.

'I would not be able to pay you,' he said slowly. 'But there was no rule against the giving of gifts.'

Lina tried to hide the flare of hope in her eyes. Maybe this was the solution she'd been hoping for. Uncle Tom might moan, but he would accept payment of her debt in jewellery or other goods, as long as he was paid.

'What would I be expected to do exactly?'

'You would come and live with me for six weeks.' Lord Whitemore held up a hand just as Lina opened her mouth to protest. 'I will, of course, ensure you are properly chaperoned during that time. Your reputation will be safeguarded.'

'My brother will still protest. He is rather protective.'

'As all good brothers should be. I will talk to him, man to man, and give him my assurances that nothing untoward will happen.'

Lina shrugged. If Lord Whitemore could persuade Raul to let her stay with him for six weeks, then she would be mightily impressed. Many people thought gypsies to have loose morals and easy virtues, but in Lina's experience the same standards were expected of the young gypsy women as every other young woman. They might not live the same conventional lives as everyone else, but if they wanted to find a decent partner to settle down with, they were expected to be untouched and unblemished on their wedding night.

'And whilst I am staying with you for six weeks...?' Lina asked.

'I will teach you to dance, to converse, how to address people at social functions.'

'Really complicated skills, then.'

'I admit you can dance, but can you dance a waltz? You can converse, but can you impress a group of society matrons with your demure manner and correct forms of address?'

Lina shrugged. This was why she had always

steered clear of the county dances in the towns and villages they visited. There were so many rules, so many opportunities for other people to look down on her, it hardly seemed worth the effort.

'These things matter. Don't ask me why, I happen to agree with you. Life would be much more fun if some of the formalities were dispensed with.'

'So I'd live with you, have lessons in dancing and how to conduct a banal conversation. Anything else?'

'At the end of the six weeks we would attend a ball together. That is the test. If you get a full dance card, behave appropriately and are successful at blending in with the other debutantes, then I will win the wager.'

'And I return to my family.'

'Exactly, and although I cannot pay you, you will be able to take all the new clothes and gifts with you when you leave.'

It probably wouldn't be enough to pay off her entire debt, Lina thought, but at least it would be a start. Something to keep Uncle Tom at bay for another few weeks.

'I will do it,' Lina said.

She gasped with shock as Lord Whitemore picked her up and spun her round. He looked boyish and carefree for a moment, the frown she had picked up on during his fortune telling wiped from his face.

'If you can persuade Raul,' she added.

'That, my dear, will not be a problem.'

Chapter Three

'You want to do *what* with my sister?' Raul asked, his fists clenching although his hands remained by his sides for now.

Alex smiled. It was a well-practised smile that normally portrayed confidence and instilled a sense of trust in the recipient. It was a smile that had served him well over the years, but today it was falling rather flat.

'I want to turn her into a lady—the perfect debutante to be precise,' Alex said bluntly, realising a direct approach would be better with the suspicious man standing in front of him.

'You want to marry her?'

'Good God, no.' Alex held up a mitigating hand. 'I am sure your sister would make any man a wonderful wife, but that is not what I am proposing.'

Quickly he outlined the details of the wager he

had accepted and the role Lina would play in the matter.

'Is this what your lot think of as fun?' Raul asked, shaking his head. 'Do you not have better things to do with your time?'

Alex stiffened at the insult.

'As a matter of fact I do. I run an estate of nearly a thousand acres, with a dozen farms and nearly five times as many residential properties. I employ over two hundred people in various roles and in addition to all that I devote a large amount of time and effort to buying and training racehorses.' Alex softened his expression and his tone as he saw the respect blooming on the other man's face. 'But I also have a sister. A particularly meddlesome sister. And I consider it well worth taking six weeks away from my other responsibilities to ensure I never have to endure her romantic meddling again.'

'What about Lina's reputation?' Raul asked.

Smiling, Alex gave the other man a reassuring pat on the upper arm. He knew he had won this argument already. Lina's brother would not bother asking about the fine details if he wasn't going to accept the proposal in principle.

'Your sister's reputation is of the utmost importance to me.' It was the truth. Alex didn't go around ruining young women's reputations, whatever walks of life they were from. He doubted this Lina was as pure and innocent as her brother liked to believe, but he would treat her like the most precious virgin for the duration of her stay. 'My sister is staying with me for the next two weeks. As she is a married woman of good reputation, I trust she will be an adequate chaperone. After that I will arrange for my widowed aunt to visit.'

'What does Lina get out of this arrangement?'

'Unfortunately the terms of the wager forbid me to pay your sister for her help over the coming six weeks, but they do not forbid me giving her gifts to reimburse her for her time and efforts.'

'Lina? Get over here, girl,' Raul called to where his sister was laughing with some villagers at a nearby table.

'So, what do you think?'

'You really want to do this?' Raul asked his sister.

She shrugged. 'It'll make a nice change from dancing and telling fortunes. And I'll be back with you in no time at all.'

'Fantastic,' Alex said enthusiastically, holding out his hand for the other man to shake.

Raul looked at the hand, then slapped Alex on the shoulder in a brotherly way.

'We don't shake hands on a deal like this,' he said, smiling and showing a set of surprisingly white teeth. 'We fight.'

'Raul, no,' Lina protested.

'Only way to know a man's character.'

'You'll get us thrown out of Pottersdown.' Brother and sister had huddled together conspiratorially and Alex had to strain to hear Lina's words.

'I'm not letting you go without this, Lina,' Raul said after a hushed but heated discussion.

Lina turned to face him and shrugged. 'He wants to fight. It's up to you.'

Alex only deliberated for a second, realising Raul was trying to figure out what sort of man he was entrusting his sister to.

'Let's fight,' Alex heard himself say.

'Good man. Ten minutes, behind the cider tent.' Raul left, whistling happily to himself.

Holding out an arm to escort Lina through the fair, Alex felt a rush of anticipation. As much as he knew he should count his blessings, these last few months he'd felt as though he'd been going through the motions and not really living, not really experiencing anything. Only the rush of excitement as he broke in a new horse or watched it cross the finish line with a new personal best speed got his heart pounding and his muscles tensing at the suspense.

This boredom he'd been feeling was entirely self-induced. Alex was well aware that his broken heart after Victoria had left had caused him to push away anything that might hurt him. And it had worked: three years on and his heart was mended, but he'd rather lost sight of the thrills in life that made it worth living.

'What should I call you, then?' Lina asked as they walked.

'You know my name. Lord Whitemore.'

She rolled her eyes, the first of many gestures he would have to persuade her to drop if she was going to fit in with the finest debutantes of the Season.

'Your real name. I'm not going to go around calling you Lord Whitemore, am I?'

'I certainly hope you are. That is the correct form of address between us.' Alex, who had always prided himself on being relaxed and informal, felt decidedly conventional and old-fashioned around Lina.

'What do people actually call you, though?' she persisted.

'Do you promise not to use it?'

'Cross my heart.'

'Alex. Well, Alexander, but I prefer Alex.'

'I suppose I'm meant to curtsy when I greet you, as well?' Lina murmured quietly.

'We can work on greetings later. I'm sure I can fill a whole morning with the proper way to greet a gentleman.'

'I'm quivering with anticipation.'

They reached the cider tent and Lina led him around the side to an open area that was partially shielded from view. Alex quickly rolled his shoulders, loosening his joints, before reaching up to undo his cravat and slip off his jacket. He caught Lina's eyes lingering on him as he rolled up his sleeves to reveal tanned forearms before a group of men sauntered around the tent.

'Ready for a beating?' one of the older men sneered.

'Pay him no mind,' Lina called. 'Raul fights fair, not like this devious coward.'

'Watch your tongue, Lina, or I'll watch it for you.'

Alex stepped forward, placing himself in be-

tween the older man and Lina. He had no desire
to be her protector, but she was under his care for
the next six weeks and he would not hear her spoken to in that way.

'Can I not leave you five minutes without you
picking a fight, Tom?' Raul called as he rounded
the back of the tent. The older man shot Alex a
dirty look, but sauntered away, taking up his place
at the back of the rapidly assembling crowd.

'Are you ready?' Raul asked.

'Whenever you are.'

'We fight until first blood.'

Alex nodded. It was all the same to him. The
muscular gypsy squaring up opposite him was obviously no stranger to a fight; indeed, it seemed his
preferred way to seal a deal or settle differences.
Alex himself had learned to box at school and had
thrown and taken a few punches in more recent
years. Added to that his work with his horses kept
him physically fit and quick on his feet. Although
he didn't expect to win this fight he was confident
he would at least be able to leave with at least his
pride intact. It wasn't really about winning or losing anyway. Alex knew it was his character that
was being tested, not his skill—whether he was the
rt of man to stand and fight or run and cower.

Slowly the two men circled each other, both light on their feet and constantly moving. For Alex all sounds of the surrounding crowd faded to a distant hum as he concentrated fully on his opponent. Suddenly Raul jabbed, a blow that was made to test Alex's reactions more than anything, and Alex easily blocked it before returning a couple of lightning-quick body blows that elicited quiet grunts from Raul.

Backing off slightly, they circled again. This time Alex struck first, a powerful blow to Raul's face that the gypsy wove away from at the last moment. Alex's fist connected, but the impact was glancing and put him slightly off balance. Raul took full advantage of the situation and began hammering down blows, forcing Alex to go on the defensive. He retreated, using his arms to protect his face, and felt the swell of the crowd behind him.

Sensing Raul's confidence at victory, Alex allowed him one more punch before feigning to the left and darting right. Before Raul could recover, he delivered a hard blow to the other man's cheek, followed by a left hook to the jaw. At exactly the same moment, Alex felt Raul's fist connect with his temple and a tearing pain in his eyebrow followed by the warm trickle of blood over his face.

Both men backed off, lifting their hands to their faces. Both sets of fingers came away wet with blood.

'First blood.' Raul grinned, wincing as the movement pained his split lip. 'For a toff, you don't fight badly. Now, let's drink.'

Allowing himself to be led to where the cider was flowing, amid handshakes and claps on the back from the dozens of spectators, Alex realised Lina was nowhere to be seen. She had a habit of disappearing—she was quick and nimble and seemed to weave with ease through the crowds. He supposed it was from a lifetime of working at packed fairs, but right now it was a damned nuisance; he wanted to finalise their arrangement and maybe just see that sparkle of admiration in her eyes.

'You will look after her?' Raul asked as the two men knocked back their cups of cider.

'I will care for her as though she's my own sister,' Alex promised.

'Then I have no more objections. No idea how you got Lina to agree, though.'

'What do you mean?'

'She hates your lot. Toffs. Always has…' Raul

paused, tapped his cup against Alex's and grinned. 'I don't think you're so bad myself.'

'What a cosy little arrangement you've landed yourself in,' Tom crowed, making Lina shudder as she caught a whiff of his horrific breath. 'Whoring yourself out to a gentleman.'

'I'm not—' Lina caught herself and took a step back. It never paid to get into an argument with Uncle Tom.

'Shall I expect payment today?'

'He's not paying me,' Lina said.

'Giving yourself away for free? Your dear mother would be turning in her grave.'

'He has promised me gifts, certainly enough to cover the debt I owe you.'

'I want the money.'

Lina shrugged. 'I will just sell the gifts and then you can have the money.'

'The deadline is still the end of the week, Lina.'

'I won't have the gifts for six weeks.'

'Not good enough. I need the money now.' There was a hint of panic in Tom's voice that made Lina pause for a second.

She closed her eyes, steeling herself for the suggestion she was about to make, and then ploughed ahead. 'If you give me the six weeks to raise the debt, I will pay you twelve pounds instead of ten.'

Uncle Tom regarded her thoughtfully. 'Four weeks and I want fifteen pounds.'

Lina swallowed nervously, but still nodded. She didn't exactly have a choice. She just hoped Lord Whitemore was generous in his gift giving.

'And I want information.'

'What information?'

'Raul tells me you will be staying with this toff. You'll be privy to his security arrangements, the layout of his house.'

A faint sensation of nausea started to build deep in Lina's gut.

'I'm not stealing anything for you.'

'I'm not asking you to steal. Just to pass on a little information. What's information amongst family?'

Lina shook her head.

'That's the deal, Lina. Either fifteen pounds and a little information in four weeks, or you pay the ten by the end of the week.'

Squeezing her eyes tight, Lina tried to suppress the image of her mother's disappointed face as she nodded.

'Good girl. I'll be seeing you in a few days.'

Chapter Four

The grass was wet beneath her feet as Lina crossed the field, hopping over a shallow ditch and scrambling up a bank before joining the road again. She had caught a ride on a farmer's cart from Pottersdown to the village of Hilstone and from there a friendly shopkeeper had assured her it was no more than twenty minutes' walk across the fields to Whitemore House. Lina had dallied, stopping to pluck some wildflowers to weave into her hair, resting on a tree stump and turning her face up to the sun and even pulling off her boots to dip her toes in the cool waters of a gurgling stream. The twenty-minute walk had turned into an expedition that lasted more than an hour, but now Lina knew she could delay no longer.

She wasn't sure why she was quite so nervous. This was what she had been waiting for: an opportunity to change her life, to do something different, be somewhere different, at least for a short time. For every one of her twenty years she had lived and worked amongst her gypsy family, travelling through England, performing at fairs in the summer and doing whatever work she could find in the long winter months. For a while she had been restless, unsure what was bothering her, torn between a desire to actually belong somewhere and a carefree and adventurous spirit that wanted to experience everything the world had to offer. She couldn't decide what she truly wanted from her life, so everything had just stayed the same.

'New experiences,' Lina murmured to herself as she stopped beside a pair of huge wrought-iron gates, pushed open to reveal a sweeping drive. Fingering the metal for a moment, she peered inside, trying to catch a view of the house.

The drive curved away to the left through immaculately kept lawns and disappeared over a dip with no house in sight. Swallowing her nerves, Lina pushed herself to enter the grounds of Whitemore House, aware of the pounding of her heart in her chest.

When the house did come into view, set back at the crest of a small hill with the drive sweeping dramatically in front of it, Lina had to stop and pause for a second. Then she laughed out loud. It was easily the biggest building she had ever laid eyes on and Raul had taken her into London twice and York once over the course of their travels. It was perfectly proportioned, one central structure with two symmetrical wings flanking it, all in a beautiful sandy-coloured stone.

After more than ten minutes of walking, Lina finally reached the front door and was self-consciously adjusting her dress as it opened before her.

A middle-aged man greeted her with a tight smile.

'Miss Lock, I presume?'

Lina nodded, her mouth too dry to speak.

'Follow me, please.' His words were delivered with a disdain that shook the nervousness from Lina. *This* was the reason she disliked the aristocracy. They were obsessed with the idea of respect and good manners, but treated anyone inferior as if they were at best a nuisance and at worst an inanimate object, to be used and discarded. Even their servants were rude.

'So are you a member of the family, then?' Lina asked, making sure she added a coarse quality to her voice as she spoke. She stepped over the threshold, trying to take in the vast entrance hall, the marble flooring and the perfectly sculpted statues that sat in recesses dotted along the walls.

'Most certainly not. I am Lord Whitemore's butler.'

'So a servant. Strange, that.'

The butler looked down at her from his superior height.

'What is strange?' he asked eventually with a long-suffering sigh.

'Well, *I* always thought servants were meant to be polite. To be a shining example to make their masters proud. But you, you're ruder than a cow that hasn't been milked for a week.'

'I beg your pardon,' the butler stammered. Lina half expected his face to turn bright red, but instead his cheeks seemed to lose colour and his lips were pressed thin. 'That sort of language won't be tolerated, *Miss* Lock.'

'Ah, but it will. See, I'm an invited guest and you are a member of staff.'

'The Marquess will hear about this.'

'Williams, what is all the noise about?' a soft, feminine voice called and was shortly followed by the emergence of Lord Whitemore's sister from one of the many doorways that led into the grand entrance hall.

'Please forgive me...' The butler was silenced by a friendly wave of the hand and Lina felt herself being swept into the embrace of the slightly older woman.

'Come, come, you must be tired from your journey. I have tea set out on the terrace. In the shade, of course, the sun does dastardly things to my complexion,' Lord Whitemore's sister gushed. The journey had taken less than three hours and Lina had experienced many more arduous days, but she allowed herself to be swept along by the other woman's enthusiasm.

'Thank you... Lady Whitemore?' Lina ventured.

'Dear me, we haven't even been properly introduced. I am Lady Georgina Pentworthy, Alex's long-suffering and completely devoted sister.'

'A pleasure to meet you, Lady Pentworthy.'

Georgina shook her head very slightly and laughed. 'Why don't you call me Georgina, my dear? Much simpler than trying to untangle which part of my name to use when.'

They walked through a room filled wall to wall with books. Lina had never seen anything like it and paused for just a second to take in the dozens of bookshelves that lined the walls, full of heavy, leather-bound books. It made her much-treasured and battered three-book collection seem rather insignificant.

'I am so pleased you agreed to come and stay,' Georgina said, squeezing Lina's arm lightly. 'These next few weeks are going to be so much fun.'

'Would it not have been better for you if I refused?' Lina asked. 'Then you would have won your wager straight out.'

'Don't tell my darling brother, but I don't really mind if I win this wager or not. It's the journey that is going to be the important part.'

'The journey?'

Georgina motioned to a seat on the terrace, behind a table that looked out over the formal gardens directly behind the house. An assortment of mouth-watering pastries and a delicate china tea set were laid out and Lina wondered if Whitemore's sister had been waiting on her arrival.

'My brother is a very accomplished man, very talented,' Georgina said slowly whilst pouring out a fragrant cup of amber-coloured tea. 'But he has buried himself in his work for the last few years and I'm hoping you will be able to coax him out.'

Lina took a sip and eyed up the pastries, relieved

when the other woman slipped two on to her own plate and motioned for Lina to take her pick.

'How am I supposed to do that?' This wager was becoming more complicated by the minute, what with Uncle Tom's expectations of her and now Georgina's hidden motives.

'He will have to take a break, look up from his work and focus on something entirely different. To get you ready to attend a London ball you will have to go shopping, go for day trips, socialise at some local functions...'

'Does Lord Whitemore not do all that already?'

Georgina grimaced. 'He does,' she said slowly. 'But suffice it to say even if his body is in attendance, his head and his heart are not.'

Taking a bite of a crisp, fresh pastry Lina closed her eyes and savoured the mouthful. She wondered if she had ever tasted anything so delicious in her entire life.

'How am I meant to influence that?' Lina asked, putting down the pastry before she spoke so she would not shower her companion in crumbs.

'Just by being here.'

It seemed like a lot of responsibility and as Lina gulped down the hot tea, she felt a stirring of unease. She liked Georgina, she seemed warm and genuine and hadn't condescended to Lina once during their conversation. Despite their obvious differences in status and wealth Georgina was talking to her as if she was a treasured friend, not a gypsy girl whose main talents were a little fancy footwork and telling lies to impressionable young girls.

'Please don't fret,' Georgina said reassuringly. 'I'll be here to guide you these first two weeks and after that I'm sure you'll run rings around my brother.'

Lina wasn't so sure. She knew she had a lightning-quick tongue, but sometimes she was too hotheaded, too fast to jump into a dangerous situation. From what she had seen so far Lord Whitemore had that easy manner of many men of his class, but also a cool, self-possessed quality and the self-assurance to go along with it. Lina wasn't sure how well her usual tricks would stand up when pitted against Lord Whitemore's imperturbable logic.

Two children came dashing across the lawn and Georgina stood to gather them in her arms. First to arrive was a boy of about five, followed by a smaller girl, who tottered to keep up, but still managed to outrun the exhausted-looking nursemaid who trailed behind.

'My darlings, how I have missed you,' Georgina gushed, peppering the two small children with kisses until both were rolling around, giggling and squirming out of her reach. 'Now, William, Flora, we have a guest. This is Miss Lina Lock. She will be staying with your uncle for the next few weeks.'

'Pleased to meet you, Miss Lock,' William said, his words accompanied by a formal little bow. His expression was serious, as was his tone, and for a second it was as though he were transformed into a miniature adult.

Flora giggled, managed to dip into the sweetest curtsy Lina had ever seen, then promptly turned bright red and hid behind her mother's skirts.

'My children,' Georgina explained rather unnecessarily. 'William is five, and Flora is three.' She turned to her son. 'Now, William, where do you think your uncle might be?'

William's eyes lit up and he was halfway across the lawn before Flora provided the answer.

'Horses. Horses. He's with horses,' she chanted, flinging herself after her brother much to the nursemaid's despair.

'Shall we go and find him?' Georgina suggested.

Lina nodded her agreement, feeling the excitement swell inside her. She'd known there would be horses on the estate—all the nobility seemed to have them to pull their carriages and to hunt with—but the idea that she might get to ride some of the magnificent animals had never even crossed her mind. She loved horses, loved feeling the wind in her hair as she galloped through the countryside, that sensation of freedom, but the horses her extended family owned were mainly slow, plodding beasts more accustomed to pulling heavy carts than being ridden for pleasure.

'Lord Whitemore likes to ride?' Lina asked casually as Georgina linked arms with her and together they followed the two children across the lawn and to the side of the house.

Georgina gave her a slightly curious sidelong look. 'Yes, my brother likes to ride,' she confirmed eventually.

They passed through a lovingly tended rose garden before entering a tree-lined walk that filtered some of the sunlight, giving the path a wonderfully dappled effect.

'If you ever find yourself searching for my brother, this is where he will be,' Georgina declared as they emerged into a large, dusty courtyard. Lord Whitemore was nowhere to be seen.

'Well, not here exactly, but somewhere with his beloved horses.'

Daintily Georgina hopped over a pile of manure and led Lina past an assortment of stables and outbuildings to where the fields stretched out before them. In the foreground was a large fenced-off area.

As they drew closer, Lina couldn't take her eyes off the magnificent, rearing beast that was snorting and stomping in the riding yard. Its coat was a beautiful chestnut brown that glistened in the sunlight and it was by far the biggest horse Lina had ever seen. Currently it didn't appear too happy, tossing its head and taking hurried little steps sideways, letting out snorts of frustration.

Lina's gaze was torn from the horse as a figure sauntered across her eyeline. He was tall and particularly muscular, something she could attest to due to the fact he wasn't wearing a shirt. Sweat dripped over his torso and as he moved Lina thought he looked rather like one of the illustrations in her most treasured book, *Greek Gods, Heroes and Myths*.

Lord Whitemore approached the horse again, murmuring softly to it words that Lina could not hear, but could see the calming effect they had on the animal. He paused when he was about two feet away, the horse still stomping nervously. Lina was mesmerised; this was the ultimate battle for power and trust, one that she could see Lord Whitemore was well practised at negotiating.

Confidently but slowly he took another step forward, laying a hand on the animal's neck and stroking softly, still murmuring his soothing words. The horse calmed, became still, and Lina saw the exact moment it capitulated and allowed Lord Whitemore to stroke it gently without any consequence.

Man and beast stood together for a few seconds before Lord Whitemore produced a simple halter.

'Enough for today,' Lina heard him whisper, and was amazed as the only recently calmed horse allowed him to slip on the halter and lead it to the edge of the pen. A stable boy quickly opened the gate, but stood back and let Lord Whitemore past rather than taking the animal back to the stables himself.

Lina watched enviously as the animal disappeared from view. She had ridden her fair share of wild horses in her time. She knew how to approach them, how to calm them and how to mount them, but she'd always chosen animals of moderate size, ones that would not cause her too much injury when they inevitably threw her. Every bone of her body wanted to be able to do what Lord Whitemore had just done and more.

'Ah, Miss Lock. I'd completely forgotten you were arriving today,' Lord Whitemore said as he emerged from the stables a couple of minutes later.

'See? There in body, but not in mind,' Georgina muttered.

Lina bobbed a clumsy curtsy, not knowing where to look as she rose. Lord Whitemore was still top-less, but as she watched he grabbed a simple white shirt that was draped over the fence and pulled it over his head. His tanned and muscular torso was still partially visible through the thin white mate-rial, especially as it clung to the sweat on his body. Lina swallowed and tried to compose herself. She didn't know why she was quite so affected by Lord Whitemore's unexpected half nakedness. In the hot summer months most of the gypsy men she trav-elled with would set up for the fairs clothed in just their trousers. Lina was no stranger to bare chests and relaxed attitudes to clothing, but something about seeing Lord Whitemore like it had set her heart hammering.

'What sort of horse was that?' Lina asked, re-covering enough to focus on what was important.

Lord Whitemore and Georgina exchanged glances.

'You're interested in horses?' Lord Whitemore asked.

'I love horses. He looked like an Arabian.'

'What have I done?' Georgina murmured as Lord Whitemore grinned. 'Another horse lover.'

'Well, these six weeks have just become a lot more tolerable,' Lord Whitemore said.

Lina bristled, but forgot her indignation as Lord Whitemore offered her his arm and started explaining the origin and breed of his latest horse.

Chapter Five

What had he got himself into? Alex let his head sink into his hands for a fraction of a second, before straightening up. This would not defeat him. He was a man who had broken in the most difficult of horses—he would not be beaten by a girl's incessant questioning and arguing.

'It's stupid,' Lina repeated. 'What does it matter if I call your sister Lady Georgina or Lady Pentworthy? Both are respectful, both give you an idea who she is.'

Alex counted to five before answering. 'But neither is correct. One more time. Lady Pentworthy would be the wife of Lord Pentworthy. Lady Georgina would be the daughter of a titled gentleman, in this case a marquess.'

'Which she is,' Lina said through gritted teeth.

'So why is it incorrect to address her as Lady Georgina?'

'She is now married to Mr Pentworthy, so she becomes Lady Georgina Pentworthy. A quirk of marrying a husband of lower rank.'

'A ridiculous quirk,' Lina muttered under her breath. 'It would be much simpler to dispense with all these stupid rules and titles and just call everyone by their actual names.'

'I will forward your suggestion to the Prince Regent,' Alex said drily.

He watched as Lina flopped dramatically back in the brown leather armchair situated by the veranda doors in the library. It was only their first day and to ease her into her lessons to become the perfect debutante Alex had suggested they start by getting to grips with how to address people. How he regretted that now.

'Maybe it would help if you spent a couple of hours familiarising yourself with the contents of *Debrett's*,' he suggested, standing and perusing the shelves until he found the heavy book he was looking for.

Lina sighed, levered herself out of her chair and followed him over to the small table.

'And what on earth is *Debrett's*?'

'It is a peerage reference book.'

Lina glared at it suspiciously.

'You do know how to read?' Alex regretted the words as soon as they came out of his mouth.

'Just because I'm not titled Lady Lina or Lady Lock or even Lady Lina Lock doesn't mean I can't read,' Lina said huffily, pulling the dusty old tome out of his hands. 'I would just prefer to read something actually interesting instead of this list of names.'

'I apologise,' Alex said, touching Lina lightly on the back of the hand. He felt her stiffen under his touch and quickly withdrew his fingers. It was inappropriate and Alex wasn't sure what had made him reach out and stroke her hand, but he regretted it immediately.

Ever since Lina had arrived at Whitemore House twenty-four hours ago the time had whizzed past in a whirlwind of activity. It was rather refreshing to have Lina question why they did certain things, to see her amusement at their customs and her awe at the splendour of her surroundings. She was loud, opinionated, sarcastic and not afraid to say exactly what she was feeling, but Alex could see there was more to the spirited gypsy girl than first appearances would suggest. The way he'd caught her running her fingers lovingly along the books on the bookshelves as he'd entered the library, how her eyes had lit up as she watched him with the Arabian horse the day before and how already she and his sister seemed the closest of confidants.

She was pretty, too. Petite and slender, her skin coloured with a hint of warm caramel and dark hair and eyes that told of a heritage somewhere in her ancestors' past. Once or twice Alex had found himself watching her lips as she smiled and her hips as she moved around the room with a lightness of foot that identified her as a dancer.

This attraction he felt was surprising. Long ago he had been a man who thoroughly enjoyed the company of women. He had kept mistresses, discreetly, of course, and dallied with a selection of both suitable and unsuitable companions. Then Victoria had come along, the woman he thought he would spend the rest of his life with. He'd gently cut off his association with his mistresses, determined to start his married life as he meant to go on: faithful to his wife. Unfortunately Victoria hadn't shared his values.

Since then Alex hadn't had the same appreciation for a beautiful woman. He hadn't reconnected with any of his old mistresses, hadn't felt that spark of attraction with anyone really. Until now.

It was completely inappropriate and unhelpful. Lina was from a different world and she was here to help him win a wager, not to become his new mistress.

'Just have a flick through,' Alex suggested, motioning to the book. 'I'll ring for some tea.' *Or something stronger.*

Dutifully Lina leafed through the pages of the book, stopping every so often to read an entry. It was quite satisfying to watch her expression turn from one of mild boredom to avid interest.

'Did you know the Duke of Hampshire has been married six times?' Lina asked.

'Unfortunately, yes. He's rather a lecherous old man, but women can't help throwing themselves at his title and money, it would seem.'

'Does he kill them off?'

Alex nearly choked on the mouthful of tea he had just imbibed.

'Well, to lose one or two is unfortunate… Six is just suspicious,' Lina said with a grin.

'I'll ask him next time I see him.'

'You know him?'

'Went to school with one of his sons. From his second marriage, I think.'

'I'd love to meet him.'

'Certainly not.' Alex realised he sounded like a pompous old man. 'Unless you're hoping to become wife number seven,' he added.

Lina fell quiet for a while, turning the pages and occasionally smiling to herself. After a few minutes, she sat back and turned to Alex. Inwardly he groaned. Normally he would praise a woman for having an enquiring mind, but there was a certain way Lina asked her questions—a tenacious stubbornness not to let any matter rest if she wasn't quite satisfied—that was exhausting. Alex didn't normally mind admitting he didn't know something; it happened rarely enough and often the subject matter was something obscure seeing that he was well educated and had an enquiring mind, but he had lost count of the number of times he'd had to concede he wasn't entirely sure of an answer since Lina's arrival.

'What would happen if I addressed someone incorrectly?' Lina asked.

Alex frowned. 'What do you mean?'

'Well, imagine we are at this ball of yours in six weeks' time.'

He had to suppress a shudder at the thought. Right now Lina was so far from being ready she'd fuel the gossips for a decade if he took her to a London ball.

'I'm imagining it…' he murmured.

'And you introduce me to some duke or duchess.'

Heaven forbid. At the moment he was wondering if he could get away with only letting Lina talk to strategically placed friends around this proposed ballroom.

'I curtsy.'

Alex had seen her curtsies; they would certainly need at least half a day's work.

'And then I address him as Duke Dorrington. What would happen?'

'I still don't understand the question.' Alex could understand the words, but wasn't entirely sure exactly what Lina wanted to know.

'Would I be hauled in front of a magistrate? Exiled to Australia? Would the ceiling of the ballroom crumble on top of me? Would the Duke expire from shock? What. Would. Happen?'

Alex had forgotten to include *prone to exaggerate* in his mental list of Lina's qualities.

'You would probably get some very hard looks

and the whispering would start as soon as you were out of earshot.'

'Oh, Lord—not the whispering,' Lina murmured.

'A woman's reputation can be ruined by just one poorly timed remark or faux pas in form of address.'

'That's ridiculous. Everyone makes mistakes.'

Alex agreed. The etiquette and rules of polite society did seem over the top sometimes.

'To you it may not be of great concern to have some gossipy matrons judging you, but imagine if you were a debutante eagerly searching for a husband. These women would be part of your social circle for the rest of your life and who knows whom they may have influence over? In a matter of minutes you could go from the most eligible young woman in the ballroom to someone to be avoided because of their vulgarity and lack of manners.'

'And if it were a man that made the mistake?' Lina asked shrewdly. 'If it were you that addressed someone wrongly?'

'I agree it is unfair, but the standards are different for men and women. I could probably call someone Lord Coward, Duke of Half-Wit, and it would be laughed off within seconds.'

Lina nodded thoughtfully, pursing her lips. 'My mother used to say that women have to hold themselves to higher standards than men. We have to have double the respect, double the strength, double the commitment.'

'She sounds like a very sensible woman.'

'She was.'

Alex heard the catch in Lina's voice as she spoke and was just rising out of his chair to offer comfort when Lina turned to him with a breezy smile.

'Enough of this,' she declared. 'Wouldn't it be much more fun if we went to see your horses?'

'And how exactly will that help me win this wager?'

'I'll practise addressing the horses as if they were lords and ladies.'

What would the stable boys think? Yet Alex felt the irresistible pull of the stables. All morning he had been eager to dash out to the yard and throw himself back into his work. Spending the time teaching Lina how to address the different ranks of nobility hadn't been as bad as he had first feared— Lina was quick and clever and had a sly humour that made the time pass much quicker. Nothing, however, could keep his mind from wandering to his new Arabian and how he would approach the next stage of its training.

'Half an hour,' Alex agreed sternly. 'Then it's back to your studies.'

Lina was up and out through the door before Alex was even on his feet and as he quickened his pace to keep up his mind was calculating training timetables and regimes.

'What is it that you do with the horses?' Lina asked as they approached the stables.

'I raise them, train them and then race them. Well, I get them ready to be raced,' he corrected himself. 'Someone else does the actual riding during the race.'

'How many horses do you have?'

'At the moment, fifteen. The number varies as I buy and sell them on. And they're not all race-horses. I have two mares that I'm hoping to start breeding soon, four Cleveland Bays for the carriage and two old thoroughbreds for general riding.'

He saw the excitement in her eyes as he spoke and knew it wouldn't be long before she had persuaded him to take her out riding. Not that Alex minded. As much as he enjoyed breaking in a new stallion or training a thoroughbred for a race, nothing could beat the feel of galloping over the fields purely for pleasure.

'And the horse I saw yesterday?'

'My latest project,' Alex said. 'An Arabian that had been giving its previous owners all sorts of problems. They haven't been able to harness or ride him, so I took him off their hands for a very reasonable price.'

'Will you race him?'

Alex shrugged. He hadn't planned to initially. A large majority of the winning horses in the big races were thoroughbreds, but Arabians certainly took some of the titles. His initial plan had been to keep the new stallion for breeding, so good were his bloodlines, but after seeing his strength and spirit Alex thought he might well have a winning racehorse on his hands.

'Can *I* race him?'

Laughing, Alex shook his head. 'Most certainly not.'

'You'd let me if I were a man,' Lina grumbled.

'I have no idea how good you are with horses or if you can even ride.'

'I can ride. Give me ten minutes with your Arabian and I will have him eating from my hand and racing like a winner.'

'Slow down.' Alex laughed, although he had to admire her enthusiasm. 'I'll make you a deal. You show me you can care for a horse, and if you impress me, I'll let you ride.'

'The Arabian?' Lina asked, her eyes shining.

'Not the Arabian,' he said firmly.

They entered the stables and Alex led her down to the very end where a gentle-natured horse was munching on a mouthful of hay.

'This is Stormborn,' he said, raising a hand to stroke the old thoroughbred's nose. 'My very first racehorse. He's retired now, but still a joy to ride.'

He watched as Lina approached the horse slowly, lifting her fingers to rub his nose and murmuring reassuring sounds. Maybe she was good with horses, but Alex couldn't risk letting her loose on any of his prize-winning racehorses.

'Clean out his stall, rub him down, tend to the saddle and harness, and then I might let you ride him.' He was certain Lina would argue; she argued about everything.

Watching in amazement as she hitched up her skirts, revealing two slender legs without any hint of embarrassment and vaulting over the stable door, Alex wondered what sort of deal he had just made. Still, Stormborn would keep Lina busy for a while and give him a chance to work with his new Arabian for an hour or two.

With a backwards glance Alex moved away to the other end of the stables, listening with half a smile as Lina introduced herself to the horse much more politely than he had ever heard her speak to another human.

Lina was in heaven. Rubbing down the old thoroughbred's shiny coat might not appeal to many young women, but Lina could not think of anywhere she would rather be. She knew Alex had set her working in a bid to both stop her from asking to ride his precious horses, thinking she would not stick out the unglamorous work, and also to give him some time to work on his Arabian.

How he had underestimated her. She would be content to clean out the stables all day. In fact, she'd go as far as to say she preferred it to practising how to address people in Alex's comfortable library.

It wasn't that she was unimpressed with his house—she doubted there was a grander, more beautifully decorated dwelling in all of England, and certainly not one she'd ever be invited into. And Alex had been an exemplary host; he'd been kind and welcoming, even if his question as to whether she could read had stung her more than she cared to admit. No, her unease came from somewhere deep inside. Lina liked to think of herself as adventurous. The whole point of this escapade was to have a more exciting life. Well, that and to pay off the huge debt she owed Uncle Tom. But now she was here, she felt the first stirrings of inadequacy and she hated it.

All her life she had ranted against the aristocracy and the way they looked down on the ordinary people. She'd gone out of her way to avoid even the lower levels of the gentry, staying away from the country dances she dreamed about attending. Now she was here at Whitemore House and Alex and his sister were treating her with such kindness, Lina had to wonder if the problem was partly to do with her.

'What do you think, Stormborn?' Lina asked. 'Am I the problem?'

The horse nuzzled into her hand, rubbing his head against her shoulder in a consoling manner.

'How are you doing?' Alex's voice came suddenly from the other end of the stable. He'd left her for well over two hours, probably expecting her to give up at some point.

Lina didn't reply, forcing him to walk the length of the stables to Stormborn's stall. She saw the surprise on his face to still find her there, especially with his favourite horse nuzzling against her shoulder.

'It looks like Stormborn likes you.'

'We've had plenty of time to get to know one another.'

'Sorry, I lost track of time,' Alex said without a hint of remorse. 'I'm sure you're keen to return to the house for lunch.'

Lina had already opened her mouth to protest when she noticed the mischievous glint in Alex's eyes. He was teasing her. Normally she was so good at reading people, but Alex she found a little harder than most. She'd been able to pick up the basics when they'd first met at the fair, but since she'd arrived at Whitemore House he hadn't given much personal information away.

'Shall we ride?' he asked, grinning at her before tossing her the heavy saddle to strap on to Stormborn's back. Lina staggered under the weight, wondering if he treated his aristocratic lady friends in such a manner. It was all very well him training her to curtsy and flutter her fan like a lady, but if he treated her like a common gypsy girl, no one would ever accept her as anything else. She nearly said something, but decided he might agree with her and put a stop to their ride in favour of another session with *Debrett's*.

Chapter Six

Lina craned her neck, desperately trying to catch a glimpse of herself in the mirror.

'Just be patient,' Georgina chastised her. 'The overall effect will be more impressive if you wait until Mary has finished with your hair.'

The wait was agonising. The maid—Mary, a shy, perpetually blushing girl who was skilled at putting together the intricate hairstyles Georgina favoured day to day—was pulling and clipping sections of Lina's hair with quick, practised movements of her fingers. Lina hardly ever wore her hair up. It was too unruly, too wild to be tamed easily, so she favoured letting the loose curls cascade over her shoulders and down her back. Today, though, Georgina had insisted.

Ten minutes later and Mary declared her work to be done.

Nervously Lina stepped in front of the full-length mirror and let her eyes travel up her body. The shoes and dress were borrowed, quickly altered by one of Georgina's army of maids, but they were the most magnificent garments Lina had ever worn. The dress was a deep crimson in colour, cut low but not scandalously so, nipped in at the waist to show off Lina's figure, and with her hair pulled back into an intricate bun, she looked as though she might belong on the arm of a marquess.

'I can't believe this is me,' Lina whispered.

'You look beautiful.'

'Thank you, Georgina,' she said, turning to the other woman as her voice caught in her throat.

'Now, don't you start,' Georgina admonished her, the tears swelling in her own eyes, 'or you'll have me weeping, and my face goes all blotchy and swollen when I cry.'

'I feel so different.'

'Let's join the others and show them what a little effort can do.'

Arm in arm, the two women left Lina's room and made their way to the staircase. Far below Lina could hear the murmur of voices and she felt her heart begin pounding in her chest. This was her first little test. She'd been staying with Lord

Whitemore for just under a week and during that time he had worked her hard, teaching her basic etiquette and manners of address. Today they had practised how to behave at a dinner party, with Alex sighing as he'd repeated the different uses of the four forks, four knives and three spoons for the fifth time. After she had grasped the basics, Georgina had swooped into the room and declared it would be much more fun if they had a real dinner party.

Alex, of course, grumbled but Lina could see he wasn't completely averse to the idea. It would only be the four of them present: Alex and Lina, Georgina and her husband, Mr Pentworthy, who up until this evening had been attending to business in London. Nevertheless, Lina felt a little nervous about it.

The two men paused as Lina and Georgina joined them and Lina watched as Mr Pentworthy greeted his wife with a warm look and a kiss on the cheek.

'May I properly introduce Miss Lina Lock?'

'A pleasure to meet you, Miss Lock.'

Like his wife, Mr Pentworthy seemed to be friendly and sincere in his greeting and Lina knew immediately that she was going to like him. She knew how Georgina adored her husband, she talked about him with love and warmth, and Georgina hadn't been wrong about much since Lina's arrival.

Lina sank into a shallow curtsy, lowering her eyes as Alex had instructed her, then looking up at Mr Pentworthy from under her long lashes as Georgina had suggested when meeting a gentleman for the first time.

'I hope your journey was not too arduous, Mr Pentworthy,' Lina said, the picture of demure womanhood. Socialising in polite company did not seem that difficult.

'Travelling is never my favourite pastime, but it is worth it to be here tonight.'

'I am glad you could make it. I've been so looking forward to meeting you.'

Alex coughed and Lina risked a glance in his direction for the first time since she'd entered the room. For some reason she'd known he would knock her off balance and she'd been nervous enough without Alex adding to her apprehension. He was dressed in a crisp white shirt and blue cravat with dark, closely fitting trousers and a jacket over the top. Lina swallowed, trying hard to concentrate on anything other than her host. Just his presence was making her feel all hot and bothered.

'Whitemore tells me you've been working hard these last few days.'

'Lord Whitemore is a tough master, but I have survived more or less unscathed.'

Alex stepped forward, placing himself almost in between Lina and Mr Pentworthy, forcing her to look at him.

'You look transformed, Miss Lock,' Alex murmured.

'Like an ugly duckling into a swan?'

'Something along those lines.'

'Do I at least look *suitable* for an intimate dinner party?'

Suitable had been the word of the week. Alex had lectured her over and over again about 'suitable' clothes to wear, 'suitable' topics of conversation, 'suitable' people to converse with.

'I'm not sure what the society matrons would think of a debutante in that dress,' he concluded after looking Lina up and down.

'Pish-posh—' Georgina breezed into the conversation '—Lina looks ravishing and she would have all the young gentlemen clamouring to escort her in to dinner.'

'Maybe the unsuitable young gentlemen…'

Lina looked up and caught the humour in Alex's eyes and felt the smile spreading across her face. He'd been a little distant the last couple of days. Whilst Lina had been reciting titles and practising enquiring about his health, she'd caught Alex staring off as if his mind were elsewhere.

'Is it the colour you object to,' Lina asked innocently, 'or the cut?'

She felt all eyes on her, but was only really interested in Alex's reaction.

'Both,' he said quickly. 'A demure debutante is only ever really seen in white or pastel shades. And she tries to leave a little more to the imagination with the cut of her dress.'

'So this doesn't allow the gentlemen to imagine what might be underneath quite so well as a shapeless dress?' Lina was enjoying herself now. The nerves she'd felt as she'd entered the room were lifting.

'You know that is not what I mean,' Alex said, his voice tight.

'I think, my dear brother, that if more debutantes

dressed like Lina has, then you would be a lot more interested in making their acquaintance.'

'You judge me to be that shallow?'

'All men are,' Georgina said lightly. 'What do you think, darling?' she asked, turning to her husband.

'I think you look beautiful in that dress, Miss Lock, but I'm sure you would look lovely in a shapeless sack, too,' Mr Pentworthy said softly, putting an end to the argument between brother and sister in such a practised way that Lina wondered how many of these disputes he settled with a well-considered sentence.

'Quite,' Alex murmured. 'Shall we go through to dinner?'

Alex placed his spoon in the bowl and sat back, watching Lina as she ate. It had been a most enjoyable evening, much to Alex's surprise. When Georgina had suggested the dinner party he had been tempted to reject the idea, but seeing as Pentworthy was returning that evening anyway, putting a more formal name to them dining together hadn't taken too much more organisation. Although no part of the wager required Lina to attend any dinner parties, he had to admit it was a good test of what she had picked up so far, in a safe and controlled environment.

'The key to reading a fortune is observing people,' Lina explained.

'I thought you interpreted the lines on people's hands or something?' Mr Pentworthy said with a frown.

'I'm letting you into treasured family secrets here—' Lina dropped her voice as she spoke '—but no one, ever, has been able to tell anything about another person by the wrinkles on their hands.'

'How fascinating. So what *do* you do?'

'Would you like a demonstration?'

'I'm not sure…' Alex began.

'Oh, yes, please,' Georgina countered. 'How fun.'

'This isn't really an appropriate topic for the dinner table,' Alex grumbled, feeling like a decidedly old killjoy in the process.

'You've already told Alex's fortune, why don't you do my husband's?'

'She knows everything about him already,' Alex said. 'You two chatter incessantly. Lina probably knows more about your husband's life than I do.'

'Well, maybe you should pay more attention, then,' Lina murmured.

He watched as she turned to Pentworthy, adjusting her position in her chair and flashing the man a sweet smile. She'd never smiled at *him* like that before.

'Would you like to know your future, sir?' she asked, her voice dropping so it sounded almost seductive to Alex's ears.

'Please, go ahead,' Pentworthy replied.

'First your name—your full name.'

'Richard Pentworthy.'

Lina took his hand in her own and caressed it for a second before turning it over and studying the lines across his palm.

'You're a powerful man, Mr Pentworthy,' Lina said. 'And a happy one. I can see you work hard for what you have, but life has not always been easy. You are married and you take your vows seriously, I would say that your wife and children are even more important to you than your work.'

'You're just telling him what he wants to hear,' Alex muttered. Lina flashed him an irritated look, before turning back to Pentworthy.

'You are a wealthy man, very wealthy, but you were not born into wealth in the same way your wife was. You've worked to get where you are today.'

'I never told her that,' Georgina whispered at Alex.

'As for the future…' She traced her fingers across Pentworthy's palm in a way that made Alex want to stand up and pull her hand away. 'I see more children, many more, in fact. You will have a large and happy family. I see success overseas. A business venture, perhaps?' Alex saw how she watched for Pentworthy's reaction before continuing. 'Yes, business—the deal you are working on at the moment—soon all those long hours will pay off. And I see recognition, perhaps in the form of a title, for all the services you have provided to the Crown.'

'That's incredible,' Pentworthy said. 'How on earth did you do all that?'

'You don't actually believe any of it?' Alex asked.

'What's not to believe?' Lina countered. 'I gave an accurate description of his life and what's important to him in the present, and extrapolated his dreams for the future.'

'You have to teach me,' Georgina gushed.

'Go through it all again, but slowly, explaining step by step,' Pentworthy instructed.

Alex sat back and folded his arms, but listened all the same. Although he was sceptical about this sort of thing he had to admit Lina must have wonderful powers of observation to describe his brother-in-law quite so accurately on their first meeting.

'I started out with a statement about your status and happiness. I know you are powerful by the people you associate with and also by the royal seal on the documents you left in the hallway. I can tell that you are a happy man by the laughter lines around your eyes. Our wrinkles never lie.'

'Such simple observations, but so effective. Go on,' Pentworthy urged.

'I can tell you work hard, as you have brought a pile of papers home with you to work on after we have finished dinner, and I know you are happily married by the way you look at your wife as if she is the only woman in the world.'

'How did you know my husband wasn't born wealthy?' Georgina asked.

'He wears very fine clothes, but there are signs of wear on the elbows and down the seams. If I'm not much mistaken, a tear in your jacket has been mended recently,' Lina said.

Pentworthy raised his fingers to the almost-unnoticeable piece of damaged material.

'You are obviously wealthy, Mr Pentworthy—you arrived in your own private carriage and your wife has the finest of clothes and jewellery—but you are more thrifty than most gentlemen, allowing your clothes to be mended instead of just purchasing new ones. This hints at a past where money was not so freely available.'

Alex shifted, leaning forward. He knew of his brother-in-law's modest beginnings and admired how Pentworthy had made his own fortune, but there was no way Lina could have known. He felt a grudging respect blooming for how she had determined that little insight.

'As for the predictions about the future, all you have to do is look at what is important to the client and build on that. In your case a larger family, an expanded business empire and recognition for the work you have done.'

'Impressive,' Alex murmured.

Lina turned to face him, her eyes shining with triumph. 'I've even converted you?'

'I'm impressed by your powers of observation.'

He watched as her cheeks flushed at the compliment and felt a primal stirring deep inside. Alex tried to suppress it, but as Lina stood, guided by Georgina, he couldn't help watching her hips sway as she walked away.

'Wait,' he called as they reached the door. 'Lina, I need to talk to you for a moment.'

Georgina shrugged, returned to the table and allowed her husband to escort her from the room instead.

'Shall we take a stroll on the terrace?'

Gently Lina placed her hand on his forearm, just as he had taught her to, and accompanied him outside.

'You did very well tonight,' Alex said as they walked side by side.

'It was hardly much of a test,' Lina said with a shrug. 'Your sister and her husband are not exactly judgemental. They are very easy to spend an evening with.'

'Nevertheless, I think we might just win this little wager of ours.'

'My behaviour wasn't too scandalous?'

'It wasn't impeccable,' Alex said after a moment's thought, but regretted it as he saw Lina's face drop. He could have just kept the tone light, congratulated her again, and enjoyed their time together, but something was gnawing at him, making him lash out uncharacteristically.

He stopped, turning to lean against a stone column to try to regain his equilibrium. Throughout the entire evening, ever since he'd seen her walk into the drawing room dressed in red and looking beautiful, he'd had the urge to pull her into his arms and kiss her. He'd barely been able to tear his eyes away from her lips and all the time he'd been imagining what her body would feel like under his, what her skin would taste like and what her breath would feel like on his neck. He wanted her more than he'd wanted any woman in a long time.

Alex didn't like this feeling—the sensation of being out of control. These last three years he had trained his mind and body to live by his strict rules, but suddenly they were rebelling.

Maybe he needed a mistress. Not Lina, of course—she was entirely inappropriate. His past lovers had mainly been young widows, but he had once been attached to an actress for a few months and before that an opera singer for nearly a year. Never had anyone he knew kept a gypsy dancer as a mistress.

Alex's eyes flitted to Lina's and for a moment he didn't care about her background. A mistress was to be kept secret anyway, so perhaps it didn't matter that Lina was from a different world.

'What did you want to talk to me about?' Lina asked. She'd turned half-away from him and was looking out over the gardens, her face illuminated by the moonlight.

'I wanted to give you this.' Alex reached into his pocket and pulled out a small package, handing it over to Lina. He felt a spark as their fingers touched that sent a shudder of desire through his whole body.

'What is it?'

'Open it and see.'

Deftly her fingers undid the small bow on the top of the box and pulled off the lid.

'It's beautiful.'

'I'm sorry I can't pay you.'

Not looking up, Lina gave a small nod, running her fingers over the sparkling silver hair comb.

'Thank you,' she said, her voice tight. Alex scrutinised her face, wondering if he'd done something wrong.

'I know it's not much.'

She shook her head. 'I think it's the most beautiful thing anyone has ever given me.'

Despite the words of reassurance Alex could tell something wasn't quite right.

'If you would prefer something else we can always return it,' he added. He didn't have much experience of buying women gifts, not recently.

'It is perfect. Thank you.'

'Allow me.' He took the comb from her, placed his hands on the thin material that covered her shoulders and spun her round so her back was to him. Against his better judgement he allowed his fingers to trail across the soft skin at the nape of her neck, wishing it was his lips instead. He felt her stiffen beneath his touch and quickly, before he could do anything he might regret, he pulled his hands away. Gently he slid the comb into the back of her hair, adjusting it so it was straight.

'Thank you,' Lina said, raising her hand to her hair and gingerly touching the comb. She turned and for a moment they were standing far too close, their bodies only inches apart. It would be so easy to lean forward, take her in his arms and kiss her until she begged him for more. Alex felt his body sway slightly, closing the gap between them, but at the last second he gained control of himself and stepped away.

'Shall we return to the others?' he asked stiffly.

He saw her hesitate. 'I'll follow you in a minute or two.'

Normally Alex would not let a young woman remain outside by herself, even somewhere as safe as his own home, but right now he had to put some distance between them and if that meant being ungentlemanly, then so be it. He knew if he stayed out here with Lina any longer, he would do something he would regret.

Chapter Seven

Lina watched Alex stroll back along the terrace and disappear inside the house and slowly willed her body to relax. Carefully she raised her hand to her hair and touched the comb again, running her fingers over the intricately decorated surface and feeling the tears spring to her eyes.

'Don't be a fool,' she whispered to herself.

The words she had said to Alex were true: this was the most beautiful gift anyone had ever given her.

Needing some time and space to clear her head, Lina carefully lifted the skirts of her dress and descended the steps into the garden. She would return to the house in a few minutes, but first she needed a moment or two to regain control of herself.

She was being foolish, spinning fantasies out of

thin air. She tried to tell herself it was only natural to feel some sort of attraction for Alex. He was both good-looking and good company, and they were spending large amounts of time together. Tonight she'd even fancied he had looked at her once or twice with desire in his eyes, but Lina knew that was probably only wishful thinking. What she did know was that her own heart pounded when he stepped close and she'd barely been able to breathe as his fingers brushed against her skin.

'Stop it,' she admonished herself. Even if he did desire her physically, nothing could ever happen between them. Their differences went so much deeper than just status and lifestyle.

'Fancy seeing you here.' The voice from the bushes made Lina jump so much she let out a shout that she only just managed to muffle at the last minute.

'Uncle Tom?'

'Unless you've got another rendezvous planned?'

'I hadn't planned one with you,' Lina grumbled.

'Now, that's not true, my dear. Remember our deal.'

Lina felt the nausea rise in her throat as she remembered the terms of the latest deal she had made with her uncle.

'You've had plenty of time to scout the place out,' Uncle Tom prompted.

She shook her head, wondering how to get rid of him, knowing he wouldn't be satisfied until she gave him something. For a second her fingers darted to the comb in her hair, but immediately she dismissed the idea of trying to buy some time with it. Alex would notice if she returned to the house without it—besides, she wanted to have a proper look at it before she gave it away. Lina knew she wouldn't want to part with the comb, but she would have to be practical in the end if it meant getting rid of the debt she owed Uncle Tom.

'It's a fine house,' Uncle Tom said, gripping her arm and pulling her off the grassy path and into the darkness. 'Lots of money kept inside for wages and the like, I'd imagine.'

'I'm not stealing for you,' Lina said, pulling her arm from his grasp and stumbling backwards a few steps.

'I'm not asking you to steal, I'm happy to do that part myself.'

Lina felt the rage building inside her. This was why gypsies had a bad name. Men like her uncle Tom who were prepared to do anything to make a quick profit.

'Raul wouldn't like it if he knew what you were doing,' Lina said. She saw the flash of anger in Uncle Tom's eyes at the mention of her brother. Raul was respected in their troupe and, despite his relatively young age, it was her brother who made the decisions as to where they went and when they moved on. He had the power to exile Uncle Tom from their travelling group and Tom knew it.

'Well, he'd better not find out then,' Tom snarled. 'We had a deal, Lina. You shouldn't have accepted the terms if you weren't happy with them.'

'Let me just pay you instead, when I get the money.'

'Why are you protecting this toff? After what his kind did to your father I'd have thought you'd be more than eager to get your revenge.'

'My father brought his situation on himself,' Lina said coldly. 'It has nothing to do with Alex… Lord Whitemore,' she corrected herself quickly.

Tom threw his head back and laughed heartily. 'I see what this sudden reticence is about—you fancy that you have feelings for this lord! Following in your father's footsteps after all.'

'I don't have feelings for anyone,' Lina said, taking a deep breath to maintain her composure. 'I just don't believe in stealing.'

'He's not going to look twice at you,' Tom gloated. 'At the very most he might use you for a quick roll in the hay, but then you'll be out on your ear and he will have moved on to someone much more suitable.'

Lina felt the tears building in her eyes, but refused to let Tom see her cry. She didn't even know why she was upset, it wasn't as though she wanted anything to happen between her and Lord Whitemore. She'd seen first-hand how lives were ruined when someone dallied with a person of superior rank and status, she knew what heartache that brought. No, the last thing Lina wanted was for any romantic involvement with Lord Whitemore, even if her heart did pound and her throat constrict when he was close by. The physical attraction she could resist; all she had to do was remind herself how her father had been broken by his short affair with Lady Farrien nearly a decade ago.

'Someone will come looking for me soon,' Lina said, turning to walk away. She felt Tom grab her by the waist and before she had chance to twist out of his grip he had her pinned up against the nearest tree.

'Consider where your true loyalties lie, Lina,'

he whispered in her ear, his warm breath making her shudder as she felt the specks of saliva hit her neck. 'And remember the terms of our deal, my dear. If you do not get me my fifteen pounds *and* the information you promised me, you won't like the consequences.'

Just as he dug his fingers into her wrist, Lina managed to slide down the trunk of the tree and, with a quick twist, wiggled out from under his arm.

'Send me a note next time the house will be empty and make sure you include details of where this toff of yours keeps his money. I don't care about vases and statues and jewellery, it needs to be money.'

'The house is never empty, there are dozens of servants.'

'But servants retire early if their master is out for the evening.'

Knowing she had some difficult decisions to make, but unsure how she could even start to untangle herself from the mess she was in, Lina turned and darted back towards the house before Tom had chance to say any more. It went against every moral fibre in her body to betray Lord

Whitemore to her uncle, but if she didn't come up with an alternative solution soon she might have no choice in the matter.

Chapter Eight

Alex glanced up from the papers he was reading in the hope that he might catch a glimpse of Lina or his sister, but he knew that was too much to hope for. Despite it seeming like an eternity that he'd been sitting in the dressmaker's, he knew in reality it had been less than half an hour.

'I don't see why my presence is required here,' Alex called, hearing the chattering voices on the other side of the curtain pause as he spoke. 'You haven't asked my opinion once in the hour we've been here.'

'Do remember that I have a vested interest in you losing your wager,' Georgina said, poking her head through the curtain. 'I might advise Lina to purchase something absolutely terrible. Hence the need for your supervision.'

'You wouldn't be so underhand,' Alex said, but

then held his hand up to correct himself. 'You *would* be so underhand, but you wouldn't allow Lina to embarrass herself in a frock that was anything but fashionable.'

'Very true, brother dearest. Anyway, it does you good to be out of the house and away from those horses you're so obsessed with.'

Alex grumbled, but returned to his papers. He knew how important truly magnificent clothes were for a debutante. If Lina attended the ball in five weeks' time dressed like the daughter of the aristocracy, then people would believe that was what she was. That was why he had insisted they ride into town and start the process of getting Lina fitted for her appearances in society. Despite all this, he hadn't expected it to take quite so long and, as far as he could tell from his position on the other side of the curtain, they hadn't even chosen the dress yet.

'Remember she needs to blend in with the other debutantes,' Alex called. 'It needs to be the latest fashion.'

Standing and stretching, Alex walked the length of the shop, allowing his fingers to trail over the selection of materials that were on display.

'It is a shame we have to buy something ready-made,' he heard Georgina say from the other side of the curtain. 'There's nothing more luxurious than a dress that fits you and only you perfectly.'

Lina gave a light, carefree laugh that made Alex smile. When she wasn't arguing with him she was good to have around. She tempered Georgina's bossiness nicely and had a quick wit that kept him on his toes.

'I think you'd look lovely in the green,' Georgina murmured. 'But really we should stick to less vibrant colours. You are supposed to be a debutante after all. Perhaps the pink?'

'Pink makes me look ghastly.'

'White, then. Although half the debutantes will be wearing white, it's so popular these days. When I was a debutante hardly anyone wore plain white.'

'White is good,' Alex called to them. It was a safe choice, guaranteed to group Lina with the other young debutantes as soon as she entered a ballroom.

'You make it sound as if it were two dozen years ago. It can only be five or six at the most.' Lina laughed.

'Six,' Georgina confirmed.

'How about this one?'

Silence followed and Alex walked to the window, glancing out into the street.

'That could work,' he heard Georgina say after a small pause. 'It's unusual, but I think it would suit you very well.'

The rest of their conversation faded into the background as Alex felt his throat begin to constrict. He tried to take a step back from the window, but his muscles failed to obey and for an awful few seconds he was in full view of anyone walking down the street.

He'd known it was her the very moment she'd rounded the corner into the high street, he recognised her graceful walk and exquisite posture as if he had last seen her only yesterday. His ex-fiancée didn't look a day older than she had three years earlier—it was as if that time had been wiped out in an instant.

Alex felt a coldness descend over his body and, willing his muscles to work again, he quickly moved away from the window. The last thing he wanted was to be forced into a polite conversation with Victoria. She'd almost broken him and the worst thing about the whole debacle was that she knew how much she'd hurt him. For Alex, a man who'd been brought up to respect strength and dignity, the humiliation of how she had almost felled him was as bad as the heartbreak itself.

As the door to the shop slowly opened, Alex cursed every deity he had ever heard mention of. Of all the shops in all the world, Victoria had to choose this one to enter today. Squaring his shoulder as if he were about to go into a fight, Alex fixed a nonchalant smile on his face. He wouldn't pretend he hadn't seen her or that he was surprised by her presence, he was better than that, even if his sinking heart might disagree.

'Good afternoon, Lady Winchester,' he said as Victoria entered the shop, trying not to enjoy the moment of panic in her eyes as she recognised his voice. He stepped forward, still smiling, took her hand and bowed formerly over it. 'I do hope you are well.'

'Qu-qu-quite well,' she managed after a few seconds.

He waited. Etiquette dictated that she should enquire after his health now, but she still hadn't rallied from the shock of seeing him.

'What brings you to Pottersdown?' he asked, his voice light and conversational.

For three years he had wondered how he would react when he saw Victoria again. He knew it

would happen. The people they socialised with—
the members of the *ton*—were surprisingly few
in number, but he'd worked hard to avoid Victoria
these last few years. Declining invitations to events
he suspected she would be attending had become
almost habit. He'd never left a ball because Victoria was there, but he had sought out the card ta-
bles quickly on the few occasions when their paths
might have crossed, knowing Victoria's views on
gambling meant he'd be safe.

'I am visiting my aunt,' Victoria said. 'Alex, I'm
sorry, I assumed you would be in London, preparing for the Season. I'd never have come if I'd
thought…'

Alex gave a dismissive wave of his hand. After
his initial feelings of dread at seeing his ex-fiancée
for the first time since she'd declared her intention
to marry his closest friend instead of him, he actually felt wonderfully unmoved by this encounter.
He'd half expected their first meeting to be much
more painful, much more strained, but he felt…
nothing. Maybe time did heal all wounds.

'You're looking well, Alex—'

'Lady Winchester.' He heard the curtain behind
him being pulled back and Georgina step out. The
venom in her voice was unmistakable.

'It is a pleasure to see you again,' Victoria said, her expression betraying her true feelings, but she quickly sank into a curtsy before the other woman could see.

Victoria and his sister had never got on, and Georgina had spent many hours detailing the punishments she thought Victoria deserved after she'd left. They'd been particularly gruesome and colourful descriptions that had made Alex wonder what sort of books Pentworthy kept in his library to fuel Georgina's imagination.

'I trust your husband is well?' Alex asked.

Lord Phillip Harrow, Duke of Winchester, had been Alex's closest friend since they'd met at Eton. Their years of friendship made the betrayal even more painful and Alex had to mourn the loss of a friend as well as the loss of his fiancée.

'He is.'

All the times he had imagined meeting Victoria again over the last few years, never had he pictured this stilted conversation. Initially when she'd left he'd wanted to rant and rave at her, make her understand just how much she'd hurt him. As time passed and his anger and pain turned to disgust at the underhand way she and Winchester had conducted their affair, Alex had imagined brushing her off with nothing more than a perfunctory greeting, slaying her with cold disdain. In reality, the situation was awkward and uncomfortable for the simple reason he had nothing he wished to say to her.

'Lord Whitemore?' Lina's voice came from behind him and Alex spun quickly. For a moment he forgot the awkwardness between him and Victoria, forgot there was anyone else in the shop except him and Lina.

As she stepped forward into the light, moving with the grace of a dancer, he heard himself take in a sharp breath. Although not unrecognisable, Lina had been transformed. Gone was the colourful gypsy girl, replaced with an elegant woman in a demure but flattering dress.

Alex saw Victoria's eyes widen in surprise momentarily before she regained control of her facial muscles and fixed her expression into one of polite enquiry.

'It is my pleasure to introduce Miss Lina Lock,' Alex said, watching cautiously as Lina stepped forward and dipped into a small curtsy. 'Miss Lock, this is Lady Winchester, Duchess of Winchester.'

To her credit Lina didn't even flinch at the title.

'Lovely to meet you, Lady Winchester.' Alex had

to suppress a smile. He'd known Lina had grasped how to correctly address titled ladies and gentleman, she'd just been toying with him when she declared the system to be impossible for a *normal* person to remember.

For a few seconds he let the two women eye each other warily. Neither knew who the other was, but Alex could sense the tension in the small shop building as the silence dragged out.

'Are you local to the area?' Victoria asked eventually, her curiosity finally winning out. 'I'm not sure I know of any Locks, but my family are originally from Yorkshire so I don't know many of the families in this area.'

Alex wondered if Lina would panic, if she would blurt out her true identity when so directly questioned. He feared for a moment they might lose the wager at the first real hurdle and, as his stomach tightened, he realised just how important this bet of theirs had become to him. When Pentworthy had first proposed it Alex had been keen, but now he and Lina had invested so much time and effort in the past week preparing for the ball in just over a month's time, he realised just how much was at stake. Holding his breath, he waited for Lina to answer.

'My family are scattered around the country,' Lina said lightly. 'Although my closest relatives are residing in Pottersdown currently.'

'So you and Lord Whitemore are neighbours. How lovely.' Alex saw the strain on Victoria's face despite her bright tone of voice. In the years since she'd left he had gone through so many emotional stages, but never had he considered how she felt about *him* after she'd eloped with Winchester. She didn't have any right to feel jealous or to wonder who he spent his time with, but the twitch just above her eye hinted that she did all the same.

'Alex,' Lina said, dropping her voice so it was low and intimate, 'what do you think of this dress?'

By the twinkling in her eye he knew she was aware of her totally inappropriate use of his first name. The little minx had picked up on the tension between him and Victoria and was ensuring he wasn't the one left embarrassed or confused by the encounter.

Lina walked slowly forward, turned in a circle gracefully and then took a step towards him, reducing the distance between them until she was standing just a little too close for comfort.

He took a moment to regard her, sweeping his eyes over the dress, the colour of smooth cream and the unusual embroidered rose pattern that snaked up one side.

'It suits you,' he said. 'I don't think I've ever seen anyone wear anything quite like it before.' There was nothing scandalous about the dress, nothing inappropriate, but all the same Alex felt the heat begin to rise in his body as he looked at her. She looked mysterious and slightly sultry, even though she had shed her flared gypsy skirt, and Alex wondered if this was why he felt that physical pull. She was so different to any woman he had ever known before—so different to Victoria, that was made especially clear as the two of them stood in front of him.

'I should be going,' Victoria said quietly. 'It was a pleasure to meet you, Miss Lock.'

The two women inclined their heads to each other before Victoria bid Alex and his sister goodbye, then quickly hurried out of the shop.

'So that was the dastardly ex-fiancée?' Lina said as she peered out of the window, watching Victoria's retreating form.

'Yes,' Alex said.

'Pretty.'

'Yes.'

'Lots of unresolved emotions there.'

Alex raised an eyebrow. He wasn't sure he was in the mood for any of Lina's much too accurate observations.

'On her part, I mean.' Lina smiled, though there was a hint of something else behind it, too. 'You obviously have dealt with her abandonment admirably, no lasting heartbreak for you.'

'Did you have to tell her every sordid detail?' Alex asked, turning to Georgina.

'Don't look at me. I haven't uttered more than three words about *Victoria*.' Georgina almost spat the name out in disgust.

Lina opened her mouth, but Alex held up a hand. He'd had enough discussion of Victoria for the moment.

'I think I'm going to go for a walk.'

Lina quickly changed out of the beautiful cream dress, reluctantly swapping it for her worn multicoloured skirt and blouse.

'I'll find Alex and meet you back here in half an hour,' she said to Georgina, who had decided to take the opportunity to get herself measured for a couple of new dresses whilst she was in Pottersdown.

Exiting the shop, she looked to the left and right,

spotting Alex a few hundred yards away, strolling slowly towards her. Quickly she went to meet him, aware that they only had a limited time for her to get him to open up a little about the encounter with his ex-fiancée.

'Come with me,' Lina said, grabbing hold of Alex's hand and pulling him down the high street. Before they had taken two steps Alex had adjusted their position, tucking her hand into the crook of his arm and slowing her pace, so they looked like a respectable couple. As she rolled her eyes, he gave her an admonishing glance. It wasn't the first time he'd had to rebuke her for not behaving like the debutante she was striving to be in public.

'We should be getting back soon,' Alex said.

'This won't take long. Anyway, you need cheering up after that little surprise trip down memory lane.'

Lina saw him smile and wondered if he would admit he found her tendency not to skirt around difficult subjects refreshing or if he would reprimand her for not observing the rules of polite conversation.

'Sit. I'll just be a couple of minutes.' Before he could protest she hurried off, glancing back to check he hadn't moved. Alex had the annoying habit of disobeying. He expected her to comply when he gave *her* an order, but wasn't very good at taking them himself. 'I told you to sit.' Lina sighed.

Alex shrugged. 'I wanted to know where you were going.'

'It was meant to be a surprise,' Lina grumbled.

'It still is.'

With a roll of her eyes she watched as he strolled on ahead of her, not even bothering to turn to see if she would catch up.

'My brother brought me here the very first time we came to Pottersdown,' Lina said as they stopped in front of a small shopfront. 'It was just after my father died and Raul was doing his very best to buoy my spirits.'

Lina pushed the door open and entered the shop. A tall man greeted them, smiling under a bushy moustache.

'Lina! I almost didn't recognise you. What would you like today?' the jolly shopkeeper asked.

'A regular customer, I see,' Alex murmured.

'I come here every day when we stay in Pottersdown,' Lina admitted. 'Two pieces of *pâté de guimauve*, please.' She turned back to Alex. 'It really is the most delicious thing I've ever tasted.'

'I concede to your expertise.'

Lina watched as the shopkeeper took two small, fluffy pieces of confectionery and wrapped them in napkins before handing them over. Alex reached for his coin purse, but Lina stepped forward first, paying the man before bidding him goodbye.

'Do you know, I don't think a woman has ever bought me anything before,' Alex mused as they strolled back towards the bench Lina had intended to leave Alex sitting on.

Lina laughed. 'Now, I don't want to get started about what is wrong with society,' she said. 'But it is rather frustrating that many women are not trusted with money of their own and as such cannot buy gifts for men they hold in high regard.'

'You hold me in high regard?'

'I was talking in general terms,' Lina said, feeling the smile dancing on her lips. 'It makes one question the whole courtship ritual, doesn't it? Men choose the women they wish to pursue, and because they choose, they are the ones to buy the gifts to woo their intended. If women had more of a choice in the matter, perhaps men would receive their share of pretty trinkets, too.'

'And what man doesn't appreciate a pretty trinket?'

'You might if you ever received one.'

They reached the bench overlooking the duck pond and sat side by side, both tasting the sweet confection and taking a moment to enjoy the flavour.

'She broke your heart, didn't she?' Lina asked quietly, unsure how Alex would react to the abrupt change of subject.

'It was a difficult time,' he replied eventually.

'Sometimes I don't think people appreciate how their actions impact on those around them.'

'Or they just don't care.'

'My father broke my mother's heart,' Lina said, watching Alex as he stared off into the distance. 'He loved her, or so he claimed, but he still betrayed her.'

'Did your mother recover?'

Lina considered the question for a little while. 'She moved on with her life, she forgave him, but I don't think she ever recovered.'

The messy subject of her parents' relationship was not one Lina often talked about. All her gypsy family knew the intimate, sordid details, so there was no need to ever discuss it, and Lina realised she hadn't really ever had any friends outside her family circle before.

'What happened?' Alex asked, turning to her.

'My father was a strong man—charismatic, I suppose. He caught the eye of a wealthy widow when we stayed in Hampshire for a while. She must have wanted something a little more alluring than her usual string of lovers.'

Lina could still remember her father sneaking off in the middle of the night. She'd been six years old and had woken to see him leaving without a backwards glance at his family.

'The widow got bored of him after a few months and my father came crawling back to the family, begging for my mother to forgive him.'

'And she took him back?' Alex asked, incredulous. Lina could see he would never contemplate letting Victoria back into his life.

'She loved him. And hated him a little, I think. She took him back, but things weren't the same. He started drinking heavily, would withdraw into himself for days on end.'

'Guilty conscience?'

'Crushed dreams,' Lina corrected. Her father had thought his life was about to change when the widow had looked his way, and for a few months it had, but he had been a temporary distraction, an oddity, nothing more. Soon the widow had become bored of her coarse new lover and looked elsewhere for her excitement. 'For a little while he thought he was going to become someone important. All his life he had been a travelling carpenter and he wanted something more, I think. When he was pushed back to reality, the dream of what could have been got to be too much. It was the disappointment that killed him.'

'It must have been an unhappy time for you.'

Lina smiled softly. 'My mother was heartbroken, betrayed twice by the man she loved—first when he left her for another woman and then when he gave up on life. But she tried to do her best by me and Raul. And we had the rest of the family to rally round, as well.'

'I'm sorry this happened to you.'

Shaking her head vehemently, Lina turned to Alex. 'I didn't tell you to gain your sympathy. I just wanted you to know that I understand.' She paused, watching Alex sink back on to the bench and his eyes glaze over slightly. 'I do not know what happened with you and your ex-fiancée, but I do know she hurt you badly. You find it difficult to trust people. Perhaps that is why you are so resistant to the young ladies your sister keeps trying to push your way?'

'Perhaps.' Alex shrugged. Lina could tell he

wasn't ready to open up about the events of his past so she didn't push any further. Hopefully it was enough to know that she understood a little of his pain.

Chapter Nine

Alex felt unsettled and he knew exactly the reason why. Seeing Victoria again had set him on edge and he hated that she could affect him so deeply even after all this time. It wasn't that he still had feelings for her—any remnants of the love he had once felt for her had been washed away when he found out the underhand way in which she'd conducted her affair with Winchester—but he was realising how many of his actions over the last three years had been influenced by what Victoria had done to him. It wasn't just the functions that he'd avoided or the desire to stay an unmarried bachelor rather than risk his heart again, it was the friendships he'd let slip. Alex could acknowledge that he'd buried himself in his work the past few years, partly that was because he enjoyed the thrill of the race, but it was also a way to avoid people.

Well, no longer. He wasn't proposing he give up training his horses, but he would stop avoiding situations just in case he came across Victoria. He'd survived his first encounter with her without serious injury, he could manage to be civil in the future, too.

'If you do not move your hand this instant, I will punch you so hard you'll be lucky to keep all your teeth.'

Alex paused outside the drawing room door, suppressing a smile.

'I assure you, *madam*, this is the correct hold for a waltz.'

'And I can assure you, *sir*, that I don't care if it is how you would hold a nun. Move your hand or I will hurt you.'

Stepping into the room, Alex saw the spritely dance teacher swiftly step away from Lina, his hands outstretched placatingly.

'I trust everything is going well?'

'She is unteachable,' Monsieur LeBon declared with a flourish.

'There is no such thing as unteachable,' Lina said sweetly, 'just an incompetent teacher.'

'I am the highest-regarded dance teacher in society!'

'Then teaching a country girl to dance a waltz shouldn't be that much of a challenge.'

'If you would follow a single instruction…'

'I've told you a thousand times. I. Do. Not. Speak. French.'

'Of course you speak French. All ladies speak French.'

'I speak Spanish,' Lina said, 'and Romani and a little German.'

The dance teacher flinched and took another step away.

'I think you'd better leave, Monsieur LeBon,' Alex said, his voice low, 'before you say something you might regret.'

With a horrified glance at Lina, Monsieur LeBon gathered his belongings and hurried out of the room.

'I apologise,' Alex said quietly.

Lina shook her head and gave him a sunny smile, but Alex wasn't fooled. The dance teacher's reaction to Lina's snippet of information about her origins had upset her.

'Monsieur LeBon is a fool…'

'It doesn't matter, Alex. People like the music and cheap labour we provide at the country fairs, but they are suspicious and distrustful of us in any other situation. We have a reputation for stealing, for taking work away from the locals. My mother always used to say it was because we lived a different lifestyle—people always are fearful when someone is brave enough to go against the accepted norm.'

Alex remembered Lina's fingers slipping into his coat the first time they had met. It was true; he hadn't been surprised when he thought she was trying to pick his pocket, he'd been more surprised when she hadn't followed through with her action.

'Perhaps I could take you through the steps of a waltz?' Alex suggested.

'It's no use. I can't dance without music. I find it impossible, always have.'

'That is easily remedied.' Alex strode from the room and into one of the numerous sitting rooms where Georgina was reading through her correspondence. 'We need your talents for a few minutes.'

Quickly, Georgina followed him into the drawing room and took her seat at the piano.

'A waltz, please, sister. Something slow.'

Georgina adjusted herself on the piano stool and placed her fingers on the keys, taking a few seconds to decide on a piece before starting to play.

'The waltz is beautiful dance, but considered by some members of society to be a little scandalous,' Alex said softly. 'The gentleman holds his partner much closer than for any other dance, but there still should be no contact except for a hand on the small of the back and the hold on the upper body.'

The waltz was a more intimate dance than many others and right now he was beginning to see how it could be both tantalising and sensual when danced with the right partner.

He placed one arm around Lina's waist and pulled her closer to him. As he watched, her cheeks flushed with colour and her breathing became more shallow. Their bodies were almost touching, but not quite. That sliver of air between them taunted Alex and he wished he could gather Lina tight to his body.

'The steps are simple,' he said into her ear, noting how she shuddered as his breath tickled her neck and not for the first time he wondered how she would react if he placed his lips on the skin just below her earlobe. 'Let me demonstrate. Follow where I lead.'

Gripping her firmly, Alex began to dance. He felt Lina stumble once or twice, her legs brushing against his as she tried to keep up, but after a few rotations around the drawing room he could tell she was picking it up. She was a talented dancer and quick on her feet, so he wasn't surprised when she relaxed in his arms and allowed her body to flow with the music.

'Certainly not unteachable,' Alex murmured in her ear.

She smiled up at him, a smile of pure pleasure, then did something completely unexpected: she closed her eyes. Trusting him completely to guide her around the dance floor, she let herself succumb to the music. Alex was a good dancer—he had never struggled to pick up a new dance or lead a partner in a waltz or a cotillion—but never could he do so with his eyes closed.

Round and round they twirled, Georgina picking up the pace as she saw Lina become more confident, until all too soon, the music ended.

Lina opened her eyes and looked up at him, her mouth ever so slightly open as she caught her breath and her skin glowing from the exertion.

'That was wonderful.'

He had the urge to kiss her, to lean down and cover her lips with his own. His fingers, gripping her waist, ached to roam over her body and explore every inch of her skin. Looking down into her eyes, he could see she felt it, too—that physical pull, the desire for two bodies to come together as one.

'I thought you said you couldn't waltz?' Georgina said.

Quickly they stepped apart and Alex saw the confusion on Lina's face before she turned away.

'I *couldn't* waltz,' Lina said with a shrug. 'What a wonderful dance it is.'

'Some of the older members of society will leave the ballroom when the musicians start to play a waltz, it is considered that controversial.'

'We were barely touching.'

Until today Alex had agreed with Lina, but now he could see how dancing a waltz might inflame a man's desires.

'If we are to win the wager, you need to fill your dance card on the night of the ball. That will mean dancing at least one or two waltzes,' he said. 'But to avoid any hint of scandal it will be better if you dance them with people you have already been introduced to or know well.'

'You?'

'Perhaps for one of them. And Pentworthy for another.'

Lina nodded, biting her lip. Whenever he reminded her of the conditions of the wager she looked nervous, as if anxious not to get anything wrong. He found how much she cared rather endearing and not for the first time marvelled at how much time and effort she was investing to help him.

'You're ready,' Alex declared.

'What for?'

'Your first country dance.' He enjoyed the shocked looks both Lina and his sister gave him. It felt good to surprise people sometimes. 'I've accepted an invitation to the Pottersdown country dance. I'm told it isn't a grand affair, but it will give you ample opportunity to practise the skills you have learnt so far.'

'You are voluntarily going to a country dance?' Georgina asked.

'What is so strange about that?'

Georgina shook her head in disbelief.

'Do you truly think I am ready?'

Alex turned to Lina and saw the worry on her face. She was normally so confident, so sure of herself, but something about his latest suggestion had worried her.

'You're ready. You can dance. You can converse about the weather and other mundane subjects.

You know how to address people correctly. What could go wrong?'

'Do I *have* to converse about mundane subjects?'

He could just imagine her regaling the ladies and gentlemen of the gentry with tales of gypsy life. Although it was tempting to allow her that freedom of speech, he knew it would not help him win his wager.

'Most certainly. That is the only way to blend in with the other debutantes.'

'What if someone asks who I am?'

Alex had considered this question time and time again. Keeping Lina's true identity a secret was vital to his final aim—passing her off as the perfect debutante. No discerning gentleman would ask her to dance if he knew of her background. Equally, he didn't want to lie outright about her origins.

'We shall say you are a family friend and that Georgina and I are sponsoring your first Season.'

Lina nodded, satisfied.

'Lina, dear, we need to decide on your dress,' Georgina gushed. 'I will meet you in your bedroom in just a moment. I need a to have a quick word with my brother first.'

Perhaps not the most subtle way to get rid of Lina, but she didn't seem to mind.

'Careful, Alex,' Georgina said once she was sure they were alone.

'Careful?'

'Lina is a pretty girl.'

'She is.'

'And she's easy to spend time with.'

'Mostly.'

Georgina sighed. 'I am delighted you have started to take an interest in the fairer sex again, Alex, but couldn't you choose someone more appropriate to become closer to?'

'I do love you, Georgina,' Alex said with a grin. 'Nothing is going on with Lina.'

'But you want it to.'

Alex shrugged. He wasn't above lying to his sister, but she must have seen the spark between them as they danced. He didn't think denial was his best policy.

'As a man, I am subject to certain desires. I respond if I hold an attractive woman close. That doesn't mean I would ever act on those desires.'

'I wouldn't want to see her get hurt.'

'I am well aware we are from different stations, different worlds even.'

Georgina laughed. 'Could you imagine the scandal if you decided to marry a gypsy girl?'

Alex stiffened as he realised he and Georgina were talking of completely different things. She was talking of marriage, a lifetime with one woman. All he was contemplating was a few enjoyable months with Lina as his mistress.

'You married a man considered beneath you.'

'I was young and in love. Anyway, Richard and I were only a few rungs apart on the social ladder.'

'I like Lina and I will admit on one or two occasions I have found myself attracted to her, but I also respect her.' Alex realised it was the truth, but a small part of him wondered if that was enough to temper the desire he felt building whenever her hand brushed against his or their bodies swayed together. Alongside that desire was a budding friendship. Not in a long time had he felt able to talk and laugh with anyone like he did Lina. She was witty and sharp, but had a kindness about her that you didn't encounter much amongst the people of the *ton*.

'I'm glad to hear it. I wouldn't want her to get her heart broken. I think she rather likes you, too.'

'What is there not to like?'

Georgina raised her eyebrows but didn't answer, instead she swooped out of the room.

Alex sank on to the piano stool and ran his fingers across the keys, picking out a few notes. He could play the piano proficiently, but he was no master of music like his sister. Too long spent on horseback rather than practising his scales meant he would never be able to play a piece by heart as Georgina just had.

Closing his eyes, he pictured Lina in his arms as they waltzed around the room. It felt right to hold her body so close to his, to feel her fingers gripping his shoulder. Georgina was right, probably nothing good could come out of a liaison with Lina, but it didn't mean his imagination wasn't already building the fantasy in his mind.

Chapter Ten

'I will only be able to dance two, maybe three dances with you,' Alex said as he helped Lina from the carriage. She pulled a face. For the duration of the journey to Pottersdown Alex had been running through the rules and etiquette of a country dance.

'What if you wished to dance only with me and I with you?' Lina asked.

'To dance three dances with the same person causes raised eyebrows and any more than that is verging on scandalous.'

'What if you didn't like a single other person there?'

'Then I wouldn't dance with anyone else, but I still could only dance with you three times.'

'What if…?'

Alex gave her a hard look and Lina fell silent. She'd learnt over the past couple of weeks that there were many rules governing these social situations. It appeared you didn't have to agree with them, but you did have to abide by them.

'Is there any time limit on how long we can converse with one another?' Lina asked.

'No. As your sponsors for the Season, it will be expected that you return to either Georgina or myself in between dances. We can then introduce you to the other attendees.'

'And if no one asks me to dance, I have to be content with just watching?' It seemed unfair to Lina that it was the gentlemen who chose whom they danced with and when, but Alex had assured her there were few quicker ways to disgrace than a lady asking a gentleman to dance.

'You will be asked to dance.'

'You don't know that.'

He frowned at her for a second and then shook his head, but didn't elaborate any further.

The country dance was being held in a large hall in the centre of Pottersdown and their carriage had been forced to stop at the other end of the square due to the large number of people hurrying towards the festivities. As they drew closer, Lina could see the doors of the hall had been thrown open and soft music drifted out into the summer evening. Groups of young women, their arms linked, rushed past Lina and Alex, laughing and talking in excited voices.

'It seems quite the occasion,' Lina commented.

'I suppose many of the young ladies and gentlemen of Pottersdown will never have the opportunity to have a London Season. This will be one of the highlights of the social calendar.'

Whilst Lina had been absorbed in *Debrett's* earlier in the week Alex had explained the difference between the aristocracy and the gentry, and how it was only the ladies and gentlemen of the aristocracy and the very top levels of the gentry who travelled to London every year to partake in the whirlwind of balls, dinner parties and social events for a few months of the year.

'Remember, it is only a month until the first ball of the Season. We will not have many opportunities to practise, so make the most of tonight. Think of this as a rehearsal, so try to fill your dance card and avoid any potentially scandalous situations.'

With her fingers gripping Alex's arm, Lina allowed him to lead her into the hall. Despite the thumping of her heart in her chest, she was excited to finally attend one of these dances and the relaxed, happy atmosphere as they stepped into the hall helped her to let go of the tension she was holding in her shoulders and summon a sunny smile.

'Lord Whitemore and Miss Lock,' Alex said to a man to his left, who promptly announced their names to the room.

Lina wasn't sure if she imagined it, but for a second people seemed to pause in their conversations and glance their way, before quickly trying to make it appear as if nothing unusual had happened.

'You're causing some excitement amongst these country girls,' Lina murmured in Alex's ear. She saw him grin quickly, before adopting a more serious expression. For the first few days of her stay at Whitemore House Lina had doubted if Alex even had a sense of humour, but as she'd got to know him more and more she realised she'd been mistaken. He had a quick, dry wit, which he covered well with a serious expression, so Lina had made it her aim to make him laugh at least once an hour and crack through the sober facade.

'Behave,' he said quietly.

'I wager at least one or two are wondering how they can lure you off into a dark corner and compromise you.'

'I'm not easily lured,' Alex said.

'But easily compromised?'

He shuddered at the thought of being forced into marriage by being caught in a compromising situation, but recovered quickly as they were approached by a middle-aged woman and a gaggle of daughters.

'Lord Whitemore,' the mother gushed. 'How lovely to see you here at our modest little country dance! It was quite the surprise when they announced your name. I don't suppose you remember little old me, but we were introduced at Mr Sotherby's ball a few years ago.'

Lina watched as Alex bowed in greeting. It was clear that he didn't have the slightest idea who this woman standing in front of him was, but he didn't seem fazed at all.

'How lovely to see you again,' he said. 'Are these your daughters? I do not think I've had the pleasure of meeting them.'

'Oh, no, you wouldn't have met them. This is Miss Annabelle Potton, my eldest. And then there is Olivia and Amelia.'

'Miss Potton.' Alex inclined his head in the direction of the eldest. 'Miss Olivia, Miss Amelia.'

Lina wasn't certain which of the younger two

was which, but it was clear Annabelle was the focus of their mother's attention today so it didn't much matter.

'Annabelle loves to dance,' Mrs Potton prompted.

'Indeed?'

'Do you dance, Lord Whitemore?'

Not the most subtle of enquiries, but Lina supposed with three daughters of marriageable age Mrs Potton had long since lost any qualms about being so direct.

'Alas, I am not blessed as one of the world's great dancers,' Alex said. 'If you would excuse me, Mrs Potton, Miss Potton, I think I have spotted my sister and it would be most remiss of me if I failed to greet her.'

Quickly he pulled Lina away.

'Not one of the world's great dancers?' Lina asked as they wove through the crowd.

Alex grinned at her. 'Well, the Miss Pottons don't need to know I'm better at waltzing than the celebrated Monsieur LeBon.'

'You could have asked one of them to dance.'

'You are sounding more like Georgina every day.' He shook his head. 'It starts with a dance, then they suggest a little air or a glass of lemonade together and before you know it they're expecting to be wooed with flowers and poetry.'

'You write poetry?'

'I've never tried, but I can't imagine it would be too difficult.' He paused for a second. 'Her hair was as soft as the finest silk, her skin as pale as a bucket of milk. Her eyes were as dark as a burning coal, her legs as long as a newborn foal.'

'That's truly terrible.'

'I'm sure Miss Potton would swoon if I recited it to her. Would you care to dance?'

Lina felt her heart soar as Alex led her to the dance floor. Already the music was starting as the couples took their places and Lina was infused with the familiar rush of energy as her body started swaying to the beat.

'Follow my lead,' Alex whispered as he positioned her a few paces away from him, in the middle of a line of women. With her eyes locked on his, Lina's pulse began to quicken. There was something sensual about dancing, even when standing a few feet apart amidst a crowd of people. It almost felt as though it were only she and Alex in the room and she wanted to reach out and pull him closer to her.

The dance began and although Lina had never

learnt the steps it was a basic country dance and she picked it up quickly, moving in the same direction as the women on either side of her. As they came together with their partners, Lina felt Alex's strong hands take hers and guide her towards the top of the line, before they came together for their dance through the middle of the couples to the bottom. The music was lively, the pace fast and soon Lina was laughing as the musicians got faster and faster with every couple that came together.

'I never imagined it would be this fun,' she panted as the music finished and Alex took her hand to escort her from the dance floor.

'That *was* fun,' Alex said, although he seemed a little surprised by his comment.

'Do my ears deceive me?' Georgina asked as she hurried over. 'My brother is actually enjoying a social function?'

'I merely commented that the last dance was pleasurable,' Alex grumbled.

'Wonderful.' Georgina clapped her hands. 'Who have you asked to dance next?'

There was a prolonged silence as Alex regarded his sister with raised eyebrows.

'You haven't won the wager yet. I can still pair

you off with eligible young ladies for the next few weeks at least.'

'My sister is under the misguided impression that she can influence who I ask to dance tonight,' Alex said to Lina.

'I don't see why you wouldn't dance every single dance.'

'If it was just about the dancing, then I agree it is an enjoyable way to spend the evening, but the romantic *politics* of asking a young lady to dance discourages many men from doing so.'

'How do you mean?' Lina asked.

'Well, I can ask you to dance without needing to worry about your expectations from me. You are aware my invitation to dance has no romantic undercurrent, but imagine if I danced with just one other young lady tonight.'

'I can't see there would be a problem.'

'People would ask why I had chosen her, was I interested in a courtship? The young lady might come to expect something more than just a dance and then when it didn't materialise she would be disappointed.'

'Then dance with lots of young ladies. No one will expect anything from you if you share out your attentions,' Lina suggested.

'That's what I always tell him,' Georgina added.

'If I suddenly start attending lots of social functions and dancing with all these unattached young ladies, then it will be assumed I am searching for a wife.'

'What is so bad about that?' Lina asked. 'It is only an assumption. You don't actually have to marry anyone.'

Alex shuddered. 'When the word is put out an eligible bachelor is looking to settle down he is besieged by ambitious mothers and dull daughters. I value my peace and my privacy too much.'

'I think you're overthinking this too much,' Lina declared after a moment's consideration.

'Too clever for his own good,' Pentworthy agreed as he wove through the crowds and joined their little group, giving Georgina a kiss on the cheek. 'How lovely you look tonight, Lina. May I have the pleasure of the next dance?'

Although he was rarely at Whitemore House, Lina had warmed to Georgina's husband on the few occasions he had returned from London to spend the evening with them. He was an intelligent man and successful from what Lina had learned from the snippets of conversation she had overheard, but he was very likeable and kind. He wasn't as good a dancer as Alex, but he laughed at himself every time he got a step wrong and kept up a stream of conversation throughout the two dances they danced together.

As they stepped off the dance floor, another man approached, introduced himself and asked Lina to dance. With her confidence growing by the second, Lina agreed. In the dances that followed, she was aware that she would crane her neck every few steps to see if she could catch sight of Alex anywhere in the hall, wishing it was he spinning her around, even while knowing she should be content with the partners she had.

'You seem a little distracted,' her latest partner commented as he escorted her to the edge of the dance floor.

'I'm sorry,' Lina said, turning to look at him properly for the first time. He'd introduced himself as Mr Gillingham, but she didn't know any more about him than his name. She'd been less than the perfect dance partner—although she'd executed the steps with precision she hadn't engaged Mr Gillingham in any small talk and now she felt a little guilty about the neglect. 'I haven't been to many dances before. I suppose I'm a little nervous.'

'Let me get you a drink, then maybe you would like to step outside for some air?'

The suggestion was a welcome one. After nearly an hour of dancing and making small talk, Lina's throat was parched and her head starting to spin. She hesitated for only a second; Alex had warned her about avoiding any situation where she was left alone with a gentleman—it was another way to be the subject of a scandal, but Mr Gillingham seemed friendly and decent and not at all like he was thinking of taking her outside to compromise her. Besides, the doors to the hall had been left open and people were wandering outside all the time.

'That would be lovely.'

They picked up two glasses of lemonade and headed for the door. Outside the air seemed wonderfully cool compared to the stuffiness of the hall and Lina felt immediately revived.

'From your earlier comment, am I to assume this will be your first London Season?' Mr Gillingham asked.

'It will. Al—' Lina caught herself just in time. 'Lord Whitemore and Lady Georgina Pentworthy have been kind enough to sponsor me for the Season.'

'You are a friend of the family?'

'Exactly.'

They strolled arm in arm as they talked, never straying too far from the other couples and groups of people emerging from the hall for a few minutes of air. Lina began to relax as she realised no one was going to expose her as a fraud and allowed herself to enjoy this experience. After these six weeks were up she would be back to her normal life. It would be foolish not to treasure every moment, even if she wished it were Alex by her side instead of Mr Gillingham.

'Please excuse me,' Alex said, flashing the four young women gathered around him a sunny smile. 'It has been a pleasure to meet you all.'

Before any of the women could protest Alex strode away, parting the crowds with his determined expression and quick pace. The evening hadn't been terrible, but the last hour hadn't been fun, either. He'd been abandoned first by Lina and then by Georgina and her husband, left to the mercy of the ladies of Pottersdown. Not that he couldn't protect himself from the gaggles of young women—he'd had plenty of practice at balls and dinner parties over the years—but it was a little tedious all the same.

Glancing around the hall as he reached the area that had been allocated to be the dance floor, Alex frowned. The past hour, throughout the conversations and introductions, he had managed to keep one eye fixed on Lina. As he'd predicted, she'd been asked to dance by a procession of young men and seemed to be having a great time. He'd known she wouldn't struggle to fill her dance card—Lina was attractive and vivacious, and men were drawn to her confidence and her beguiling smile—but she had followed his rules and not danced more than twice with the same man. Last time he had glanced her way she had been smiling at a smartly dressed young man as he led her from the dance floor, then they had disappeared.

With a growl of frustration Alex spun around slowly and searched the hall. There were swarms of people, mostly organised in little groups, but he had the advantage of being at least a head taller than most of them so could peruse the room quite easily. After a minute Alex was certain Lina wasn't there, which meant she had stepped outside with her latest dance partner.

Quickly he pushed his way to the door, feeling

the cool breeze as he left the hall. The occupants had spilled out into the town square and if Lina and her escort were out here amongst the other guests, there would be no impropriety, but Alex felt his muscles tense all the same.

He saw them underneath a tree in the middle of the square. Lina was laughing in the carefree, light-hearted way that Alex liked so much, although now it was directed at this other man it made him want to storm over and pull her away.

'Alex.'

He spun, surprised to hear the familiar voice behind him. 'Victoria.'

'I didn't realise you would be here.'

He shrugged. It was a fair assumption to make, he didn't normally attend country dances.

'Did your husband accompany you?' Alex asked, his eyes straying past Victoria to where Lina was perched. Had he seen her sway a little closer to her escort?

'No.' A moment's hesitation. 'He stayed in Hampshire.'

Alex wondered if he sensed there might be a strain in their relationship, but then realised he did not want to know. Once Victoria's pain would have been his pain, but she'd chosen her path, pushed him away and he had come to terms with it. Now he did not want to know if her marriage was a happy one. They were not friends and they never would be.

He heard Lina's laugh again and stepped forward.

'I'm keeping you from Miss Lock,' Victoria said, a hint of sadness in her voice, placing her hand on his arm.

Alex stopped and saw her look up at him hopefully.

'Please excuse me, Victoria. I hope you have a pleasant evening.'

Swiftly he walked away, closing the gap between him and Lina within a few seconds. She was turned half-away from him, but seemed to sense as he approached, stiffening and the laughter dying on her lips.

'Lord Whitemore,' she greeted him formally. Although she'd been doing nothing wrong Alex could see a hint of guilt in her expression.

'I was worried, Miss Lock,' Alex said.

'I never wished to cause alarm.' Lina's companion stood and turned to Alex. 'I am Mr Gillingham, it is a pleasure to make your acquaintance, Lord Whitemore.'

Alex gave a stiff nod of greeting before turning back to Lina.

'Come, it is time we left.'

'But it is still early.'

'You will thank me for the early night in the morning.'

'Can we not...?' The question died on her lips as she met his eye and instead she turned to Mr Gillingham. 'Thank you for a most pleasurable evening, Mr Gillingham,' she said sweetly. 'I very much enjoyed our time together.'

Alex knew she was just doing it to annoy him, but he could hardly suppress the growl in his throat when Lina fluttered her eyelashes at the young gentleman. As she placed her hand on his forearm, Alex started to stride away, forcing her to almost run to keep up.

'What a lovely gentleman,' Lina mused. 'So polite.'

Alex grunted.

'He is a keen rider. Goes out with the hunt every month.'

'Enough about Mr Gillingham.'

'I think tomorrow we need to work on your manners, Alex,' Lina said primly.

They walked back to the hall in silence and spent

ten minutes trying to navigate the crowd whilst searching for Georgina and her husband. Throughout their search Lina walked passively by his side, but he could sense she would tell him exactly what was on her mind when they were in private.

'Enough,' Alex declared when they still hadn't found Georgina after two laps of the crowded hall. 'Home.'

'You've been reduced to sentences comprising of just a single word,' Lina observed.

Ignoring her comments as they made their way to his carriage, Alex tried to let some of the simmering feelings go, but found it was almost impossible. Seeing Lina enjoying herself with Mr Gillingham had made him feel something he hadn't felt for a very long time: jealousy. He'd wanted to storm over and snatch her away and keep her all to himself. It was ridiculous—Lina wasn't his to covet. In four weeks' time she would be out of his life and moving on with her family. And he would be... Well, his life would return to normal. Once he'd won the wager he could concentrate on what was really important: training his racehorses.

'*I* was the model of propriety this evening,' Lina declared as he helped her up into the carriage.

'And I?' Alex asked, raising an eyebrow as he

settled into the seat beside her. It was a snug fit and Lina had to wriggle over a little to make room.

'You were rude.'

'Forgive me?'

She huffed, then looked at him slyly. 'Were you jealous?'

'Of Mr Gillingham?'

'You certainly acted as though you were jealous.'

'I acted as any responsible sponsor would on finding the young lady they were chaperoning had disappeared outside with an unknown man.'

'There were plenty of couples outside.'

'Has anyone ever told you that you're exceedingly argumentative?'

'Has anyone ever told you you're arrogant and self-important?' Lina countered.

'My sister tells me most days.' Alex smiled. 'I take it as a compliment.'

Lina exhaled sharply as if biting her tongue and turned towards the window. Although he'd never admit it out loud he'd begun to like how argumentative she was, how she was never afraid of voicing her opinion. It might make their relationship a little more fiery, but underneath that it was a testament to how much she cared about what they were doing, how she had started to care for him.

That was a hundred times more valuable than an easy life.

The ensuing silence gave Alex a chance to study her profile; the soft lips, round cheeks and thick, shiny hair. It would be so easy to turn her to face him and kiss her. He didn't think she'd protest, he'd seen the way she responded when their hands touched or when he held her to dance. Perhaps he should allow himself this one pleasure. He'd held himself so tightly, been so strict for so long. Maybe it was time to start indulging in a little of what he desired again.

Chapter Eleven

The room was warm despite the wide-open window and it was a relief when Lina was able to slip out of her dress and let her body breathe. She was clad in a variety of petticoats and a thin chemise, which Georgina had assured her were absolutely necessary under her dress. Although she was tired, and a part of her just wanted to flop down on to the bed, she felt unusually restless and knew she wouldn't be able to sleep.

Bending down to slip off the silky petticoats, Lina heard a creak behind her and spun quickly, her arms flying up to protect herself.

'Hush,' Uncle Tom said as he advanced from the shadows.

Lina backed away. Tom was a relative, her father's uncle, but that didn't mean he'd ever been kind or sentimental about their bond. He was here now for a reason and by the cruel glint in his eyes Lina didn't think it was anything positive.

'You've been a very naughty girl, Lina,' Tom said, stalking towards her, his hand hovering just above his waistband as if suggesting he had a weapon tucked away just out of sight.

'I've still got two weeks to get you your money,' Lina protested.

'You have.'

The hard plaster of the wall behind her pressed against her back and Lina glanced around the room, searching for something to protect herself with.

'But you have broken the second part of our deal.'

Lina knew very well she was supposed to have let Tom know when the house was empty. The country dance was just the opportunity her uncle was waiting for to strike and she'd deliberately let the occasion slip by.

'I wasn't sure if Mr Pentworthy was going to ac-company us all to the dance or stay here until the very last moment,' Lina said with a shrug, trying to project a bravado that she didn't feel. 'Anyway, you've got in here without my help, you could easily be helping yourself to the valuables downstairs now instead of threatening me.'

'There's one slight problem with that,' Tom said, stepping closer so there was now only a foot between them. Lina refused to cower backwards, but couldn't help but flinch as Tom's breath hit her face. 'I need money, not goods.'

Lina frowned. Tom had never been particular before about what he stole: money, valuables, jewellery—it was all the same to him.

'Why?'

'What does it matter to you why? You need to find out where your toff keeps his money and then inform me when the house will be empty.'

It didn't make sense. Tom could have stolen a few silver candlesticks in the time he'd been up here threatening her. Understanding slowly dawned.

'You've been caught, haven't you?' Lina asked. 'The magistrates have got their eye on you and if they find you with any more stolen goods, you'll hang. Money can't be easily traced.'

'Never you mind,' Tom said, but Lina could tell she had come to the correct conclusion. No wonder Tom had been pushing Raul to move on to a different county—he wanted to be somewhere he wouldn't be known. 'I'm giving you one last chance, Lina. Find out where he keeps the money and sort out an opportunity for me to get my hands on it.'

There was a desperation in Tom's eyes and Lina wondered what other trouble Tom had got himself into. He'd always been a greedy, thieving scoundrel, but he wouldn't normally risk breaking into a titled gentleman's house to make a little money.

'Is it worth the risk?' Lina asked softly.

Fury flashed in Tom's eyes. 'I don't need any judgement from a whore like you.'

Holding her hands out in a placating manner, Lina tried to move farther away, but she was hemmed in by furniture and her back was firmly up against the cold wall.

'I need some payment for your debt now,' he said, his voice low.

'I've got two more weeks until the deadline.'

'The deadline has changed.'

Quickly Lina whipped the silver comb from her hair. It wasn't expensive enough to cover all her debt, but it was a start.

'Take this.' She offered the comb.

Tom hesitated. 'It's not enough and I need money, not trinkets,' he said eventually.

Without hesitation Lina launched herself forward, screamed as loud as her lungs would allow and plunged the teeth of the comb into Tom's arm. Raul had taught her to act fast and never look back if being attacked, and it had served Lina well over the years.

Tom shouted in pain and anger, lashing out, but Lina was too quick for him, ducking under his swinging arms and rushing for the door. Footsteps in the corridor made Tom falter, but as the door crashed open he dived for the window and threw himself out.

Lina kept running, her body careening into Alex's solid form, and immediately she felt his arms around her.

'What happened? Are you hurt?' Alex asked, tilting her chin up so he could examine her face.

'There was a man,' Lina said breathlessly. 'He jumped out of the window.'

Alex darted over to the window and peered out.

'Is he there?' Lina asked.

'Across the lawn,' Alex shouted, directing the two footmen who had just arrived in the room to chase after the intruder. Turning back to Lina, he took her in his arms. 'Did he hurt you?'

She shook her head. The sensible thing to do would be to tell Alex everything: Uncle Tom's identity, his plans to involve her in his scheme to steal Alex's money, the hold he had over her. But looking up at the concern etched on Alex's face, she knew she couldn't. He'd throw her out, assume she was just the same as her criminally minded relative and Lina wasn't ready to leave yet. Soon it would be time to bid Alex and this life goodbye, but she would do anything she could to have a few more weeks, a few more days even.

It was almost laughable, given her views on the aristocracy before she'd met Alex. She hated their superiority, their customs, the need for everything to be ordered and structured. She hated the way they used and discarded the lower classes, hated how not everyone was created equal. Alex was doing the same with her. He was using her to win a wager, just as he might a horse, and after he had won she would be discarded. She knew all this, but still she didn't want her time in Whitemore House to end.

For the first time in ten years she was starting to understand how her father had felt. There was something captivating about Alex that made her wish for one more dance, one more ride together. Even though Lina knew nothing could ever hap-

156 An Unlikely Debutante

pen between them, nothing meaningful anyway, she couldn't stop the fantasy building in her mind.

'What did he want?' Alex asked.

'I don't know. He just appeared.'

Carefully, as if she were made of delicate silk, Alex led her to the bed and sat her down, positioning himself beside her and taking her hand. He didn't seem to be aware of her state of undress, but the concern in his eyes made her heart leap. Behind the wall he had erected to shield his heart from any further pain was a caring and loving man. She loved how he had stayed to check she was safe instead of chasing after the intruder as many men would. He recognised the comfort she got from his presence and quietly gave her exactly what she needed in that moment. It was hard not to find herself falling for him, just a little.

'You're safe now,' he reassured her. 'No one will hurt you.'

'Stay with me,' Lina whispered as she closed her eyes and laid her head on Alex's shoulder.

'I'm not going anywhere.'

It was funny how something could be pure torture and pure bliss all at the same time, Alex mused. The light was just starting to filter through the gap in the curtains, heralding the start of another beautiful summer's day. Alex hadn't slept all night after Lina had alerted him to the intruder in her bedroom, then asked him to stay with her. For a while they had just sat in silence, Alex's arm draped around her shoulders, her head resting in the crook of his elbow. Their positioning was too close and there was an intimacy between them as they sat propped together on the bed, but Alex could see nothing was further from Lina's mind than seduction.

It was just him who found the warmth from her skin and the gentle, sleepy movements of her body against his almost too much to bear.

'Good morning,' Alex murmured as Lina opened her eyes and looked up at him with a sleepy smile.

The fact that she did not leap to her feet and start spouting some nonsense about the impropriety of them spending the night together highlighted the difference between Lina and most women of his acquaintance. Lina could acknowledge nothing scandalous had happened between them and for her that was enough.

'I'm sorry I fell asleep on you.'

'I didn't mind.' To his surprise Alex found it was the truth. He hadn't slept at all, his muscles were stiff and his arms aching from holding Lina up-right all night, but he realised he wouldn't swap a good night's sleep for the time he had spent with Lina.

Careful, he told himself. Georgina was right, nothing of substance could happen between him and Lina. It would be better not to let the desire he felt deep inside creep up to the surface. Even worse was the tenderness he was experiencing as he watched Lina stretch and wake up. Desire was one thing, but a deeper connection was an entirely other matter, one that he needed to shut down immediately. Already in the past few days he had caught himself smiling whenever Lina came into a room, seeking her out to ask her opinion on something he had just read or saying something controversial to prolong a conversation and hear the passion in her voice as she spoke. Every day he found out something new about her that he admired: her inquisitive nature, her ability to laugh at herself, her shrewd understanding of how far she could delve into the details of his past. Right now he didn't want to contemplate the time when the wager was over and Lina would leave his house and his life for good.

'I've been thinking about the intruder,' Alex said,

trying to steer himself on to a safer subject. He noticed how Lina dropped her gaze and scrunched her hands into the bedsheets as he brought up the subject of the mysterious intruder. 'It seems strange he was in this part of the house and not downstairs, where most of the valuables are kept. Are you sure he didn't say anything to you?'

Last night he hadn't pushed her too hard with questions—he'd seen she was upset and reasoned she wouldn't have much information to give anyway, but in the long hours he'd spent mulling over the events of the night before, he had realised that a few things didn't make sense.

Lina shook her head. 'He just appeared from the shadows and rushed at me. I had just taken my comb from my hair so I stabbed at him with that and screamed. That's when he dived for the window.'

It was exactly the same story, exactly the same words she'd used as the night before.

'And you didn't recognise him?'

Again Lina glanced away as she shook her head and fiddled with the sheets. There was something she wasn't telling him, but he couldn't work out what.

He could interrogate her, but what would be the

point? Whoever it was had made his escape and pressing Lina for information she did not want to give would just jeopardise his relationship with her. He'd find out eventually what had happened. It was just a case of letting the dust settle before he asked the more probing questions.

'I will tell the servants to be vigilant and ensure there is always someone downstairs, even at night.'

'Thank you.'

'I'll leave you to rise and see you at breakfast. It is Georgina's last morning with us, she's leaving at midday to return home.'

'I will join you downstairs shortly,' Lina said.

Alex glanced back as he reached the door. She looked so small and forlorn sitting on the bed, hugging her knees, that he had the urge to return and sweep her into his arms, but reason won and instead he walked out of the room and closed the door firmly behind him.

Chapter Twelve

'Do you have to leave?' Lina asked, hugging the other woman tightly.

'I wish I didn't, but I need to return home before we travel to London for the Season. Alex will look after you and I shall be seeing you in a few weeks.'

'It's been a pleasure,' Alex said, kissing his sister on her cheeks, 'and an ordeal of course.'

'Pish-posh. You've barely noticed I'm here. You spent more time with those horses of yours than with me.'

Despite her words Georgina hugged her brother tightly and Lina could see the tears in her eyes as she pulled away.

They walked out to the waiting carriage, and as Alex helped his sister up, Lina saw her bend down and whisper something in his ear. She was too far away to hear all Georgina said, but she did hear the last words.

Be careful.

A knot formed in Lina's stomach. Surely they couldn't know the truth about the intruder last night, or the awful bargain she had made with Uncle Tom that would have her betraying Alex when Tom called in the debt?

'Goodbye,' Georgina called as the carriage lurched away, waving from the window.

'Peace at last,' Alex said with a grin.

'You'll miss her.'

'Don't ever tell her that.'

'What are we going to work on today?' Lina asked as they strolled back into the house.

'How to avoid scandal in the ballroom. We only have a month until the first ball of the Season, and to win the wager there can be no hint of scandal surrounding you.'

Smiling, she rolled her eyes. 'My behaviour last night was not scandalous.'

'It could have been. If Mr Gillingham had suggested walking a little farther from the crowds, would you?'

Lina considered the question. Strolling arm in arm with a gentleman did not seem scandalous to her, even if you were alone. The problem only came if the gentleman in question tried to force something that she did not want, but Lina had years of experience extricating herself from those sorts of scenarios. In her world, a woman was expected to keep faithful to her husband, but there wasn't this need to be completely separate from the opposite sex until marriage. Lina had often been left alone with the men of her acquaintance and nothing was thought of it.

'If nothing happens between a woman and a man when they are alone together, why is it an issue?' she asked.

'You only have the couple's word that nothing happened.'

'Suspicious lot, aren't you?'

'If you are brought up with these rules, they don't seem so ridiculous.'

'I don't understand why you wouldn't want to spend some time alone with someone if you are considering spending the rest of your life with them.'

'Marriage between members of the *ton* is a very peculiar affair,' Alex said, staring off into the distance. 'You have to remember that most of the time love or affection doesn't factor in a match. Marriages are about social elevation, money and connections.'

'I can't imagine spending my life with someone I didn't at least care for a little.'

A relationship had never been very high on Lina's list of priorities. None of the men she travelled with were remotely interesting to her, and after seeing her mother's heartbreak at the hands of her father Lina was wary of giving away so much of herself. Quickly she glanced at Alex. She couldn't deny the attraction she felt for him and he was a man she could see herself falling for, but even the idea was ridiculous. Men like Alex did not do anything more than dally with women like her. Any other notion was pure fantasy and Lina knew she had to abandon it before she got carried away.

Alex shrugged. 'I suppose it depends what you want out of a marriage. Many married couples live completely separate lives, sometimes even in separate houses. They do their duty, produce the heirs, then carry on as they did before they were married.'

'That wasn't how it was for you and Victoria,' Lina said quietly.

'No.' There was a long pause and after a while Lina thought he would say nothing more. 'I cared for Victoria and look where that got me. Maybe

there is something to marrying for mutual benefit, not love.'

Lina felt her heart sink at his words. Alex was a
kind man, a good man, he deserved a future filled
with happiness and she could not see how a loveless marriage could make anyone happy.

She opened her mouth to protest, to try to argue
a case for love matches, but Alex had already left
her, stalking off through the house into his study
and closing the door firmly after him, their lesson
for the day apparently forgotten.

Lina prowled through the downstairs rooms,
trying to find something to occupy herself with.
Eventually she settled into one of the comfortable
leather armchairs in the library, a stack of books
by her side. She opened the first and tried to concentrate on the words, but found she was reading
each sentence two or three times and it still wasn't
going in.

'Silly man,' she murmured to herself. Alex might
think he was unaffected by the sudden appearance of his ex-fiancée, but his reactions suggested
otherwise. He had loved Victoria very much, that
was apparent, and Georgina had confirmed that
he'd been devastated when his fiancée had called
off the wedding and left to marry his best friend.

No one could go through such heartbreak and be completely unmoved the next time they saw the woman they used to love, not even someone as strong as Alex.

She also hated the way he was talking about marriage, about the benefits of taking love out of the equation. Lina might only have known Alex for a few weeks, but she could see such a union would only make him unhappy. Seeing the sag in his shoulders and frown on his face made her want to shake him, to grab him by the arms and shout and scream that just because he had been hurt once didn't mean he couldn't love again.

'A happy man is a reasonable man,' Lina said out loud, one of her mother's phrases popping into her head. If she could distract him from his worries, take him out and cheer him up, then he would be in a better frame of mind to be challenged on his views of marriage. There was a chance she could just plant the seed that one day he might be ready to love again, because she couldn't bear the thought of him being unhappy for ever.

Slowly she replaced the book on the top of the pile and stood, gazing out over the beautiful gardens illuminated by brilliant sunshine. August was almost over, but every day the weather seemed more glorious than the last. Perhaps she could provide the distraction Alex needed and get to spend the day out in the fresh air rather than cooped up learning how not to disgrace herself in the ballroom.

Before she could change her mind, Lina hurried out of the library and downstairs to the kitchens. It was like a maze underneath the house, corridors running for what seemed like miles in different directions, nooks and crannies filled with mops and buckets and assorted cleaning equipment. Lina had ventured downstairs a couple of times, but had received a cold reception from most of the staff. She knew her encounter with the butler on her first day at Whitemore House would have been exaggerated and retold many times until she was a rude gypsy criminal, out to con and deceive their beloved master.

With her head held high and her expression flinty, Lina entered the huge kitchen. The cook and a solitary kitchen maid were kneading dough, whilst Jim, the young lad who did the odd jobs around the house, was lugging bags of flour from one side of the big room to the other. For the size of the house Alex had relatively few servants, but Georgina had explained that he rarely entertained and as such only needed the bare minimum for himself and his infrequent guests.

'Can I help you, Miss Lock?' the cook asked, after eyeing Lina suspiciously for a few seconds.

'I would like a picnic packed for this afternoon. Lord Whitemore and myself are going for a ride out and will not be back for the midday meal.'

'This is the first I've heard of it.'

Lina smiled sweetly. 'I'm sure it is, we only decided a few minutes ago.'

'What about the beef I've got in for lunch?' the cook asked stubbornly.

'I could put it back in the cold storage, Mrs Witherly,' the eager, young kitchen maid suggested.

The cook uttered a noise that was halfway between a sigh and a growl.

'I've got this dough to see to,' the cook said, kneading the floury lump with her reddened fists. 'And now you want me to make up a picnic, as well?'

'I'm happy to do it, Mrs Witherly,' the kitchen maid said, flashing Lina a conspiratorial smile.

'No, you've got your work to see to.'

'Lord Whitemore will be disappointed,' Lina said, turning as if to leave. The cook and other senior staff might dislike her, but they were devoted to their young master and never wanted to disappoint or inconvenience him.

'I suppose I could put together a few cold cuts and some bread,' Mrs Witherly said slowly.

'Thank you.'

Before the cook could change her mind, Lina left the kitchen and hurried back upstairs. Now came the difficult part—persuading Alex that they could take time away from practising polite conversation and forms of address to go on a ride to lift his spirits.

With a groan Alex stretched his neck from side to side, feeling the crack at the extremes of movement and the wonderful release that came afterwards. The pile of papers in front of him hadn't seemed to have diminished at all and for once he couldn't concentrate on the intricacies of running the large estate. He also had Mr Tobias Tomlinson visiting tomorrow to discuss which horses to enter into which races over the coming year and to go over the jockeys he had hired. Tomlinson was a talented horseman and was better at picking out a winning racehorse than anyone else Alex knew. He worked solely for Alex and together they made a formidable partnership in the horseracing world.

Normally he would be excited by the prospect of planning out the racing calendar, but this morning he couldn't get the discussion with Lina about marriage from his head.

He knew he was likely never to marry. He'd gone down that path before and it had led to heartbreak and destruction. If he did ever decide to find a wife, it would not be a love match. Desire and a little affection were fine feelings for a mistress, but they were not enough to base such a momentous decision on.

Still, he felt unsettled by the conversation. Once he had been so idealistic. He'd been determined not to follow his peers into loveless marriages, certain that there was more to life than seeking a wife with the largest dowry. This loss of innocence pained him.

'Can I come in?' Lina asked. She moved so quietly sometimes that he was surprised to see her holding the door half-open.

'I've got some papers to finish dealing with,' Alex said. It was true, although he doubted he would make any useful decisions whilst he was in this mood.

'I'm sorry if I said something to upset you earlier. Sometimes I speak before I think through what I'm saying. Raul always tells me I need a filter as the words come out of my mouth.'

'Nothing to apologise for,' Alex said.

'Good.'

Far from retreating from the room, as had been Alex's intention when he'd given his curt reply, Lina almost skipped over to his desk, skirted around the large wooden piece of furniture and perched on the edge just a foot away from him.

'I have a request,' she said, her eyes shining.

He waited for her to proceed, feeling his mood lifting a little already. It was difficult to stay gloomy with Lina grinning at him.

'I have been working very hard these last two and a half weeks,' she said, pausing as if daring him to contradict her. 'So much so that I was able to attend a country dance and not cause a scandal.'

Alex felt the smile dance on his lips and quickly fought to maintain his sober expression. 'That is true,' he conceded.

'As a reward, I thought we might take those lovely horses of yours out for a ride.'

Alex glanced out of the window. It was beautifully sunny, the sort of day that was made for riding through the countryside, not sitting in a stuffy study.

'I do have rather a lot of work to do.'

'It'll be waiting for you when we return.'

'Aunt Lucy should be arriving this evening, there are things that I need to prepare for her stay.'

'Delegate. You're good at that.'

'We need to ensure you are ready for the ball in London.'

'That's weeks away and I'll work doubly hard tomorrow. Give me this one afternoon.'

'It *is* a lovely day,' Alex said and was rewarded by Lina launching herself at him.

'Be ready to leave in half an hour,' she instructed. 'I will sort out everything else.'

Chapter Thirteen

Already Lina could see Alex's spirits lifting as they saddled up the horses and checked the animals over prior to their ride.

'I'm sure there's a riding habit of Georgina's somewhere in the house,' Alex said, studying her as she swished her skirts out of the way of Stormborn's dancing hooves.

'Why on earth would I want to wear one of those restrictive garments?'

'It'll make it easier to ride.'

Lina stared at him with raised eyebrows. 'Have you ever ridden in one?'

'Of course not.'

'Me, neither, but I think they are designed for ladies who ride side-saddle.'

Lina gathered up the brightly coloured material of her skirts as she led Stormborn out into the yard. She'd changed back into her everyday outfit, a plain white blouse on top with a skirt made of a mix of materials below, all brightly coloured and attractive to the eye. It was comfortable and practical and Lina was used to riding horses in it.

She felt Alex come up behind her, sensed his body just a few inches from hers and realised she was holding her breath. More and more this was happening; her body would react to his closeness even though her mind knew nothing could ever develop between the two of them.

Carefully he boosted her up, helping her to arrange her skirts once she was in the saddle, his fingers brushing against her thigh and making her shiver with anticipation, but of course it was an accident and as quickly as the contact had begun it was over.

'Let him lead,' Alex counselled as Lina loosened her grip on the reins. 'He's a headstrong horse who runs better when you give him a bit of freedom.'

Alex mounted, vaulting up on to a large black stallion as if it were no more effort than hopping over a muddy puddle. It was incredible what strength and agility riding horses could build; Alex had immense physical strength mainly due to his time training the racehorses in his stables.

They set off, riding in a companionable silence for a while. It took a few minutes for Lina to get used to Stormborn's long stride, but soon she was sitting comfortably and ready to increase the pace.

'Shall we race?'

Alex looked around him for some landmark to race to. 'First one to that copse of trees?'

It was easily half a mile away, a good distance to test out both the horses and riders.

'What are the stakes?' Lina asked. She knew she should know better than to enter a wager whilst on horseback, but with the sun on her face and the wind in her hair she felt carefree and daring.

'If I win, then you show me your tattoo.'

Lina stiffened. 'What makes you think I have a tattoo?'

'I caught a glimpse of it when you first arrived and hitched your skirts up to vault over the partition in the stable.'

Alex was grinning and Lina felt herself blushing.

'Ladies don't have tattoos,' she said as primly as she could. 'Only soldiers and seamen mark their bodies like that.'

'If I win, you show me your tattoo,' Alex repeated firmly.

'And if I win, you let me ride your Arabian.'

'Deal.'

Before Alex could beat her to the start Lina spurred Stormborn on, encouraging him into a gallop up the gentle incline. She leaned forward as the majestic animal sailed over a low hedge, not slowing as the climb became steeper. Behind her she could hear the thundering of Alex's horse, but Lina didn't dare look back. The copse of trees was close now, only a hundred feet away, and for a moment Lina thought she might just beat Alex, but suddenly he was past her, his eyes focused on his destination, the wind lifting his hair and making his shirt billow.

There were only a few seconds between them, but Alex was the indisputable winner.

'I wonder what a gypsy girl would have tattooed on her leg?' he mused as they allowed the horses to slow to a leisurely walk.

Lina ignored him, knowing she would have to show him the tattoo she'd had done at the tender age of fourteen when her family had visited the port town of Southampton. The idea of lifting her skirt up over her legs to reveal the patch of skin high on her thigh wouldn't normally faze her, but knowing it would be Alex's eyes travelling over her bare skin made her hot with anticipation.

'Are we still on your estate?' Lina asked, eyeing the rolling countryside that stretched out before them. They hadn't come across any wall or boundary, but she couldn't imagine all this land could belong to one person.

'The estate stretches another two miles west,' Alex said, pointing in the direction they were travelling. 'Most of the land to the south and east is farmland, but out to the west it is undeveloped and natural.'

'How can one person own so much?' Lina murmured quietly.

'When so many own so little?'

She glanced at him to see if he was irritated by her question, but there was no anger or annoyance on his face.

'When I first inherited, it took me a while to appreciate just what owning an estate such as this one meant,' he said, looking out into the distance. 'Most people see money and riches, fine clothes, fine houses when they think of the aristocracy, but running an estate is so much more than that.'

Lina remained quiet, she could see this was a subject he was passionate about and wanted to hear what he had to say. She loved listening to him talk, hearing the conviction in his voice, and she appreciated how persuasive he could be in an argument.

'I provide work for two hundred people, either directly or indirectly. I own many of the houses in the village and have the responsibility of maintaining them whilst keeping the rents low enough for people to afford. My farms are a reliable source of crops for the local area and the dairy at Home Farm is the largest in the county.'

It was impressive. She wondered how one man kept on top of it all.

'Over the years I've seen how people who own less, who have less money or property or livestock, look at me, but I always ask how they would fare with this responsibility. Yes, I live in a fine house and wear fine clothes, but I also provide jobs and homes and sustenance for so many, as well.'

'You speak so passionately,' Lina said quietly. 'I admire that.'

Alex looked at her, holding her gaze for a long few seconds, and Lina found she was unable to look away. Every day she spent in Alex's company she found out something about him that made her like him more and more. She'd realised long ago that the facade of boredom he'd projected at the Pottersdown Village Fair when they'd first met was

just that: a facade. Underneath that was a passionate, caring, driven man. It was hard not to admire
him, probably a little more than she should.

'Here's the perfect spot,' Alex said, indicating
an area under the shade of a tree with views down
to the shimmering lake below. Quickly he slipped
to the ground, secured his horse and then turned
back to Lina. Before she could begin to dismount
his hands were around her waist, lifting her off
the horse and to the ground as if she weighed no
more than a bale of straw.

There was a vice-like pressure around her chest
as Alex's hands lingered on her waist for a second
longer than was necessary, then he turned away
and the contact was lost. Trying to distract herself, Lina spread out the blanket under the tree,
smoothing out the wrinkles until it provided a soft
and comfortable place to sit. Alex was rummag-
ing through the saddle bags, assessing the picnic
Mrs Witherly, the cook, had provided.

'You're so nosy,' Lina said, jostling him to one
side and taking the bags from him.

'I've yet to meet a man who isn't interested in the
contents of his next meal,' Alex said with a shrug.

Taking her time, with Alex hovering over her,
Lina set out the feast. Despite her initial reluc-

tance to make up the picnic, the cook had evidently not wanted to disappoint her employer. There was enough food for six people, all beautifully packed and smelling delicious.

'For two and a half weeks I've lived your life-style,' Lina said as she finished laying the last of the food out. 'Now you are going to spend the afternoon as a gypsy.'

Alex kicked off his boots and sat down, resting his back against the trunk of the tree.

'If I'd known you feasted so well, I'd have run off to join a group of travelling gypsies years ago,' he said, tucking in to a slice of meat pie.

'This afternoon is not all about the food,' Lina said, grinning as Alex eyed her suspiciously.

'You're not going to whip a fiddle from the saddlebags, are you? Or make me carve a chest of drawers?'

'We have a rich and varied culture, and all you know about us is that many of our men are talented carpenters and we like music.'

'That's not true,' Alex said, biting into a radish. 'I know gypsies hail from all over Europe and farther East. I know music and dancing is important to your culture, and that you move about the country, staying in each place for a few weeks to a few months at a time.'

'Impressive,' Lina said, her voice dripping with sarcasm.

'Educate me. Tell me something about your people that I wouldn't know.'

Lina considered for some moments. Her heritage was truly mixed, with her mother being of Spanish descent and her father coming from one of the oldest gypsy families in Europe. He used to boast he could trace his ancestry back to the original Romani people. His family had been travelling through Europe for centuries and her father had visited twelve different countries in his lifetime.

It was hard to put any of that into words, hard to describe the sense of belonging, the sense of being part of something much bigger.

'Do you know what my favourite part of our lifestyle is?' Lina asked eventually.

Alex shook his head, leaning forward as he waited for her to answer.

'Sleeping under the stars.'

'The idea is appealing, but I would have thought the reality less attractive. I can see how it might be enjoyable in the balmy summer months, but I can't think of many nights in winter I would give

up my snug bed to sleep in the freezing temperatures and buffeting winds.'

'Lying in the open, looking up at the skies, seeing the stars twinkling in the darkness, that is what
I enjoy most about my life.'

'What if it rains?'

'In the summer we often will just shelter beneath
our carts...' Lina paused, wondering whether to
open up to Alex further. Over the last few weeks
she had gleaned a lot of information about his life,
picking up various facts and anecdotes from different people, but he didn't know all that much
about hers. He'd asked the odd question and she'd
told him the bare bones of the story of what had
happened to her mother and father, but any further details she had kept close. She supposed the
secrecy came from her expectations of other people. Throughout her life she'd been shunned and
looked down upon because of her roots, so she'd
learnt to keep a lot to herself.

'When I was young my mother used to point
out all the stars to me,' Lina said eventually. 'She
said that was how we stayed connected with our
kin from around the world. Each star represented
a member of our family, so I only had to look up
at the night sky to know wherever I was in the

world, there were thousands of my kin looking down on me.'

'That's a lovely sentiment,' Alex said.

Glancing sideways at him, Lina was relieved to see the serious expression on his face. It had been difficult to share such an intimate detail about her life, but Alex hadn't laughed or ridiculed her. She liked that he knew when to be serious, just as he knew when a little humour was needed for light relief.

'Of course we don't sleep outside much in winter,' Lina rushed on. 'Often Raul will negotiate a spot in a barn if the men are doing some farm work. I don't think I've ever had to sleep outside in the snow.'

'Good,' Alex said. 'I don't want to be worrying about you the next time we have a frost.'

For a while they ate in silence, enjoying the feast Mrs Witherly had packed and the beautiful views. The afternoon was unusually hot, even for August, and even in the shade of the tree Lina could feel her skin glowing with heat and moisture.

Already bootless, Alex soon loosened and discarded his jacket and cravat, and Lina knew he would have shed his shirt if she were not present. At the thought Lina felt her cheeks blush and hoped the soaring temperatures were enough of an explanation for the sudden flushing.

'What else have you got planned for our afternoon of gypsy life?' Alex asked as he finished his meal, leaning back against the tree trunk and closing his eyes.

'I hadn't planned an afternoon nap,' Lina said, nudging him with her foot. 'Perhaps a dip in the lake?'

As she'd expected, this suggestion had Alex's eyes shooting open.

'It would be rather refreshing,' he said slowly.

Lina stood, ignoring the pounding of her heart as she looked down at the shimmering water of the lake. She'd swam in plenty of lakes in her lifetime—in her mind it was the best way to cool down after a long day's work. Normally she would swim with her cousin Sabina and some of the other young girls. Then they would strip down to their undergarments and dive into the water without any inhibitions, but never had she swam with a man and certainly not a man she found as attractive as Alex.

Before she could change her mind, and without looking to see if Alex was following her, Lina set off down the hill towards the cool water of the lake. She was feeling reckless and giddy with anticipation. Nothing could happen between her and Alex, but that didn't mean she couldn't dream.

Chapter Fourteen

Alex watched as Lina half ran, half skipped down the hill. She was almost at the edge of the lake before he moved. Everything about this was a bad idea, but he knew he wouldn't be able to stop himself.

'It's a hot day,' he murmured to himself. 'There's nothing wrong with wanting to cool off with a swim. It's perfectly innocent.'

There was nothing innocent about the thoughts running through his head. He was already picturing how Lina would slip out of her clothes and wade into the water, her skin puckering and tightening in the cool, refreshing water.

Behave, he told himself. Despite the mounting attraction he'd felt for Lina over the past few weeks his sister's words were still ringing in his mind. She'd warned him again to be careful—dallying with Lina would just end in heartbreak and animosity.

Trying to keep his movements slow and measured, Alex reached the lake just as Lina began unlacing her dress.

'Help me?' she asked, turning her back to him and indicating the ties that held the high waist of her skirt in place.

Alex had undressed many young women in his youth, although not in the past three years, but he felt a light tremble to his fingers as he pulled at the ends of the ties and loosened the fastenings of Lina's skirt. Despite the warm day Lina had several layers on, as young women were expected to wear, whatever the weather, but still he could feel the heat of her skin as his fingers trailed across her lower back.

'Thank you,' Lina said, turning around. They were standing close, too close for propriety, but Alex knew their proximity would be the least scandalous thing that happened this afternoon. It was unheard of, stripping down with a young woman to go swimming, but Alex knew good manners and society's expectations for his behaviour would not be enough to stop him from diving into the lake after Lina.

'Turn around,' Lina instructed him.

Alex didn't move, instead tugging at his own shirt, pulling it over his head. He saw Lina's eyes flit to his chest, saw her lose the battle with her self-control as her eyes roamed over his body.

'Are you sure you don't need any more help?' he asked. 'I wouldn't want you getting tangled in all those underclothes.'

The idea of slowly stripping every layer from Lina's body created a surge of desire, and although he knew she'd say no, he desperately wanted her to say yes.

'Turn around,' Lina instructed again.

This time he complied, turning slowly so his back was towards the lake. The rustling of material fuelled his imagination as he waited for Lina to undress behind him, all the time fighting the ungentlemanly urge to turn and peek.

After what felt like an eternity of anticipation he heard a quiet splashing sound and a soft yelp. It was excuse enough to turn and seek out Lina with his eyes, just to make sure she wasn't hurt, of course.

She was clad in a thin chemise that ended just below the knee. With the sunlight shining down, the outline of Lina's body was just about visible through the fabric. Alex felt his body tightening in response and had to fight the urge to sweep her from the water, pull the chemise over her head and lay her down on the grass with his body covering hers.

'You looked,' Lina said, accusingly. 'Turn around.'

'You screamed.'

'I exclaimed quietly. The water is rather cold. Turn around.'

She took a few more steps into the lake before looking to see if he had complied with her order.

'You're still looking.'

'It seems I have lost the ability to turn away,' Alex murmured quietly.

With a huff Lina waded farther into the lake, the water now up to mid-thigh level and dragging on the hem of her chemise.

Quickly Alex stripped off his breeches, took a few steps to his left where he knew the lake was deeper and dived straight in. The coldness almost took his breath away and as he opened his eyes under the water everything was brown and murky. He allowed himself a leisurely glide through the water, feeling his body adjust to the cold and his muscles flex as he began to swim. He surfaced near the middle of the lake, enjoying the burn in his lungs as he sucked in a deep breath to replenish what he had used.

'I thought you wanted a swim?' he called over to Lina, who was still slowly wading towards him.

'It's a little colder than I imagined.'

'Nonsense, it's refreshing.'

Swimming closer, he debated whether she would forgive him if he pulled her down. The idea of their bodies entwining under the water was too enticing as Alex paused beside her.

'Don't do it,' she warned.

'What?'

'Whatever it is you're thinking about.'

Alex grinned, gripped her firmly around the waist and pulled her down, making sure at no point her head went under the water. Lina screamed as the cold hit the upper part of her body and wriggled free from his embrace.

'That was cruel.'

'You were taking too long getting in. I used to do the same to Georgina when we were children.'

'I might not have wanted to be dunked under.'

'I kept your head dry.'

Lina muttered something under her breath, flipped over on to her back and began kicking her legs, propelling herself through the cool water.

From his position, bobbing on the surface, Alex had a wonderful view of the swell of her breasts through the wet cotton of her chemise. Willing himself to be a gentleman and look away, he found his eyes would not obey the command.

'You swim well,' Alex commented as he pulled himself through the water beside her.

'Raul taught me. Neither of my parents could swim, but Raul and I, and a few of our friends, will often cool down in a lake or a pond on a hot day.'

Alex felt an unexpected stab of jealousy at the thought of these friends swimming with Lina, seeing her with her chemise plastered to her body. Although he knew the presence of her brother would mean nothing untoward had ever happened, he still didn't want anyone else enjoying this experience with Lina.

'I learnt to swim here,' Alex said, realising he hadn't told Lina much about himself or his past. She knew a lot about him, from gossiping with his sister and the servants, but he didn't often share much about his life. 'My father used to bring me and Georgina on hot days. Sometimes our mother would join us, too.'

'Your mother would come in for a swim?' Lina asked, her eyes wide.

Alex nodded. 'My mother wasn't a conventional marchioness. She and my father were very much in love, they used to spend much of their time together and Father could persuade her to do almost anything.'

'Including swimming in a lake.'

'Exactly. We used to return home dripping wet and Mother would hurry us all upstairs before too many of the servants saw us.'

'It sounds like you loved your mother very much.'

'She was kind and very much involved in our upbringing. We had a nursemaid, of course, and later I went off to school, but our parents were of the opinion that we were their children, so it was their responsibility, and their pleasure, to bring us up.'

'You must miss them.'

Alex lay back in the water and allowed his feet to float to the surface. 'I do miss them. I miss my father's sage advice and my mother's warm affection.'

As they bobbed side by side, Alex wondered what his parents would make of his arrangement with Lina. His father would often make small wagers, challenge his wife or children to a race or a game of croquet, with the loser having to shoulder some small household task. His mother, however, would caution him just as Georgina had. She would worry about Lina getting hurt and about her son forming an attachment to someone that could not last.

Glancing over at Lina, he felt a swell of affection. She was argumentative and sometimes irritating, but over the past few weeks he had enjoyed the vitality and energy she'd brought to Whitemore House. If he wasn't so damned attracted to her, he would class her as a good friend, but Alex knew a friendship could not work when one party imagined the other naked and in his arms multiple times a day.

Perhaps he had dismissed the idea of making Lina his mistress too quickly. Although it would complicate their arrangement regarding the wager, especially since his widowed aunt was arriving to chaperone them this evening, a few weeks with Lina in his bed might just satisfy the physical craving he had for her. His mind started to run away from him as he imagined sharing breakfast with Lina every morning, spending long afternoons out riding, talking and laughing as they did so easily together, and falling into bed and satisfying their desires every night. With a jolt, he realised that sounded more like marriage than a relationship with a mistress and quickly tried to get his fantasies under control.

'You look rather serious,' Lina said. 'A penny for your thoughts?'

'I was thinking how beautiful you look wet.'

Lina jerked with surprise, the movement causing her head to dip under the water, and she came up spluttering. Alex was immediately by her side, one arm looped around her waist. The fabric of her chemise clung tight to her body as Alex resisted the temptation to let his fingers roam over the curve of her waist.

'You must know you're beautiful,' he said, looking down into her eyes.

She gave a miniscule shake of her head, but Alex could tell it was just a reflex, she was too affected by his proximity to answer properly.

'I'm sure many men have told you how beautiful you are,' he murmured. 'How could they not?'

With his free hand, he smoothed back the wet strands of hair from around her face, letting his fingers dance across the skin of her cheek and down to the line of her jaw. Perhaps just one kiss would slake his desire, perhaps then he would be able to think clearly and rationally.

'How could they not be enchanted by your smile? Bewitched by that sparkle in your eyes?'

Still Lina did not say anything, but Alex could feel her chest heaving against his body and knew more than anything she wanted to be kissed. Surely if he wanted it and she wanted it, there could be nothing wrong with one quick kiss?

Before his conscience could rear its head, Alex lowered his lips on to hers, kissing her gently at first until he felt her rise to meet him. As her body pressed against his, he could no longer hold back and kissed her as he'd wanted to for so long. Unable to stop himself, he laced his hands around her back, pulling her even closer, until he wasn't sure where his body ended and hers began.

'Alex,' she moaned as he pulled away slightly so he could kiss the angle of her jaw and her thrown-back neck. The sound of his name from her lips stoked the fire that was burning inside him and it took all of Alex's self-control to stop the encounter going any further. He would not seduce her, not here, not now. He respected her too much for that. But maybe just one more kiss…

As her lips met his, Alex felt a jolt all through his body. It was as though he'd been asleep these last few years and kissing Lina, touching Lina, was finally waking him up.

Her lips were velvety, soft and warm despite the coolness of her skin and Alex knew he could lose himself in her kiss if he wasn't careful. Reluctantly he pulled away, loving the desire he could see burning in Lina's eyes and the way her body was still pressed against his.

They stood, still submerged up to their shoulders in the middle of the lake, and for a few seconds neither of them could string together a coherent sentence.

'You're shivering,' Alex said, noticing the goosebumps on her skin for the first time. Quickly, before Lina could protest or before he could think his actions through, Alex scooped her into his arms and began to wade through the water. As their bodies rose out of the water, there was an initial chill, despite the high temperatures. Alex knew once they were dry they would be warm, but he increased his pace a little so Lina would not suffer. As they reached the water's edge, he made the mistake of glancing down. Lina's cotton chemise, normally white, was now almost entirely transparent, revealing the olive skin below. He could see every curve, every swell and undulation, and he felt his resolve not to seduce her falter.

The water had pushed her chemise up to the top of her thighs and with one finger Alex was able to trace the simple bird she had tattooed in blue ink on her perfect skin. He heard her gasp as his fingers lingered over the outline.

For a second their eyes met and Alex could see the battle between desire and sensibility in Lina's mind. He knew one kiss, one stroke with a solitary finger, and she would be his, completely, entirely, just as he had imagined a thousand times these last few days.

Reluctantly Lina wriggled free from his arms and quickly gathered up her clothes, holding them in front of her as a shield.

'We should dress,' she said, valiantly trying to keep her eyes from wandering over his body.

'We should.'

Neither moved.

'We might catch a chill.'

'We might.'

Still they both stood, a few paces apart, but unable to pull their eyes from one another.

'You should turn around,' Lina said eventually.

With great effort Alex managed to comply and

turned to look out over the lake. After a few seconds, he heard Lina turn, too, and begin the process of shedding her soaked chemise and donning her dress and petticoats. Trying to distract himself from the knowledge Lina was standing completely naked just a few feet away, Alex shed his own soaked layer and pulled on his breeches.

Far from slaking his desire for Lina, their kiss had just heightened it. Now his mind was filled with images and memories and fantasies. He desperately wanted to kiss her again, to taste her sweet mouth, to run his lips over her jaw, her neck, down on to her breasts. He yearned to feel her body underneath him, writhing in pleasure as he entered her, see her face as she climaxed with him deep inside her.

Just these thoughts were enough to make Alex consider another cold swim.

He'd never set out to seduce Lina, never intended to make her his mistress when he'd accepted the wager Pentworthy had proposed, but now Alex knew it would be almost impossible to keep his hands off her for another four weeks. Perhaps the best thing for everyone involved would be to make her his mistress, just for a short time. That way he would be legitimising their intimacy, and hopefully by the time he won his wager he would be able to think a little more clearly when Lina was close. After all, none of his other mistresses had kept him interested for more than a few months. Then again, no one intrigued him quite like Lina.

Chapter Fifteen

Lina dressed quickly, pulling at the material of her petticoats, blouse and skirt as they stuck to her damp body. She felt jittery and longed to turn and look at Alex to see if she could tell what he was thinking.

The kiss had been sublime, something she'd been secretly longing for and not daring to hope might happen. Even now her lips were tingling and every inch of her skin was burning from the memory of his touch. She desperately wanted him to sweep her up into his arms and kiss her again, even though the rational part of her knew it could never happen.

She and Alex could not have a future. Despite some people's perceptions of gypsy women being of loose morals, it could not be further from the truth. If anything, gypsies had stricter rules when it came to intimate contact with the other sex than most people. Nothing more could happen between her and Alex—unless, of course, he asked her to marry him and it was more likely a cow would fly through the sky than that would happen.

'Come,' Alex said, taking her arm gently, gathering her wet chemise with his own wet clothes and leading her back up the hill. He was still shirtless and as they walked, Lina's arm brushed against the solid muscles of his chest, each contact making it a little more difficult for Lina to concentrate. 'Sit,' Alex instructed, as he busied himself hanging the wet clothes over a branch to dry. Only once this was done did he pull his shirt over his head and then sit down beside her.

Lina's heart thumped in her chest as he leaned towards her, pushing a stray stand of damp hair from her forehead and tucking it behind her ear.

'I have a proposition for you,' Alex said, his voice low and his lips curved up in a small smile.

Frowning, Lina nodded to indicate she was listening. She had no idea how they were going to resolve the tension between them. Every time she looked at Alex her skin flushed and prickled. She couldn't go on like this for another four weeks. The alternative, leaving and returning to her family and friends, was even worse. The idea of never seeing Alex again, never looking into those deep brown eyes or walking arm in arm as they talked and teased each other was heartbreaking. She knew she was falling for Alex. It was impossible not to when it felt as though they had been made for one another—she loved his determination and focus, as well as his wit that had her smiling all day long.

'I think it is a proposition that will benefit us both greatly. We will have to be careful, discreet, but I am confident we can make it work.'

With her heart sinking, Lina realised what he was suggesting.

'Be mine, Lina, for the next few weeks at least. After that we can re-evaluate, decide whether we'd like to prolong our liaison further.'

'You want me to be your mistress?'

Alex edged closer and ran his fingers down the side of her cheek and along the angle of her jaw, stopping at her chin and tilting her face up to his. Before she knew what was happening, his lips were on hers again and Lina felt herself losing grip on reality. Surely something that felt so good couldn't be wrong?

Summoning all her resolve, Lina pushed Alex

away. He looked surprised, but recovered quickly, grinning at her in the way that melted her heart.

'We can work out details later,' he said, waving his hand to indicate some point in the future where he envisioned them sitting down and working out what she would get for disgracing herself as his mistress.

'You want me to become your mistress?' Lina said again, this time the anger rising in her voice.

'It makes sense, Lina, I can't stop thinking about you, I see you every time I close my eyes and I've spent the last week fantasising about the fun we would have in the bedroom together. You can't deny the attraction between us.'

She couldn't deny it, but the thought of becoming Alex's mistress, anyone's mistress, was repulsive to her.

'You have so little respect for me?'

This stopped Alex's caress of her cheek and his hand dropped from her face into his lap.

'I respect you greatly, Lina.'

'No,' Lina said, shaking her head vehemently. 'You don't. You don't ask a woman you respect to disgrace herself, to sully herself for a few weeks of fun in the bedroom. That does not indicate respect between two people.'

She stood, burying her hands in her skirt so Alex would not see them trembling. She felt sick and her head was spinning, but she just needed to get away.

'I do respect you,' Alex said, more firmly, his face setting into a harder expression. 'I have had a few mistresses over the years and I have respected all of them.'

'Great. Wonderful. Fantastic. The answer is no.'

With quick strides Lina hurried over to where Stormborn was watching the exchange with interest. Within thirty seconds she had untethered him and used the tree to help her mount unaided.

'Where are you going?' Alex asked.

'Away. Anywhere but here.'

'Lina, don't be foolish.'

She almost screamed. How could such a kind and intelligent man be so obtuse and unfeeling? He had asked her to debase herself, to give herself to him for a few weeks of pleasure, and then he would discard her like a used pair of old boots. Of course Lina wished something more could happen between them, something beautiful and passionate and intense, but not like this. She couldn't believe he had even asked.

Before she could say something she might regret, Lina urged Stormborn forward and into a gallop down the hill. The lake loomed ahead of her and she wished she could turn back time and be floating in the cool waters with Alex, before any mention of being his mistress had been made.

As the wind whipped through her hair and the sun warmed her face, Lina forced herself to breathe deeply. Only once she was sure Alex was not following her did she let the tears start to fall down her cheeks.

'Foolish, foolish girl,' she muttered, allowing Stormborn to slow to a trot.

Throughout her stay at Whitemore House Lina hadn't foreseen this turn of events. She knew what happened when someone of Alex's rank dallied with someone of hers. They might have a few weeks of fun and pleasure, but then Lina would be pushed away, back to her own world, her self-respect and the respect from those around her gone for ever, whilst Alex suffered no consequence from his little indiscretion. It was unfair, but that was the way of the world. It was what had happened to her father and he had never recovered, and Lina knew in matters of sex, women were vilified much more than men, no matter whose fault it was.

Perhaps she should just return home, run back to Raul and Sabina and all the people she'd known for her entire life. She was angry with Alex and didn't know if she wanted to face him again, but mostly she was angry with herself for not seeing this coming. Never had she thought he might ask her to become his lover, his mistress, so when it had occurred her defences had been down and she'd been vulnerable.

Turning Stormborn's head, Lina set off in a south-westerly direction, but then paused. She was angry, certainly, and hurt, but these last few weeks she'd been trying to control her impulsive decisions, trying to think things through without the cloud of emotion. Taking the time to consider whether the best thing for her to do was abandon Alex and his wager was important, not a snap decision.

'What do you think, Stormborn?' Lina asked, stroking the friendly horse between the ears. 'Should I go home?'

The very thought of leaving Whitemore House, leaving Alex and never seeing him again sent a stab of panic through her heart.

She was in an impossible situation. If she stayed, it would be with the knowledge that Alex cared so little for her and her reputation that he would ask her to become his mistress. If she left, she would be returning to her old life, with the same old routines, same old boredom—and Uncle Tom would want to collect the debt she owed him.

Lina allowed Stormborn to lead for a while, knowing her decision would not be an easy one and would probably take time. The horse picked his way through the long grass of a meadow, stopping occasionally to bend his head and tear a mouthful of wildflowers to munch on.

Whilst she had been debating what to do with herself for the next few weeks Lina had lost track of what direction she'd been riding in and now wasn't sure which way led back to the house, but as they progressed through the meadow Lina caught a glimpse of the road on the other side of the hedge, winding its way through the countryside.

'Help!' A hoarse cry floated on the still summer's air and Lina straightened in the saddle immediately. 'Help!'

Looking around, Lina could see no obvious source of the plea for help and quickly pushed Stormborn forward towards the road.

'Help!' The cry got a little louder and was followed by a sob of pain.

'Hello?' Lina shouted, feeling a little foolish, but not knowing what else to say.

A gap in the hedgerow loomed and then Lina and Stormborn were on the dusty road, Lina's head swivelling in both directions. Just around the bend a carriage lay at a strange angle, two wheels missing and the side smashed in. Reining in Stormborn, Lina quickly dismounted, taking care to hold on to the horse's bridle in case something spooked him. The horses that had pulled the carriage were nowhere to be seen and Lina could see the straps had been cut to free them. The coachman was also missing and Lina could only assume he had freed the horses so they would not pull the damaged carriage in their injured and frightened state and then gone to look for help.

'Hello?' Lina said again, poking her head in through the window, bracing herself for what sight might greet her eyes.

'Praise the Lord!' a woman in her mid-fifties exclaimed, tears falling down her cheeks.

'What happened? Are you hurt?'

Many gypsy women were skilled healers and the recipes for salves that were passed from generation to generation were a source of pride amongst the gypsy community. Lina had never learnt more than the basics, but even a child could tell there was something wrong with this woman's left leg. Just above the ankle the leg ballooned into a tense swelling which was already an angry purple colour. The clenched teeth and short, gasping breaths hinted the woman was in considerable pain.

'My leg,' the woman said. 'I can't move.'

'Has your coachman gone for help?'

'I sent him to the house, but he's on foot and heaven only knows how long he'll be.'

'Whitemore House?' Understanding finally dawned on Lina. This was Alex's widowed aunt, their chaperone for the next couple of weeks. She was due to arrive sometime that evening, but must have decided to make the journey a few hours early.

Quickly assessing the situation, Lina realised there was not much she could do on her own. This poor woman would need a few strong men to help lift her from the carriage and another form of transportation to deliver her to the house.

'I will ride to the house and get help,' Lina said. 'I'm sorry to leave you, but I think it will be the quickest way to get you out of here.'

'Thank you, my dear.'

Taking the older woman's hand and giving it a squeeze, Lina wriggled herself back through the window and remounted Stormborn. Urging him forward, she sped down the road, hoping she was heading in the right direction for Whitemore House.

Chapter Sixteen

Alex prowled around his study, picking up various pieces of paper that needed his attention, but unable to focus on anything. Lina still hadn't returned. It had only been thirty minutes since he had got back to the house, but he'd hoped he would find Stormborn back in the stables and Lina rubbing him down. Neither horse nor woman were anywhere to be seen.

Flopping down into his chair, he wondered if she had left for good. He wouldn't put it past her; he'd seen the hurt and anger in her eyes as he'd suggested she become his mistress. Never had he expected such a violent reaction.

Alex understood her reluctance. She'd told him how her father had been used and then discarded by a wealthy, titled woman looking for some amusement. Lina was concerned that would happen to her. All he needed to do was be clearer in his offer, show her how they could enjoy each other's company for the next few weeks and then both continue with their lives enriched and emotionally unscathed by the experience. If they both went in with their eyes open, knowing this affair would have an end date, it wouldn't hurt either of them.

A small voice in the back of his mind scoffed at him. Already he was panicking that he might not ever see Lina again, that he'd driven her away with his proposition. The idea he could give her up after they'd become even closer was difficult to accept, but of course he would have to. No matter how much he liked Lina, how much more he liked *himself* when Lina was around, the only way they could realistically be together was if she became his mistress. He might dream of a future where Lina stayed on at Whitemore House for ever, where they were bound together by law, but that couldn't be anything more than a dream.

Running a hand through his hair, Alex wondered if he was being selfish. He knew there were different standards for men and women. A titled, unmarried gentleman was almost *expected* to have a mistress or lover, whereas for an unmarried woman to be entangled with a man there were often consequences. But they would be careful. No one from Lina's normal life would ever know anything had happened between them.

The thundering of hooves approaching the house made Alex smile in relief. He had not lost her yet. She must have returned for a reason and he was fairly certain that reason was the mutual attraction they shared.

'Alex!' Lina shouted, her voice panicky and breathless. 'Alex!'

A surge of concern powered his stride and he was out through the front door within a few seconds.

'There's been a carriage accident, on the road from Pottersdown. I think it's your aunt, she's hurt quite badly and trapped. You have to come now.'

The initial relief he had felt at seeing Lina safe and unharmed was replaced by worry. Aunt Lucy was a wonderful if slightly eccentric woman, who Alex would hate to see hurt.

'She will need at least a few people to lift her out and a carriage to transport her here.'

'Williams!' Alex shouted for his butler who was hovering in the background. 'Send out the grooms on horseback and ask the footmen to follow on foot, ask Peterson to ready the carriage and make his way to the road to Pottersdown as soon as possible.'

He dashed to the stables where one of the stable boys was in the process of taking the saddle off Ebony, the horse he had ridden during his trip with Lina. Quickly he resaddled the horse and vaulted up. Lina had already started back down the drive on Stormborn by the time he reached the front of the house and he pushed Ebony to catch up. Behind him he heard the footmen and grooms hurrying to follow.

He and Lina rode side by side as they turned from the drive on to the road, neither saying anything. Now wasn't the time to bring up their argument from earlier that afternoon. Perhaps once Aunt Lucy was safe and settled they might be able to discuss things further.

As they sped towards the scene of the accident, they passed the coachman, who waved and pointed and assured them he would be back to help within minutes. And then Alex saw the carriage.

'Aunt Lucy,' he called, jumping from Ebony and throwing the reins to Lina.

'Darling boy, help your poor aunt out of this wreck, wouldn't you?'

Despite the obvious injury to her leg Alex was

relieved to see his aunt hadn't lost her wicked grin and the sparkle in her eyes.

'You do know how to make an entrance, Aunt Lucy,' he scolded her softly as he pulled himself in through the window of the coach after ascertaining the door would not open.

'I like to keep you on your toes, young man.'

Crouching in the enclosed carriage, Alex took a moment to find his balance on the tilted floor before moving in to look at his aunt's leg.

'You won't be dancing this Season,' he said quietly. Aunt Lucy had hitched up her skirts to her knee and the entirety of her lower leg was swollen and discoloured. He was no doctor, but he was certain she had broken it, possibly in multiple places.

'Nonsense,' Aunt Lucy said, gritting her teeth as Alex gently tried to move her leg from where it was wedged against the buckled seat. 'I'll be waltzing with the young gentlemen in a few weeks, mark my words.'

Outside Alex heard the clatter of hooves as the first of the grooms arrived and wondered how best to put his men to work. They would have to lift Aunt Lucy out of the carriage and for that to happen it would be easiest if they could remove the door since it couldn't be opened.

'Histon, ride to the village and fetch the doctor,' Alex instructed. Aunt Lucy was going to need something for the pain before they attempted to pull her out. 'Paulson, Yates, set to work removing this door. It's wedged shut and we need it off before we can even attempt to get Lady Grenville out.'

'It won't be long, Aunt Lucy,' Alex said, turning back and once again trying to lift her swollen leg from where it was wedged.

'Tell me,' Aunt Lucy said, dropping her voice to a conspiratorial whisper. 'Was that pretty young thing that found me the young lady Georgina has told me all about in her letters?'

'Yes—Miss Lina Lock.'

'I can see why you might need a chaperone.'

Alex found his cheeks flushing for the first time in years. Aunt Lucy always had been direct and after the episode in the lake earlier in the day Alex had something to feel guilty about.

Gently he worked his hands underneath his aunt's leg, manoeuvring slowly to cause as little pain as possible.

'She's from a gypsy family, Georgina tells me.'

'That's right.'

'I once *knew* a man from the circus, but never a gypsy.'

'Aunt Lucy!'

'Try not to be so uptight, dear. I'm fifty years old and I've been married three times. I think it's safe to say I'm familiar with the opposite sex.'

Wriggling his fingers, he pushed against the bowed piece of wood that seemed to be pinning her leg in place. If only he'd had smaller hands, more delicate fingers, he might've been able to wriggle them underneath the wood and dislodge it.

'Lina,' Alex called, lifting his head so he could see when she arrived at the strangely angled window.

'First-name terms. I see I really will need to keep an eye on you two.'

'Can I help?' Lina asked.

'I need you to try to move this piece of wood,' Alex explained quickly. 'Aunt Lucy's leg is trapped and my fingers are too large to get underneath. You'll have to climb in.'

He watched as without hesitation Lina vaulted into the carriage, more like a cat than a human. It was a snug fit inside with the three of them and Alex had to hold Lina as she put her feet on the angled floor so she would not slide into Aunt Lucy. He felt her stiffen as her body brushed against his and wondered if she would pull herself from his grip. Instead she rallied, found her balance, then crouched down next to Aunt Lucy.

'Wriggle your fingers underneath and see if you can dislodge the wood,' Alex ordered.

'So bossy,' Aunt Lucy murmured to Lina, as if they were the best of friends already.

Lina crouched, inspected Aunt Lucy's leg and then leaned over, craning her neck to see how it was pinned.

'It needs moving from underneath,' Alex informed her. The look she flashed him was pure ice.

'That may be so,' she said primly. 'But I need to ascertain what angle to push at, where there will be the least resistance.'

'Just push the wood away.'

'That clearly didn't work for you.'

'Only because my hands are too big.'

'Or you were going about it all wrong.'

'Put your hands under Lady Grenville's leg and push the wood away,' Alex instructed firmly.

'When will you realise you're not always right and you don't always know best?'

'When it is the truth. Right now, you're wasting valuable time.'

'This is beginning to sound like a lovers' tiff,' Aunt Lucy interjected.

'We are not lovers,' Lina said so loudly the grooms outside must have heard.

'Yet,' Alex whispered softly in her ear. It was provocative, especially given the fire Lina was spitting at him already, but Alex reasoned things could not get much worse.

Leaning over Aunt Lucy, with one hand tucked beneath the trapped leg, the other braced against the offending piece of wood, Lina pushed gently.

'You'll have to push harder...' Alex began to say, but trailed off as Lina shot him a triumphant look as the wood moved easily upwards and away from Aunt Lucy's leg.

'Clever girl,' Aunt Lucy murmured, her face screwed up with pain.

Alex quickly grabbed the wood, moved it away and steadied his aunt's injured leg. Voices outside indicated the doctor had arrived and Alex eased back, knowing he and Lina would have to vacate the carriage to let the medical man in.

'We'll be just outside,' he reassured her.

With the angle the carriage was at and the over-crowding with the three bodies inside it was difficult to decide how to get him and Lina out without hurting Aunt Lucy any further.

'I'll have to lift you out,' he said to Lina, already

placing his hands on her waist. Immediately she wriggled free from his touch, as if she couldn't bear his hands on her. Alex had to hide a grin at her reaction to him. She was angry—angrier than he'd ever seen her before—but she was also worried about her primal reaction to him. He knew he could have her melting in his arms with a few soft kisses and she knew it, too. It made her livid and jittery every time he came close.

'I climbed out before.'

'There was more room then.'

Lina studied the gap she had to wriggle through and the available space before eventually conceding.

Gently Alex placed his hands on her waist again, taking his time before lifting her up and through the carriage window. He felt her transfer her weight to someone outside and within a couple of seconds her feet had disappeared and one of the grooms appeared at the window.

'We'll have the door off in a couple of minutes, my lord.'

Giving Aunt Lucy's hand a squeeze, Alex pulled himself through the carriage window. Already Lina was talking to the newly arrived doctor, explaining what had occurred and the problem they were facing.

Not for the first time, Alex admired Lina's ability to take control of a situation. Most women of his acquaintance allowed the men in their lives to sort out any problems or difficulties that came their way. Even Georgina, who was fiercely independent for a woman of her rank, would stand back and defer to Alex if she were here. Lina didn't even consider not getting involved—it was one of the things he was so drawn to about her.

'Lord Whitemore,' Dr Jacobs greeted him as he approached.

Alex shook the doctor's hand and indicated the carriage. 'Can you help?'

'Let me examine Lady Grenville quickly, but from Miss Lock's explanation it sounds like a splint will be needed before we even attempt to move your aunt. If the leg is broken, any movement will be very painful, but I do have one or two medicines that might help with that.'

They watched as Dr Jacobs made his way over to the carriage and peered inside.

'Thank you for helping,' Alex said quietly to Lina.

'Your aunt seems nice.'

'She is. A little scandalous in the eyes of society, but she has a heart of gold.'

They lapsed into silence, watching the men work at removing the carriage door.

'Will you stay?' Alex asked, finding he was holding his breath as he waited for Lina to answer.

She remained silent for over a minute, her gaze fixed on some point directly ahead of her, her eyes barely blinking.

'For now.'

Trying to exercise some restraint, Alex refrained from shooting his fist up in the air. Instead he murmured, 'I'm glad.'

Now he had a chance. A chance to win his wager—but more important, a chance to spend a little more time with Lina and hopefully even a chance to persuade her they both could enjoy a closer relationship over the next few weeks.

Chapter Seventeen

Lina tapped lightly on the door, listening for the invitation to enter before she turned the doorknob and slipped into the room.

Far from the dark and stuffy sickroom she had imagined, Lady Grenville's bedchamber was light and airy, with the windows thrown open and a cool breeze blowing through, making the curtains billow.

'Come, come,' Lady Grenville gushed. 'Don't be shy. Come and sit beside me.' She patted a spot on the bed that wasn't covered with piles of books and writing materials.

'I don't wish to disturb you, Lady Grenville,' Lina said, feeling a little nervous. 'I just wanted to enquire how you were.'

'In agony, darling girl, but I'm told that's perfectly natural when one has a broken ankle.'

'Did the doctor say how long it will take to heal?'

Lina had never broken a bone. Despite her often-reckless antics, she always seemed to land on her feet relatively unscathed.

'I'll be in bed for at least six weeks, possibly eight. Then it all depends how well the bone has knitted together. It's ghastly, I've been laid up for less than a day and I'm going out of my mind with boredom already.' Lady Grenville's speech was accompanied by wild and animated hand gestures and Lina found herself warming to the overly dramatic middle-aged woman. 'You must promise to keep me company, dear girl.'

'Of course. Although I'm sure Lord Whitemore will not let you get bored.'

'But he is a man and men have the most peculiar ideas as to what constitutes entertainment.'

'Does this mean you will not make the Season in London?' Lina asked.

Lady Grenville grimaced and shook her head sadly. 'Alas, probably not. I've been looking forward to donning my finest dress and dancing the night away all year, but I think I may have to wait until next year to grace the ballrooms of London with my presence.'

Both women were silent for some moments, lost in their own thoughts.

'What is it like? A London ball?' This was a question she'd been eager to ask someone for a while, but when she had put it to Alex, he'd just shrugged and said it was a house full of people who danced and talked. Hardly enlightening.

'It's divine, Lina. I may call you Lina?'

Lina nodded.

'And you must call me Aunt Lucy. Everyone does.' She paused, adjusting her position on the pillows, leaning back with a dreamy, faraway look in her eyes. 'The women are dressed in the finest of silks and satins, their hair coiffed, their necks and arms and ears dripping with jewels. The men, oh!' Aunt Lucy gave a deep groan. 'They look so handsome in their evening dress.'

Already Lina could begin to picture the scene. It was enticing, but she knew she did not belong there.

'The ballroom is decorated with candles and flowers. And as people arrive, they will gather in groups, conversing, with the musicians playing in the background. Then the dancing begins. Waltzes and cotillions, glorious dances executed with precision—at least at the beginning of the evening.'

'It sounds wonderful.'

'It is, my dear. The London Season is where young women go to find a husband, so everyone is immaculately presented.'

'And immaculately behaved,' Lina murmured.

There was a mischievous twinkle in Aunt Lucy's eyes. 'Not so much. Plenty of marriages have started with an illicit kiss stolen at a London ball. You will have a fantastic time.'

Lina shook her head absent-mindedly. She wasn't sure she would still be around then. A London ball would be a wonderful thing to experience, and this was a once-in-a-lifetime opportunity, but she still hadn't decided if she was staying another night, let alone continuing with Alex's wager.

'Are you worried you won't fit in?' Aunt Lucy asked.

'I won't, but that's the whole point. Someone like me shouldn't be in attendance somewhere like that. The whole idea is to *appear* to belong,' Lina said, her voice a little melancholy.

'Think of it as an adventure,' Aunt Lucy said, patting Lina's hand. 'How wonderful to be someone else, just for one night. To live another life, without any repercussions.'

That was what Lina had hoped for when she'd

agreed to this crazy wager of Alex's—the chance to live a different life for a few weeks, to experience something new with the knowledge that once the ball was over and the six weeks were up, she could happily slip back into her old life with no lasting consequences. The problem was, as time went by Lina didn't know if she would be able to go back. These past few weeks had changed her, made her want more from life, made her see the endless possibilities in the world. How could she return to dancing and telling fortunes at country fairs in the summer months and finding odd jobs to bring in money in the winter?

More important, how could she return to a life without Alex?

As soon as the question hit her, Lina tried to suppress it, afraid Aunt Lucy might read her mind if she allowed her doubts to stay on the surface for too long. She didn't have a life with Alex now, so there was nothing to lose, nothing to mourn. They had shared some moments of laughter and fun, some moments of closeness and compassion, but there was no relationship there and never would be. The idea of becoming his mistress was not one Lina would entertain and, even with her very basic knowledge of marriage etiquette, she knew a marquess *never* married a gypsy.

Even with this knowledge, Lina couldn't stop her heart from pounding whenever Alex came close. She found herself laughing when he laughed, hurting when he hurt...

'I thought I might find you here,' Alex said, strolling into the room and giving his aunt a peck on the cheek.

'I was considering a brisk walk around the estate followed by a ride on one of those fabulous beasts of yours, but thought I'd better save some energy for healing my poor broken ankle,' Aunt Lucy said, pulling her nephew in for a short embrace.

Alex sat down on the bed, positioning himself so he was directly next to Lina. Their thighs were almost touching, just the layers of clothing separating them, and already Lina could feel the heat beginning to rise in her body. This morning at breakfast she'd managed to time her appearance to coincide with the arrival of one of Alex's horse trainers, and as such they hadn't spoken about their kiss and the proposal that had followed afterwards.

'Good morning, Lina,' Alex said softly, leaning in as if they were the only two in the room.

'Lord Whitemore,' Lina greeted him coolly and

stood abruptly, crossing over to the window and pretending something had caught her eye in the gardens.

'What a beautiful day,' Alex observed, coming up behind her, standing so close she could feel his breath on her neck. For an instant Lina wanted to lean back, to allow him to envelop her in his arms and feel his body pressed against hers. 'The perfect day for a swim.'

'I wouldn't want to spoil this day with a dip in a cold lake,' Lina said, turning and facing Alex, trying to pretend his proximity wasn't affecting her.

'I don't think it would spoil it at all. In fact, I would wager it would improve it tenfold.'

'Have you ever considered that you accept wagers too quickly?' Lina asked, knowing she was hardly the person to judge, but luckily Alex did not know about her catastrophic bet with Uncle Tom.

'What a wonderful idea,' Aunt Lucy interrupted, clapping her hands. 'You two should go and enjoy the day together. I may be stuck in my sickbed, but there's no reason you two young things shouldn't go and have fun.'

Lina peered at the older woman, trying to work out if Alex had primed her to suggest an outing.

'Take a trip to that lovely big lake and dip your toes in the water. I'll want to hear all about it later.'

'I would feel too guilty, leaving you here alone,' Lina said quickly.

'Nonsense, Aunt Lucy doesn't mind. The doctor said she needs to rest.'

'Perhaps I will rest today, as well,' Lina suggested, already knowing deep inside that she would not win this argument. 'Yesterday was a particularly eventful day.' She'd been thinking about the carriage accident and all the drama that had ensued after she'd discovered Aunt Lucy trapped and injured on the Pottersdown Road, but saw Alex's grin out of the corner of her eye, no matter how much she tried to avoid looking at him.

'It was an eventful day,' he murmured. 'Sometimes it is best to discuss what has occurred, so any wrongs can be put right and any misunderstandings cleared up.'

Lina eyed him suspiciously. She doubted he was going to apologise—he didn't think he had done anything wrong—but maybe this was his way of telling her they could move past his proposition and return to their easy companionship whilst they prepared for the London ball where Lina would make her debut.

'A stroll through the gardens would be lovely,' she conceded.

'Don't do anything naughty,' Aunt Lucy said as they headed towards the door. 'I might be laid up, but I still am your designated chaperone.'

'We won't do anything you wouldn't do, Aunt Lucy,' Alex promised.

'You wicked boy,' Aunt Lucy called, her laughter following them out through the door.

'Aunt Lucy has been married three times.' Alex bent low to whisper in Lina's ear. 'And she's had a multitude of lovers.'

'And you thought she'd make a suitable chaperone?'

'The perfect chaperone.'

Alex hummed to himself as he leaned against the wall, waiting for Lina to emerge from the house. She'd returned inside to fetch a parasol to give her skin some protection from the sun. Although Lina had a naturally caramel skin tone, the hours she spent in the sun every day made her face and arms freckle. Over the past couple of weeks Georgina had encouraged her to stay in the shade as much as possible and carry a parasol when walking in the sun. As expected, Lina had grumbled, but soon she'd become accustomed to avoiding the sunlight and Alex thought her freckles were fading a little.

'I think this is about Victoria.' Lina burst out through the doors on to the terrace, already half-way through the sentence before she met Alex's eye.

'Victoria couldn't be further from my mind right now.'

'Nonsense. You saw her for the first time in three years less than a week ago and again a few days later. Of course she's preoccupying you.'

Alex picked up Lina's hand and placed it in the crook of his arm, taking his time and ensuring Lina didn't pull away before he replied.

'Victoria is married. Victoria eloped with my closest friend. Victoria inspires nothing but bad memories. I could go on with the reasons I am not thinking about Victoria. But I *am* thinking about you.'

'Please stop,' Lina said quietly.

'If only it were that simple,' Alex said with a theatrical sigh. 'You have awoken something deep inside me, Lina—something that I fear will not be put to sleep easily.'

'Lust.'

'Desire,' Alex corrected her. 'There is a world of difference.'

Desire and a whole lot more. Never before had he yearned for someone's company as he did Lina's. They only had to be apart for a few hours and he would find himself searching for an excuse to seek her out. Desire he could deal with; anything deeper was not something he wished to explore.

'I will not be your mistress.'

'I understand your reticence, truly I do.'

She looked up at him with hope in her eyes. For a moment Alex felt guilty about pressing her like this, but he knew she desired him just as he desired her. It was obvious in every movement, every look. If he could just get her to see things differently, to understand that a liaison did not have to end in disaster if they both entered into it with their eyes open, then they had a chance of spending a few glorious weeks finding pleasure in each other.

'If that were true, you would never have asked it of me.'

Alex considered this for a few minutes as they continued their stroll through the gardens. He knew he could be a touch self-centred and found it difficult to compromise on his desires, but that was common amongst men of his class.

'Your family was ruined by an ill-fated affair between your father and a titled lady. She used him for her pleasure and, when she was done, disposed of him as if he didn't matter at all. Naturally you are wary about the same thing happening.'

'There's so much more to it than that,' Lina grumbled, although Alex had been quite proud of his little summary.

'Then tell me. I'm willing to be persuaded this is a bad idea.'

'I shouldn't have to persuade you.'

'And you don't have to, I'm just asking you to indulge me. Let me get to know you better, understand you better.'

For a while they continued in silence, walking past the rose garden and into the shade of the stumpery. It felt almost mystical with the upturned tree stumps surrounded by luscious ferns all in a cool natural tunnel made from the dense vegetation above and protected from the heat of the sun.

'A relationship between two people should be based on the principles of equality,' Lina said slowly. 'Any relationship—be that friendship, intimacy, marriage—only works if the two people are equal.'

'Nonsense. I know many happily married couples who were not born equal. Take Georgina and Pentworthy as an example. She is the daughter of a marquess. He is from much more humble origins.'

Lina shook her head. 'Equality comes in many forms, not just rank and wealth. Georgina may have had a more privileged start, but her husband is intelligent, driven and successful. This elevates him to her equal.' She paused, looking at him to check he was following her before ploughing on. 'When Pentworthy came and asked for Georgina's hand, did you hesitate?'

'No.'

'Despite him not holding a title and at the time not being as wealthy as your family.'

It was true; there had been richer suitors, and even an earl interested in claiming Georgina as a wife, but Alex hadn't tried to persuade her away from her choice.

'He is her equal and she his. That is why their marriage works so well.'

'You are my equal as well, Lina. You must know that.' She hesitated at this and he pressed on. 'And what has that got to do with you not wanting to be my mistress?'

'We're *not* equals. You have all the advantages, the money, the power, the social contacts, and I have none of that. It means any relationship we would have would be very one-sided, very unbalanced, and when it came time to move on I would be the one left hurt and disadvantaged by our liaison.'

'Wealthy men keep mistresses all the time,' Alex protested, wishing he had a better argument to throw at her. Yesterday Lina had been so angry and emotional, but today she was rational and eloquent. It made it difficult to argue with her.

'And most of the time it is those mistresses that get hurt. A man will move on when the relationship ends. He might gain a little reputation as a rake, but this is laughed off. Men will be men after all. The woman is scorned, cast out from polite society.'

'I would never let you get hurt, Lina,' Alex said quietly.

The pain and longing in her eyes was almost enough to prompt him to kiss her right there and then, but he managed to hold back. He wished he could embrace her, fold her in his arms and protect her from everything the world could throw at her.

'I wish I could believe that.'

'We're in our own little world here, Lina. No one would ever know.' He bent forward and tucked a stray strand of hair behind her ear, letting his fingers linger on her neck. 'A few weeks of pleasure, of enjoying each other's company to the full, and when you return home no one would be any the wiser.'

He could see his words were persuasive, not because they were new or revolutionary, but because she wanted him almost as much as he wanted her.

'Answer me one question, Lina,' he said, taking her hand in his own and raising her knuckles to his lips. Slowly he kissed them, watching to see if she pulled away. 'If all the complications and the possible repercussions were taken away, would you want this?'

For the longest moment Lina looked at him, the dappled sunlight dancing across her face. Almost imperceptibly she nodded her head and Alex's heart soared. Her eyes, her lips, her body, every part of her hinted at her attraction to him, but now he had the confirmation that he craved, now he had the permission to pursue her.

'I believe we've been looking at this all wrong,' Alex said, invigorated. 'We've been thinking about the negatives. I am going to focus on the positives.'

'P-positives?' Lina managed to stutter, looking completely overwhelmed when he plucked a pretty purple flower and handed it to her with a flourish.

'Positives. Like the time we would spend together, the fun we would have.'

'We spend time together already.'

'Not like this.'

Already Alex's mind was racing. He would bombard Lina with attention, show her exactly what they could be enjoying together. If his predictions were right, he didn't think it would be more than a week before they were falling into bed together.

Chapter Eighteen

Lina felt her whole body melting. It was incredible what sensations one solitary little finger could elicit and secretly she wished for more. Alex was seated next to her in the carriage, declining the spacious seat opposite her and deciding instead for the proximity that allowed him to touch her surreptitiously.

She felt his finger trail to the base of her neck before circling its way up again, eliciting an involuntary shudder of pleasure as he reached the point where her neck met her skull.

'Just think how good my lips would feel,' Alex murmured.

'You're relentless,' Lina managed to whisper, trying to stop her head falling back involuntarily, inviting his lips in.

'I *always* get what I want.'

'Always? That's not healthy.'

'Well, maybe not always,' Alex conceded. 'But this time I have very good motivation.'

Second by second Lina felt her resolve crumbling. Fixing her eyes on the moving scenery outside the carriage window, she tried to focus on the rolling hills, but within a minute her mind was back to the subject of Alex and his completely indecent proposal.

'You will behave during this trip?' Lina asked.

'Shouldn't I be asking you that?'

'I'm not the one trying to seduce you.'

'If only,' Alex whispered, his breath hot on her neck.

Lina felt the heat rising in her body and quickly she darted across the carriage and settled herself in the middle of the seat opposite. To remain so close to Alex would be admitting defeat. She still didn't want to be his mistress, still didn't want to ruin herself, but every time he was close to her reason seemed to fly out of the window and she struggled not to lean in and kiss him.

'Alex, I'm being serious. You won't disgrace me whilst we are away?'

The levity departed from his face and suddenly Alex was completely serious. 'Do you have to ask?'

Slowly Lina shook her head. That was what made this so painful: she knew he would never force anything between them. The kiss they had shared had been completely mutual. She'd wanted it as much as him. Ever since, he'd pursued her, tempted her, taunted her, waiting patiently until she could endure it no longer and gave in.

Until recently she'd prided herself on her strength of resolve, with her family often labelling her stubborn. That was all that was getting her through the torture of being so close to Alex, knowing he wanted her, but not being able to act on the fire she felt every time he looked at her with desire in his eyes.

'Tell me about the races,' Lina said, wanting desperately to distract Alex from his primary mission of seducing her.

Sitting back on his seat, a small smile on his lips and a glazed look in his eye, Alex took his time before speaking.

'Newmarket is arguably the finest racecourse in the country and the race days are huge social events. The horses and jockeys are eager to perform and all the hard work of the past year comes to fruition.'

'You watch your own horses race?' Lina asked.

'There will be seven races throughout the day. I have horses in two of the races. The rest of the time it is about assessing the competition, scouting for any horses I may wish to purchase, deciding which of my horses will enter which of the races going forward.'

She loved the enthusiasm in his voice and fire in his eyes as he talked about his horses. It was easy to admire a man who was so driven, so passionate about something.

'And there are spectators there, people who don't own racehorses?'

'Indeed. It's a lucrative business. Newmarket has a good reputation, so there will be plenty of ladies and gentlemen in attendance, socialising and enjoying the horses. And of course many people go to bet on the outcomes of the races.'

They lapsed into silence for a while, Lina looking out the window and enjoying the scenery, and Alex no doubt planning how to seduce her best at the races.

Nearly an hour later the carriage slowed as they approached the entrance to the racecourse. In front of them was a line of coaches, curricles and carriages either parked or stopped for a few moments to let the passengers out. Streams of people were heading towards the racecourse, both the women and the men dressed in their finest clothes, as if this was an occasion to impress. Lina smoothed down her cream dress, the one Alex had purchased her a few weeks ago, and adjusted the bonnet that was perched on her head. It was the first time she'd worn such a contraption and it felt strange and uncomfortable pinned to her hair, but Alex assured her she looked the part of a young debutante and that it was good practice for the challenges yet to come.

'Alex!' a voice called as their carriage drew to a stop directly outside the entrance. Lina saw Georgina hurry across to them, her husband strolling along behind, offering a few words of greeting to the people he passed.

With Alex steadying her, Lina stepped down from the carriage, noticing how he pulled her close, tucking her hand into his elbow.

'Lina, you look so well,' Georgina gushed. 'I hope my ghastly brother has been looking after you.'

'I'm treating her like a queen,' Alex said quickly.

Not quite like a queen—even Alex might balk at the idea of propositioning royalty.

'I fear I am going to lose this wager,' Georgina said. 'You look like the sweetest debutante of the Season.'

'And taste like it, too,' Alex murmured so only Lina could hear.

She refused to blush or feel embarrassed, instead fixing Alex with a steely look.

'You'll be a sensation at the Wilcox ball in two weeks' time.'

Lina's heart sank, in spite of herself. Was it really only two weeks away? That was no time at all. Two more weeks to spend with Alex, two more weeks to live this life, then it would be back to reality—back to dancing and travelling and dancing some more.

They bought tickets and passed through to the spectators' area, stopping every few feet for Georgina to greet an acquaintance or exchange words with a friend.

'Perhaps I could whisk you off to the stables,' Alex whispered in Lina's ear whilst Georgina and Pentworthy were preoccupied speaking to an elderly couple.

'To see the horses?'

'Amongst other things.'

'I'd like to see the horses.'

'And the other things?'

'My cousin always tells me there's no harm in looking,' Lina said, a mischievous grin on her face. The festival-like atmosphere here at the racecourse was infectious and Lina wanted to let all her responsibilities slide away for a few hours. What could be the harm in enjoying Alex's attention? It wasn't as though anything could happen between them with all these people around.

Alex almost dragged her through the crowds towards the stables, calling a quick excuse over his shoulder to Georgina as they went.

'Good morning, my lord,' Richardson, one of Alex's horse trainers, greeted him.

'Good morning, Richardson. How are Hercules and Dawnbreaker today?'

'In good spirits, Lord Whitemore. Feisty and raring to race.'

'This beautiful creature is Hercules,' Alex explained as he approached the first horse. 'Won six races in the past year. He's a real champion.'

Lina stepped forward slowly, not wanting to spook the animal before the big race. He eyed her belligerently, but made no other move.

'And this is Dawnbreaker. He's young—possibly

too young to race—but he's fast and eager. It's his first time competing today.'

'They're both magnificent horses,' Lina observed, wondering how much money Alex had spent on the two beautiful animals. It was probably more than she would ever see in her life, but as a horse lover herself she couldn't deny it looked like money well spent.

'I'm just going to check the starting positions and times,' Richardson said, exiting the stalls and leaving Lina and Alex by themselves with the two horses.

'Alone at last,' Alex said as he came up behind Lina and looped an arm around her waist.

Over the last few days after Alex had vowed to persuade her to become his mistress, he'd pursued her relentlessly. It had taken all of Lina's strength and determination to resist him. Here in the darkness of the stable, she felt her resolve slipping. Just one kiss wouldn't hurt, one moment of feeling his body against hers.

When she didn't pull away she felt him drop his lips on to the back of her neck where her skin was exposed beneath the back of her bonnet. There was a jolt that shook her entire body as he trailed his lips ever so gently across the nape of her neck and Lina had to bite her lip to stop herself from crying out.

'Thirty minutes until race time,' Richardson announced loudly as he re-entered the stalls. Lina pulled away from Alex quickly, busying herself inspecting Dawnbreaker to hide how unsettled he had left her.

'We'd better go and place a bet,' Alex announced, taking her by the hand and leading her away from the stables. 'Here, choose your winner for the first race.' He handed her a crisp note and pointed her in the direction of the impeccably dressed men lined up in booths in front of the racetrack.

Lina inspected the list of horses racing first, picked out Dawnbreaker's name and went to place her bet. Although she could have picked any horse she liked the sound of, as an unknown horse Dawnbreaker had the highest odds, and Lina always liked rooting for an underdog.

She returned to Alex's side, betting slip in hand.

'Who did you go for?' he asked.

She showed him and watched as the warmth blossomed in his eyes. Before Lina knew what he was doing, he pulled her closer and gave her a peck on the cheek, having to duck his head under the brim of her bonnet to reach her skin.

'Alex!' they heard Georgina hiss from behind them. 'You can't do that in public.'

Quickly she inserted herself between Lina and Alex, gripping on to Lina's arm as if to protect her from any further improprieties.

'She bet on my horse,' he said.

Georgina surveyed the crowd for a few minutes, watching the faces and levels of interest in their fellow racegoers.

'I think you're safe.'

'Safe from what?' Alex asked, leaning against the rail that separated the spectators from the race-track.

'Scandal. Notoriety. Unwanted attention,' Georgina snapped. 'It may be none of my concern what goes on between you two in private, if you are sensible enough to keep it discreet, but you cannot parade your affair in public.'

'Nonsense, Georgina,' Alex said with a laugh. 'Nobody saw us. And besides, half the gentlemen here are with their mistresses. It's not scandalous, just a fact of life.'

'We're not—' Lina began to say, but Georgina was already ploughing on with her reprimand.

'That's as may be, but they do not go about kissing or pawing them in public, and they're not under the same scrutiny as you. You're a marquess, for heaven's sake, probably the most eligible man in England.'

'We're not—' Lina tried again, but this time Alex started talking at the same time.

'Then it shouldn't matter if I strip Lina naked and consort with her right here in the middle of the racecourse. I'd still be eligible, still be good enough for the daughters of the *ton*.'

'Don't be so flippant,' Georgina hissed. 'You might be eligible, but many women would be put off by such a flagrant display of affection in public. What if one of those is the woman you're destined to spend your life with?'

'Unlikely. She eloped with my closest friend, remember?'

Lina felt his words as if they were a blow to her abdomen. Her denial of an affair between her and Alex died on her lips for a third time as his words registered. Despite his protestations, despite his flippancy when it came to the subject of Victoria, she'd known there was still a maelstrom of feelings for his ex-fiancée buried inside—and that he viewed Lina as no more than an outlet for his desires.

In the silence Lina felt the tears building in her

eyes and knew she had to escape before she made a complete fool of herself. Of course she'd had her reservations; she'd known nothing meaningful could ever happen between her and Alex, but deep down she supposed she'd nurtured a tiny flame of hope. With those few words, Alex had extinguished it. He'd had his perfect woman once and she'd left—Lina was nothing more than a pleasant distraction for him.

'We are *not* having an affair,' Lina said at last, far too loudly, spinning and fleeing through the crowd before she could gauge anyone's reaction.

Faces and bodies blurred in front of her as the tears began spilling down her face and Lina dipped her head, hoping the bonnet would be enough to save her from too many pitying looks.

'Lina! There you are. I'm glad I found you,' Pentworthy said, sitting down beside her on the grass.

She turned to look at him, offering a weak smile, but unable to summon anything further.

'I apologise for Georgina,' he continued. 'She can be rather blunt and, for a woman who spent her childhood being taught how to be the picture of demure womanhood, sometimes she lacks diplomacy. Here.' He took out his handkerchief and offered it to Lina.

Dabbing her eyes, Lina tried to rally. It would do no good to wallow in self-pity; truly there was no reason for her to be sad. She hadn't lost anything— at least not anything that she'd ever truly had.

'Love can be painful,' Pentworthy observed after a few moments of silence.

'I know Victoria hurt Alex more than he cares to admit.'

'She did,' Pentworthy said slowly. 'But I wasn't talking about Alex.'

Not wanting to acknowledge the truth behind his words, Lina kept her eyes fixed firmly on her knees.

'Did you know I was in love with Georgina for two years before she even knew who I was?'

This made Lina look up. The relationship Georgina and her husband shared was so strong, so close, she had always imagined it had been built on a solid mutual affection.

'Our paths crossed at various social functions, but I was not considered a suitable suitor so Georgina barely noticed me. She had lots of men clamouring for her attention and I got lost in the melee.'

'So how did you get her to notice you?'

'One night I was a little in my cups so my confidence was improved and I asked her to dance at a ball. Instead of making inane small talk about the weather and the dancing, I talked to her like the intelligent woman she is.'

'I can see that would work with Georgina.'

'She still doesn't know I was in love with her for years before she even noticed me.' Pentworthy paused, taking a deep breath before continuing. 'So I know what it is like to fall in love with someone who seems unattainable.'

'I'm not in love with Alex,' Lina said quietly. It seemed the right thing to do, to protest against this absurd idea.

Pentworthy shrugged. This was one of the things Lina liked about Georgina's husband; despite being a successful and driven man, he wasn't pushy.

'It's been more wonderful and more difficult than I first imagined, living this life for the past few weeks. I wanted new experiences, to do something other than live my same old humdrum life, at least for a little while, but I didn't think I would find the idea of going back so difficult.'

'You'll miss Whitemore. And the lifestyle.'

'Perhaps it's just the lifestyle I've fallen in love

with. I thought I hated the ways of the upper classes, but who wouldn't be swept away by the beautiful houses, the exquisite dresses and a life of leisure?'

For a moment Lina considered whether this was true. She had enjoyed the time she'd spent at Whitemore house—perhaps the deeper feelings she thought she had for Alex were in fact simply a manifestation of her desire not to return to her old lifestyle.

'I suppose you need to ask yourself if you would enjoy the balls and the outings and all the trappings of upper-class life without Whitemore there by your side to guide you through.'

Of course she wouldn't. It was Alex's dry observations, Alex's gentle teachings, Alex's reassuring presence by her side that made the whole experience enjoyable.

'What does it matter anyway? In two weeks, I will be back with my family and this little interlude will seem like nothing more than a surreal dream.'

'Perhaps.'

What did it matter if she was falling for Alex? He had made it quite clear that he desired her, that he wanted her in his bed, but never had he hinted at deeper feelings. She knew he cared for her, but for them to have any kind of a future together it would have to be love. There were too many differences and obstacles to overcome, only very strong feelings would be enough motivation. Alex liked her, he desired her, but he did not love her. Lina wasn't sure if he would ever let himself love again after his experience with Victoria and he certainly wouldn't consider opening his heart to someone as unsuitable as her.

'Only you can know what is in your heart,' Pentworthy said, patting her on the hand. He shrugged as if this were all a simple matter to contemplate, not something rife with important implications. 'If it's merely the lifestyle you enjoy, then you will return to your old life and slowly things will get back to normal. If you *are* in love with Whitemore, then you need to decide what you will do about it.'

'There is nothing I *can* do.'

'There is always something you can do,' Pentworthy replied softly.

'I'm very sorry for my behaviour,' Alex said sheepishly, aware that Lina's red eyes hinted at the possibility she'd been crying.

Pentworthy had sought him out a few minutes earlier and informed him where he could find Lina. Alex had headed straight over here, although as he'd walked the last few feet he wished he had taken a few moments to consider what he was going to say. Thankfully Lina didn't seem to want to talk about the argument with Georgina or his outburst, offering him a tight smile and the opportunity to move on.

'I think the first race is about to start,' she said, leading Alex through the crowd to get a better view.

As they approached the rail that separated the racetrack from the spectators, the horses were just being positioned in their starting stalls. Alex felt the familiar thrill of anticipation he experienced every time one of his horses raced, but today it was dampened a little by a definite feeling of guilt over how he had upset Lina. Looking back, he probably shouldn't have leaned in for a kiss, albeit a friendly peck on the cheek rather than a full kiss on the lips. It wasn't how a gentleman behaved in public, even towards a woman he was trying to persuade to become his mistress.

'Dawnbreaker is in stall number three.' Alex pointed towards the magnificent animals and their riders all lined up in a row.

'Does it make a difference what position they start in?'

'A little. The farther away from the inside rail the horse is, the bigger the distance it has to run, which is why the riders will try to get to a position as close to the inside rail as possible once the race has started.'

'So position three is worse than position one and better than six?' Lina asked.

'Exactly. How much of a difference it makes is questionable, but often the odds of the horse in the first stall are lowered because of this bias.'

Surreptitiously, he glanced at Lina. On the surface she seemed calm and collected—she appeared interested in the horses and eager for the race to begin. Perhaps a little too eager. Normally Lina would be laughing and joking, questioning him about every little detail, picking up on any gaps in his knowledge. Right now, Alex thought she was trying to act normal, trying to convince him she was unaffected by the scene earlier in the afternoon.

Part of him wanted to turn Lina to face him, look her squarely in the eye and promise her he was over Victoria. Surely the encounters he'd had with his ex-fiancée over the last few weeks proved it? But he'd seen the hurt in Lina's eyes when he'd mentioned Victoria; when his angry and uncensored mind admitted that once he'd thought he was destined to spend his life with her.

The other slightly uncomfortable realisation was just how much Lina was beginning to care for him. Only a woman with deeper feelings for a man would react in the way Lina had. Maybe it would be for the best if he gave up his pursuit of her.

As Alex contemplated this option, he wondered if he *would* be able to stop now. Of course desire was something he could rein in, but he couldn't deny there was something else pushing him to pursue Lina. He wanted her in his bed, but even more than that he wanted her in his life. The idea that she would leave for ever in a couple of weeks was unbearable. If she stayed as his mistress, then she would stay in his life.

Careful, he cautioned himself. Desire was one thing, but asking Lina to stay because of deeper feelings they shared sounded more like marriage than an affair.

'Look!' Lina said, grabbing his arm with one hand and pointing with the other.

The race had started, all nine horses building up speed at an impressive pace, their hooves churning up the grass and their riders bent low over their backs.

'Go, Dawnbreaker!' Lina shouted, completely caught up in the moment, unaware of her surroundings or the fact that other people were staring.

Alex envied this ability of Lina's to do what she wanted without caring what other people thought of her. He was able to do the same to an extent, but it wasn't a natural state of affairs for him, he had to work to go against his upbringing and not be bothered by other people's opinions.

Lina grabbed his hand, squeezing it with excitement as the horses raced past their position, Dawnbreaker vying for the lead position. Watching carefully, Alex saw how his horse remained completely focused, ignoring the other animals around it, not becoming distracted by the crowds or the noise. A surge of excitement began to build, travelling down his spine, and he observed Dawnbreaker and his rider take the lead, slowly but surely increasing the distance between them and the horse in second position. If he wasn't very much mistaken, he was watching a champion racehorse win his first race.

'He's won!' Lina cried as Dawnbreaker crossed the finish line clearly in the lead.

She threw her arms around Alex, hugging him for a second before he felt her body stiffen as she must have remembered Georgina's reprimand from earlier in the afternoon.

'Congratulations,' Lina said, pulling away and offering her hand for him to shake instead.

Feeling strangely bereft without her lithe body pressed against his, Alex took her hand and raised it to his lips.

'Shall we collect your winnings?' he asked.

'My winnings? Oh, from the bet I placed. How exciting!'

Quickly Alex led Lina through the crowds, instructing her on how to collect her winnings after presenting her betting slip at one of the numerous booths.

'Alex, there's thirteen pounds here,' Lina whispered quietly as they stepped away from the booth. 'This can't be right.'

'It is. As Dawnbreaker was unknown and untested in a big race environment, the odds were twelve to one. I gave you one pound to bet, so you get twelve pounds in return plus the pound you bet originally.'

'It's so much money.'

She caressed the notes for a moment before holding them out to him.

Carefully he plucked one note from the pile before pushing the rest back towards her.

'I'll take the original stake... You get the winnings.'

'Alex, that's too much.'

'You chose which horse to bet on, the money is yours.'

He watched as she flicked through the banknotes again as if she couldn't quite believe her eyes. She tried to form a word with her mouth but nothing came out. Alex could see the tears building in her eyes. It was easy to forget that twelve pounds might be enough to change someone's life.

Chapter Nineteen

The sky was overcast as they said their farewells to Georgina and Pentworthy, the brilliant sunshine of earlier in the day a distant memory.

'There's going to be a storm,' Lina observed, looking at the sky with a knowing expression.

'Probably just a little rain.'

'There's a storm building,' Lina insisted. 'Tonight or tomorrow. Feels like a big one.'

'How can you tell that?'

She gave him a small smile, not her normal cheeky grin, but at least it was better than the emotionless facade she'd adopted for most of the afternoon. 'You don't spend twenty years sleeping under the stars and not develop a feel for the weather.'

When he thought about it he supposed it was a vital skill, knowing when it was safe to sleep outside and when it was prudent to find shelter some-where.

As Alex helped Lina into their carriage, he felt the first heavy raindrop fall on his head and before he could climb up after her a few more splattered his jacket. With a quick glance at his coachman and groom, who sat huddled at the front of the car-riage, he satisfied himself both men were suitably protected against the weather. It appeared it was only him oblivious to the impending storm.

'Did you enjoy your day?' he asked as he settled on the seat opposite Lina. It felt a lifetime since he'd been squeezed in next to her on the way to the races and although he would like nothing more than to sit with his arm draped casually around Lina's shoulders again, her expression told him that was not a good idea.

'Yes, thank you.'

'I appreciated your company.'

They fell silent. It felt awkward, too stiff and formal, and Alex cursed himself once again for the foolish words he'd spoken earlier in the day. The excitement of the first race, with Dawnbreaker winning and Lina collecting her first racing win-nings, had helped in knocking down the protec-tive barrier Lina had raised between them, but that change in mood had been short-lived. For the rest of the afternoon she'd remained polite, replying to his enquiries with a word or two, but never initiating a conversation of her own. She seemed lost in her own mind, preoccupied, and Alex knew that could not be a good thing.

'I was thinking of moving to my London house next week. Would this suit you?' Alex asked, hating the way he felt unsure about his plans for the first time in many years.

Lina shrugged. 'Whatever you think best.'

'That way we will have a little while before the Wilcox ball and the final challenge of the wager.' His heart sank a little at the prospect, but he continued, 'I need to visit my tailor and you will need at least one new dress. It will also give us the opportunity to take in an opera and anything else you'd like to do whilst we're in London.'

Another shrug, this time accompanied by a weak smile.

'Perhaps a trip to Astley's,' Alex suggested.

'Astley's?'

'Astley's Amphitheatre. There is a circus there, mainly great feats of horsemanship, riding standing up, that sort of thing.'

'Of course I've heard of Astley's.' Lina's hushed

voice belied the excitement on her face. 'I've always wanted to go.'

He saw the flames of excitement in Lina's eyes that she could not dampen no matter how hard she tried. For a moment, he pictured her trying to emulate the performers at Astley's and shuddered as he realised it was exactly the sort of thing she *would* try to do.

'Only if you promise never to try the tricks you see,' he added quickly. The idea of Lina galloping through the countryside hanging upside down from the stirrups made his stomach churn with worry.

'Will Aunt Lucy accompany us to London?' Lina asked after a few minutes of silence.

'No, her leg will heal better if she stays at Whitemore House—a long carriage journey wouldn't be practical or comfortable. I will ask Georgina to reside with us when we arrive in London, I'm sure she will be amenable.'

'I wouldn't want to inconvenience her.'

For a moment Alex felt a surge of hope, wondering if Lina was suggesting she would prefer to stay with him alone, but one look at her subdued visage and the hope dwindled and died.

Deciding to sit back and stop trying to force the

conversation, Alex closed his eyes. Things would seem better in the morning. Hopefully Lina would have time to work through whatever it was that was concerning her and tomorrow they could return to their normal, easy relationship.

Outside, the rain was pounding on the carriage now and whenever they travelled over an exposed stretch of road, the carriage rocked from side to side as it was buffeted by the wind. The trees groaned and rustled, their branches creaking. It was a foul night to be out and Alex spared a thought for the coachman and groom braving the elements to hurry them home.

'We're slowing,' Lina said when they'd been travelling for nearly an hour. It should still be another hour at least until they reached Whitemore House, probably more in these conditions.

Alex leaned forward, peering out of the window into the darkness, trying to see if there was a fallen tree or something similar blocking the way.

'There are men on horses, my lord.' The groom's voice carried down to them on the wind.

Time seemed to slow as Alex's senses heightened. Men on horses blocking the road on a night like this meant nothing but bad news. Highwaymen and robbers had become less of a problem over the past few years, but they did still exist and an encounter could be deadly.

'Don't get out of the carriage unless absolutely necessary,' Alex instructed Lina, squeezing her hand to try to convey the importance of his words. Most highwaymen were ruthless men without any scruples when it came to killing. The punishment for highway robbery was death, so they were already risking everything. It didn't concern them if their victims were left alive or dead.

There was a chance these men in the road ahead weren't highwaymen, but Alex couldn't think of another reason to be stopping carriages on a night like this.

'Can we push through them?' Alex shouted as he leaned out of the window. The horses had slowed to a walk and he peered into the darkness, trying to make out the forms in the road ahead.

'The road's too narrow,' the coachman answered after considering for a few seconds. 'They've got guns, my lord. If they fire, it'll spook the horses and who knows where we'll end up.'

'Be ready,' Alex instructed, referring to the pistol the coachman kept in a small box up next to his seat. 'Stop the carriage, I'll get out. If you see an opportunity to break through, then go. It is most important to get Miss Lock to safety.'

'But, my lord—' the coachman began to protest.

'That's a direct order,' Alex said, pulling his head back into the carriage as it slowed to a stop.

'Be careful,' Lina said, her face pale and her expression worried.

Alex gave her a reassuring smile and had just flung open the door when he felt her arms around his neck. Before he knew what was happening, Lina's lips met his and she was kissing him deeply, almost frantically. She had an irresistible pull over him and Alex nearly forgot the line of men on horses waiting outside and the danger they presented. Only when Lina pulled away did he regain his senses and manage to push himself from the carriage.

'Is there a problem, gentlemen?' Alex shouted to be heard above the wind. Six pairs of eyes regarded him from the darkness, all sitting confidently on their horses.

'Don't move,' one of the men shouted.

Alex froze, knowing it would be foolish to get himself shot before the men had even dismounted.

'Remove any weapons you are carrying and place them on the ground.'

'I'm not in the habit of carrying a gun around the countryside,' Alex said. He knew it was best not to antagonise the men in front of him, but he wasn't going to start stuttering and stammering in fear, either.

'Is there anyone else in the carriage?'

Alex hesitated. There was no point lying, but he would much prefer they left Lina alone.

'Just a young woman. She has no money or valuables upon her person.'

Two of the men conferred quietly, appearing to argue over their next course of action. Alex shivered as the rain began to soak through his jacket and shirt; he'd only been outside for a couple of minutes and already he was soaked to the skin.

'Stay where you are. No sudden moves or we shoot. That goes for you, too.' This last instruction was directed towards the coachman and groom, who remained hunched over at the front of the carriage.

One of the horsemen dismounted, giving the reins of his horse to his closest companion, then crossed slowly to the carriage. Alex took the opportunity to study the men in front of him. It was strange to have so many; often highwaymen worked alone or in pairs, but it was uncommon to have six mounted bandits. More people to share the profits with—but he supposed there was safety in numbers, as well. All the men wore heavy over-coats, hats and had a piece of material pulled up over the lower half of their faces so only their eyes were visible from below the brims of their hats. It would make identification impossible. This buoyed Alex's spirits a little; if the men were planning on killing all witnesses they would be much less concerned about concealing their identities. The fact they were so covered up gave Alex hope they might survive this encounter.

Turning slowly, Alex watched as Lina was pulled roughly from the carriage, stumbling and thumping the highwayman on the shoulder as he dragged her along.

Despite the danger in the situation Alex had to stifle a smile. Lina wasn't the sort to go quietly when manhandled, even when her assailant was armed and dangerous and she was at a disadvantage.

Alex caught her as the highwayman thrust her towards him, looping an arm around Lina's waist both to steady her and to stop her doing anything foolish like rushing and attacking the mounted men.

'We have five pistols trained on you both,' the

leader of the men said, having to raise his voice to be heard over the wind. 'If you make any sudden moves, you will be shot. If you do not comply with our orders, you will be shot. If you attempt to escape, you will be shot.'

As the man was speaking, Alex could feel Lina shivering, although he couldn't be sure if it was from cold or fear. Given the warm weather the last few weeks and the beautiful sunshine earlier in the day when they'd set off on their journey to the races, Lina was dressed only in her cotton dress with a light shawl draped over her shoulders. Hardly appropriate attire to be out in a storm.

'May I give my companion my jacket?' Alex asked.

'No. Very slowly I want you to gather all of your valuables and money and pass it to our comrade here.'

Alex was carrying his coin purse and a thin stack of notes—winnings from their time at the races. He also had a pocket watch, but didn't like to adorn himself with copious valuables like some young men seemed to. Lina would have the twelve pounds she had won by betting on Dawnbreaker, but nothing more. Overall it would be a small loss, nothing he couldn't live without. Certainly nothing worth risking Lina's life for.

Slowly he reached into a pocket and withdrew the coin purse and the stack of banknotes held together by a silver clip. These he handed over, at the same time manoeuvring himself very slightly in front of Lina. It wouldn't be enough to protect her from all six bullets if they were fired upon, but it might give her a fighting chance of diving for cover should one of the highwaymen become twitchy with his trigger finger.

'And you, miss,' the man in front of them growled, gesturing for Lina to hand over any valuables.

'I don't have anything,' Lina said, her voice defiant. 'And even if I did, I wouldn't hand it over to you.'

'Show some manners, or I might just have to shoot you.' The highwayman took a step closer to Lina and Alex quickly stepped in between the pair, unsure if he was more worried about the man hitting Lina or Lina hitting the man. Not that he wouldn't deserve it, but it was a way to ensure that they got shot and rolled into a ditch.

Behind him he heard Lina mumble something

about manners, but luckily the wind blew her comment away from the highwayman's ears.

'You've got my money,' Alex said placatingly. 'Now, just let us go on our way.'

The men on horseback glanced at each other, as if trying to decide what would be the best course of action. Before they could come to an agreement, Alex saw movement out of the corner of his eye. His coachman, a middle-aged man who'd been travelling the roads of England long enough to know most hold-ups didn't end well, shifted slightly in his seat. Quickly Alex took another step closer to Lina, grasping her by the shoulders as he saw the coachman raise the gun and aim at one of the highwaymen. As the pistol fired, Alex didn't wait to see if it hit the mark; even if the one man was dead there were five more to shoot back. He pulled Lina sideways, flinging them into the ditch at the side of the road. Just before they disappeared into the icy water that lay at the bottom of the ditch, Alex felt a searing pain across his biceps which caused him to jerk and fall awkwardly. He recovered at the very last moment and managed to roll so he cushioned Lina's landing.

For a few seconds the commotion from the road above them stilled as their heads dipped under the water, and as they re-emerged, Alex could hear confusion and the clattering of hooves.

'Stay here,' he instructed, knowing the cold, dirty water wasn't the best place to spend more than a few minutes, but for now it was safer than the unknown situation up on the road.

'Be careful,' Lina whispered as Alex poked his head above the rim of the ditch.

It was chaos. Horses were rearing, men shouting, and as Alex hauled himself up to join the melee, another shot was fired.

Spooked by the unnaturally loud gunshot, the horses tethered to the carriage had sprung into action and Alex could see both the coachman and the groom desperately trying to control them. It was to no avail, and he watched the carriage head straight for the group of highwaymen, scattering them as it ploughed through their line at speed.

The remaining men struggled to calm their horses—two had been thrown in the commotion and were visibly torn between remounting and being able to defend themselves with their pistols. One decided to remount, and the other, with a quick glance at his companions, followed.

'Let's get out of here,' someone shouted.

Alex almost cheered at the idea. He was standing unarmed and battered against six armed men. He didn't have a chance if they decided to come after him.

The first of the highwaymen spun his horse and cantered away into the darkness, four more hot on his heels. Only the man who'd taken their money, the man who'd threatened Lina, remained for a few extra seconds, his pistol aimed at Alex from his position on the back of his horse.

There was nowhere for Alex to go. Either this man would shoot him or he wouldn't. At this range, he would have a fifty-fifty chance of hitting his target, and seeing as Alex was unarmed there wasn't much risk to the highwayman if he tarried for a few seconds longer to fire the shot.

Alex had always wondered what thoughts might assail him as he looked death in the eye and he was surprised that only images of Lina filled his mind. Lina smiling as she teased him. Lina slipping into the water of the lake on the estate. Lina dancing in his arms at the country dance.

Looking straight at the man in front of him, Alex shrugged, as if to indicate he was ready to take his chances. He saw the minute movement as the man's finger squeezed the trigger, heard the bang as the powder propelled the bullet forward. The bullet went wide, very wide—thanks in no small part to Lina leaning out of the ditch and poking the horse the highwayman was seated on with a fallen branch just a moment before the shot was fired. The horse reared, danced forward and backwards a few steps, then shot off down the road so quickly the highwayman nearly lost his seat.

In an instant Alex was kneeling down, pulling Lina out of the ditch. She was shivering violently, covered in mud, and her dress was sticking to her body in a way that looked very uncomfortable.

'You're bleeding,' she said through chattering teeth.

Alex glanced down at his arm. His jacket was torn and the shirt underneath was soaked with blood. He recalled the stinging sensation as he flung himself and Lina into the ditch and realised he must have been shot.

Despite her obvious discomfort, Lina did not hesitate in pulling his jacket from his shoulders and tearing the ripped material of his shirt to get a better look at the wound. In the darkness it was difficult to see, but he felt her fingers probing softly.

'I need to bind it, try to stop the bleeding.'

It felt rather nice to have Lina's fingers dancing across his skin, even if the wound did not burn and sting now, he'd become aware of it. Deftly, as if she dealt with bullet wounds all the time, Lina tore strips of his ripped shirtsleeve and fashioned them into a makeshift bandage, which she wound tightly around his biceps.

'That'll do for now.'

'How about you?' Alex asked, catching her hand as she was about to step away. 'Are you hurt?'

'Just a little bruised,' Lina said with a shrug.

Many women of his acquaintance would be in hysterics by now. Many men, too. Lina was cold, uncomfortable and a little shaken by the evening's events, but her demeanour was calm and he knew she would not be swooning or collapsing or engaging in any other form of unhelpful behaviour.

'Where's the carriage?' Lina was peering into the darkness, scrunching up her eyes as if in the hope of being able to see in the dark.

'It won't be far. McManus is an experienced coachman. He'll have brought the horses under control without too much trouble.'

'Shall we start walking?'

They'd just been robbed, fired upon, forced into freezing water and battered by the storm raging overhead and Lina was calmly suggesting they set off to find the carriage.

'You're very practical in a crisis,' Alex said, draping his jacket over her shoulders. It was wet, torn and probably provided only minimal protection from the elements, but any small advantage could be vital on a night like this.

'Would you prefer me to collapse to the floor, crying and screaming?'

'Most certainly not.'

He held her by the shoulders for a moment, raising one hand to brush the damp tendrils of hair stuck to her face away.

'Thank you for saving my life,' Alex said softly, looking into her dark eyes and seeing a flash of warmth.

'It seemed the right thing to do.'

Before he could stop himself, he dipped his head and kissed her. Later he might blame the excitement of the evening, the residual sensation of danger, of throwing caution to the wind, but right now he knew he kissed her because he wasn't able to *not* kiss her.

Despite the chill of the rest of her body Lina's lips were wonderfully warm. She still tasted of the strawberries and wine they'd indulged in a few hours before at the racetrack and as her tongue flicked out to meet his, Alex felt his desire swell and grow.

'Are you hurt, my lord?' The voice was carried on the wind and Alex recognised it as belonging to the groom, Kitsworth.

Lina hurriedly stepped away from him, taking her warmth with her, but Alex caught her hand to stop her from going too far.

'Kitsworth, what happened?' Alex called as the groom rounded the bend in the road.

'The carriage is damaged, my lord.'

'Are you injured? Or McManus?'

'No, my lord. McManus is checking the horses over now.'

Quickly Alex and Lina followed the groom back down the lane, their heads bent against the driving rain. The wind had picked up again and the trees were creaking ominously on either side of the road.

The carriage had come to a halt about half a mile from the site of the ambush. Despite the coachman's best efforts, it had careened out of control and was now lying at an angle, half in the ditch to the side of the road. Alex was reminded of the horrible accident Aunt Lucy had been involved in and realised they had been lucky neither he nor Lina had been inside.

'Horses seem fine, my lord,' McManus shouted over the sound of the wind and rain.

Alex surveyed the scene. There was no way they would get the carriage back on the road tonight without extra help. All four of them were soaked to the bone and Lina especially looked pale and as if her body had nearly reached the limit of its endurance.

'Did we pass any houses on the road before the ambush?' Alex asked.

'There was a cluster of houses a few miles back,' McManus said.

Alex grimaced. Despite the blood still seeping from his arm he was confident he would still be able to ride a horse a few miles, but he doubted Lina would be able to manage it. If he didn't get her somewhere dry soon, she would certainly catch a chill or even something worse. 'Take the horses,' Alex instructed his coachman and groom. 'Ride to the nearest village or house, wait for the worst of the storm to settle and then see if you can borrow a carriage to transport us home.'

'Where will you go, my lord?' McManus asked.

'There looks to be a barn on the other side of that field.' Alex motioned off into the darkness. He was taking a risk—the barn might be locked or have fallen into disrepair, but he would just have to hope for the best. Lina needed to be somewhere dry and sheltered, and there weren't many other possibilities.

As the two men readied the horses, Alex stepped closer to Lina. She was shivering violently now, unable to conceal just how cold she was.

'Do you think you can make it across that field?' Alex asked.

'Race you,' Lina replied, managing to summon a faint smile through chattering teeth.

Chapter Twenty

The barn loomed over the muddy field, large and dark and silent. Lina felt her leg muscles burning as she struggled the last few steps and watched as Alex gripped one of the doors and swung it outwards. Almost crying with relief, Lina allowed Alex to pull her into the barn, collapsing to the ground as he slammed the door closed behind them.

The silence that followed was eerie and unexpected after what felt like hours of howling winds and groaning trees. Even better than the silence was the lack of driving rain beating down on their bodies, adding weight to their already soaked clothes.

'We need to get warm and dry,' Alex said.

Lina knew what he said made sense. If they stayed in their wet clothes, they would at the very least catch a chill, maybe something even worse, but right now she wasn't sure if she could summon the energy to stand, let alone undress.

'We have nothing to change into, nothing to dry ourselves with.'

'Stay here,' Alex instructed, disappearing into the darkness before Lina could protest.

Rustling and creaking sounds followed as Alex moved around the barn, and Lina wondered what he was looking for. The wooden building was sizeable, with a hayloft above them, and as Lina's eyes adjusted to the gloom she could just make out the silhouettes of pieces of farm equipment down here on the ground floor.

Triumphantly Alex returned, brandishing two pieces of material.

'What have you found?'

'Two blankets. They smell of a farm—I think they're horse blankets for the winter, but it's better than nothing. We can bathe tomorrow when we get home.'

Right then a dry, soft horse blanket sounded like heaven.

'Can you make it up into the hayloft?' Alex asked.

Lina knew she was the one who should be looking after him, he'd been shot after all, but she was so cold and exhausted she felt as though her body had shut down. Nodding, she gathered her soaking-wet skirts and let Alex direct her to the ladder. She stumbled as she reached for the first rung and immediately Alex's hands were around her waist, steadying her.

'Just climb slowly,' he instructed. 'I'll be right behind you.'

The air felt a little warmer as they entered the hayloft, and Lina was surprised to see there was a substantial amount of hay on the small, elevated platform despite there not being any animals kept below. The farmer must have moved his livestock elsewhere for shelter during this storm, or at least Lina hoped so—she didn't wish anyone, man or beast, to be out unprotected in this weather.

A small amount of light filtered in through a tiny window in the roof of the barn and through it Lina could see the thick clouds still covering the sky. For a moment she wondered about McManus and Kitsworth, the coachman and groom. They had a long ride ahead of them in this foul weather, with no guarantee of shelter at the end. She just hoped some villager or farmer took pity on them and provided them with a fire to warm themselves by.

'Take your clothes off,' Alex instructed.

He'd climbed up silently behind her and was now busy moving around some of the hay to make room for them.

'I've got nothing to change into,' Lina protested weakly. She knew Alex was right—even standing naked was more sensible than remaining in the sodden dress and petticoats she had been wearing. The cold, wet clothes would prevent her skin from warming naturally from within as her core temperature rose now they were under shelter.

'I promise not to look.'

'All night?'

Even in the darkness she saw him grin.

'Well, maybe one peek.'

'Hand me one of those blankets,' Lina said, and slowly Alex did.

She wasn't naturally shy, had never had a problem about stripping down to her underclothes in front of friends and family, but as she tugged at the first of the ties on her dress, a warm and prickly sensation spread right from her toes to the top of her head.

'You should be undressing, too,' Lina said.

'I'll need help with my shirt, it's a little difficult to move my arm.'

Lina paused, her dress half-undone, but in no danger of going anywhere; the water had done a good job of ensuring it was firmly stuck to her body. In two steps she was by Alex's side, lifting up the bottom of his shirt, peeling it off the taut muscles of his abdomen and chest. Slowly she manoeuvred his arm through the ripped sleeve and then allowed her fingers to dart across his skin as she lifted the sodden, bloodstained shirt over his head.

'Thank you,' he said and Lina had to force herself to step away.

She continued with the ties of her dress, eventually loosening it enough to be able to push it down over her hips and step out of the heavy material. The chemise and petticoats she wore, normally a brilliant white, were now almost transparent and stuck to her skin scandalously.

Quickly Lina glanced up. Alex was in the process of unfastening his trousers, something that made her pause herself. He looked at her, unable to stop his eyes falling to her body, and even in the darkness Lina knew it was as if he were looking at her naked.

Five seconds passed, and then ten, before eventually, with what must have taken iron-strong self-control, Alex turned around, leaving her to take off her underclothes in private. At the same time he took off his trousers and Lina had to resist the very primal urge to go and wrap her body around his.

Trying to remember all the reasons why dallying with Alex was a bad idea, Lina quickly peeled off her chemise and petticoats and wrapped herself in the blanket Alex had given her.

You're from different worlds, she told herself. *Once he gets bored of you, he'll move on and you'll be heartbroken. Mistresses are disposable. It's not an equal relationship. You'll be ruined and all for a few weeks of pleasure.*

Right now a few weeks of pleasure sounded like heaven, but Lina had to acknowledge that she was developing deeper feelings for Alex and so the pain when he moved on to another women would be too much to bear.

'Let me look at your arm,' Lina said. Stepping closer to Alex was probably not the best idea, but she couldn't let him bleed to death just because she didn't trust herself to keep her hands off him.

He held out the injured arm and carefully Lina peeled the makeshift bandage off, noticing how Alex gritted his teeth to stop from wincing. The wound had stopped bleeding, but still looked red and raw, a half-inch-deep gash across his biceps.

'Can you move it?'

Slowly Alex flexed the biceps, his face contorting with pain, but he managed to complete the movement.

'I think you'll heal just fine. We can get the doctor to look at it when we get home.'

Within a few minutes Lina had bound the wound again, knowing it was important to keep it fully covered to try to prevent infection.

'You're icy cold,' Alex said, his fingers gripping her own.

It was an effort to keep her teeth from chattering and her feet felt like blocks of ice, but it was hardly surprising seeing as they'd spent the past hour drenched to the bone with dirty ditchwater and rain.

'We need to get you warm.'

Lina had visions of thick, luxurious blankets and a crackling fire to warm her toes by.

Instead she watched as Alex rearranged the hay in the loft.

'We need to share body heat.'

'How?'

'I'll lay the blanket I'm wrapped in on top of the

hay and we will both lie on top of it, covering ourselves with your blanket. We can pull some of the loose hay on the blanket as well to give us extra insulation.'

'We're both naked.'

'I think we can both be adults about this. It's for survival, not any amorous purpose.'

Lina nodded, her eyes widening as Alex dropped his blanket from around his waist and laid it on the hay. It was dark in the barn and she couldn't make out much, but her eyes sought out the contours of his body all the same.

'Lie down,' he instructed.

Loosening the blanket wrapped around her body, Lina lay down, feeling Alex's fingers pulling at the material as she did so. By the time she was comfortable and supine, the blanket had been spread to cover her with a space left directly next to her for Alex.

Lina realised she was holding her breath as he slipped under the blanket. For a moment he busied himself pulling clumps of hay on top of them to add another layer of insulation, but after a short while he stilled, and there was just the sound of their breathing and the hammering of the rain on the roof of the barn.

'Your teeth are chattering,' Alex observed.

'I'm still cold.'

'Come here.'

Gently he turned her so she was facing away from him, looped an arm around her waist and pressed his body against hers. Lina stiffened. She could feel all of him and she wanted nothing more than to roll over and welcome him into her body.

'Just relax,' Alex said, his voice a little hoarser than usual. Lina felt anything but relaxed. A strange heat was building just below her abdomen and spreading through her body. She had to physically suppress the urge to wriggle and writhe against Alex, subconsciously wanting more skin-to-skin contact, more sublime sensations as Alex's fingers grazed her arm.

She could feel his manhood, hard and solid against her buttocks, and knew this was just as difficult for him as it was her.

Desperately she searched for some distraction, anything to quell this building sensation of inevitability between them.

'You thought Victoria was the woman you were destined to spend your life with,' Lina blurted—and regretted it immediately.

* * *

Alex stiffened. With Lina's body pressed up against his, every curve, every inch of exposed skin teasing and tantalising, he was finding it difficult to concentrate on anything except maintaining control of himself, but Lina's words registered after a few seconds.

'Victoria?' he asked, unsure where the topic had come from.

'Earlier this afternoon when you were arguing with your sister, you said Victoria was the woman you'd been destined to spend your life with, or something along those lines.'

The argument was still fresh in his mind. Georgina couldn't help but meddle in affairs that didn't concern her, but this time he had to admit she had been right. It had been careless and wrong to kiss Lina in public, even just a little peck on the cheek. Throughout his life he'd been taught to adhere to the rules of society. Some men didn't see a problem with parading their mistresses in public, snatching a kiss in the shadows of the opera house or letting a hand stray somewhere it shouldn't whilst dancing a waltz. Alex wasn't that kind of man—or at least he hadn't thought he was. Kissing Lina on the cheek hadn't been a conscious decision, it had just *happened*, and Alex knew he'd been as power-less to stop it as he had the storm raging overhead.

'I'm not sure—' he began.

'Don't try to deny you said the words.'

Alex sighed, Lina seemed to have rallied a little, recovered some of her normal tenacious nature.

'You might tell the world you're over Victoria, but you're not.'

He started to speak, but Lina rushed on.

'It is perfectly natural to still care about some-one even if they hurt you. I think it is just a shame you won't admit to yourself that your affection for Victoria and the heartbreak you suffered is holding you back from moving on in matters of the heart.'

'I don't love Victoria,' Alex said firmly. Lina re-mained silent and he considered the words he'd just uttered. Even when being completely honest with himself he believed he was speaking the truth. 'I think it is hard to move on, to stop caring about someone when they've spent a long time in your heart. No matter how much someone hurts you it is difficult to forget all the good times, all the happiness.'

'I'm sorry it worked out this way,' Lina said qui-etly.

'I'm not. If Victoria could hurt me as she did,

then it is a blessing she left my life before she could do any more damage.'

'Do you truly believe that?'

'Yes.'

Alex remembered the empty feeling he'd had when he'd first encountered Victoria in the dressmakers after three years apart. Perhaps if he was honest with himself, he hadn't felt as little as he admitted. Certainly he'd felt empty and emotionless, but that in itself was significant—it was his mind's way of protecting him from further heartbreak.

'Did you believe you were destined to spend your lives together?'

'I was very young…' Alex started.

'It was three years ago, not fifteen.'

'I was naive. Victoria was the first woman I'd ever loved and I suppose I assumed she felt the same about me.'

Lina shifted against him, her body starting to warm as they shared their heat, her buttocks pressed up against him in a way that made it difficult for him to concentrate.

'And because she hurt you, you've decided never to risk opening your heart to love again.'

'You're starting to sound like my sister.'

'I want to understand, Alex.'

He sighed. He didn't know how he felt, didn't know why he rejected all the eligible young women he came across at first glance. Perhaps if he was honest, he might admit he was trying to prevent himself from getting hurt again.

'I don't ever want to be out of control like that again. To give anyone that power over me.'

Lina was quiet for a few moments, her body still against his. 'That, I can understand.'

As the silence stretched out, only broken by the pounding of the rain on the roof of the barn, Alex felt as though he needed to say something more, to explain his reasoning, but the truth was he didn't know that he understood it himself.

'If Victoria was free, not tied to your friend in marriage, would you want to be with her again?' Lina asked, her voice no more than a whisper.

'Definitely not. I could never trust her, never enjoy myself with her.'

Not like I do with you, a little voice in his head added. He did trust Lina and he certainly enjoyed spending time with her.

The blanket shifted as Lina rolled over, facing him in the darkness, her delicate hands resting on his chest. Alex had to stifle a groan as her breasts brushed against his arm, but did allow his hand to drape over her waist and rest in the small of her back.

'I hope one day you are able to love again,' Lina whispered softly, burying her head into the space between his shoulder and his jaw. 'I just want you to be happy.'

The rain had stopped by the time Lina woke up and dawn was just breaking, sending the first rays of sunlight through the small window in the hay-loft. For a few moments she felt peculiarly content and she wriggled and stretched with her eyes closed.

'Good morning.'

Lina froze, noting the warm body next to hers, the soft skin and hard muscle underneath. As she remembered the events that had led to the night in the barn, her eyes shot open and she was on her feet in an instant, pulling the blanket to wrap around her as she rose. She was completely naked, and had spent the entire night with her body pressed against Alex's for warmth. For a moment she remembered how good it had felt to have his arm draped across her waist, to have her body nestled against his, and she had to physically shake herself to stop from collapsing back on to the blanket and asking Alex to make her his.

Glancing down, her eyes widened. Of course he was completely naked, and she'd just whipped the blanket from him, exposing every inch of his body. She knew she should look away, but her eyes were transfixed, locked on his naked form, and nothing would entice them to move.

Alex grinned, winked at her and then rose slowly, taking his time to brush the stray bits of hay from his body before wrapping the second blanket around himself.

'We should dress,' Lina said quickly, picking some hay from her own hair.

'Or we could just give in to our desires and fall back under the blankets...'

She studiously ignored his last remark, knowing it wouldn't take much to persuade her to do exactly as he had suggested. Her body was taut with desire. Just one touch, one carefully placed finger, would have her begging and moaning for Alex to ruin her.

Their clothes were still a little damp, but no longer dripping with dirty water. Lina grimaced as she straightened out her chemise and petticoats before putting them on. They were a grimy grey

colour with streaks of mud, an unpleasant re-
minder of the events on the road the night before.

'We can bathe when we get home,' Alex said, a
half-smile on his face as he watched her expression.

He was clad in trousers now, just his top half-
bare, and Lina risked a quick look. With his torso
exposed, his body streaked with dirt and the makeshift bandage around his upper arm, he looked
like some warrior of old, again reminding her of
an illustration in her favourite book, *Greek Gods,
Heroes and Myths*.

The idea of relaxing in one of the gigantic bath-
tubs at Whitemore House brought a smile to Lina's
face, too. Over the past few weeks she'd enjoyed
lying back in the warm water, spending time lath-
ering her hair with fragrant soaps and scrubbing
her skin until it glowed. Of course she'd had baths
before, but the tin tub filled with cold water her
family owned didn't quite make for the same experience.

'Could you help me?' Alex asked, indicating his
ripped shirt and the bandage on his arm.

Lina pulled her own dress over her head before
approaching Alex. The more layers of clothing between them the safer she felt. If too much of her

skin touched his, she wasn't sure she would be able to keep a clear head.

Carefully, she helped Alex manoeuvre his arm into his shirt, lifting it over his head and down over his chest, her fingers accidently grazing the solid muscles of his abdomen. Lina stepped away as if she'd been burnt, turning to fiddle with the ties on her dress to cover the deep blush she could feel was spreading across her cheeks.

'McManus and Kitsworth should return for us soon,' Alex said. 'If you can make it, I think we should go back to the road, return to the carriage and wait for them there.'

Lina nodded. Despite the few hours of sleep they had managed to get she still felt exhausted, but she would be able to rest once they were safely home. Right now it was most important to get out into the open, where she was less likely to throw herself at the man she desired with every fibre of every muscle in her body.

Chapter Twenty-One

'What an adventure you've had!' Aunt Lucy exclaimed, her eyes shining as Alex finished telling her about their eventful journey home from the races. He'd glossed over the part where he and Lina had spent the night in each other's arms, completely naked, with just one another's bodies for heat. Although Aunt Lucy was a free spirit when it came to matters of the heart and matters of the bedchamber, Alex didn't want to embarrass Lina by giving his aunt too many details.

They'd arrived back at Whitemore House just before lunch, exhausted and filthy. Luckily, as they'd returned to the damaged carriage on the road near the barn McManus and Kitsworth had arrived on horseback, with a friendly farmer driving his cart behind them. The coachman and the groom had spent most of the night trawling the local area, desperately trying to find someone who would open their door to two strange men in the middle of the night in the storm. Alex was pleased he'd taken Lina to shelter in the barn rather than ride for help the night before. He'd been unsure about his decision, but seeing the pale, drawn faces of his coachman and groom, he knew he'd made the right choice.

On arriving home he'd first instructed McManus and Kitsworth to take at least a week off to recuperate and then he'd sunk into a hot bath, making sure not to get his injured arm wet. Lina had still not emerged from her bedroom, where every so often a maid would disappear with a fresh bucket of hot water, so no doubt she was still soaking in the tub that had been carried into her room. An hour ago the doctor had arrived and quickly cleansed and sutured Alex's wound, declaring he should make a full recovery as the bullet had only grazed him, passing cleanly through the skin and top layer of muscle.

'It was certainly an eventful night,' Alex said, leaning back in his chair. He felt tired, his eyes heavy and his body weary. He hadn't slept a wink, finding it impossible to relax with Lina's body pressed against his, having her so tantalisingly close but unable to act out his deepest fantasies. Every time she'd shifted, every time she'd wriggled in her sleep, Alex had fought to maintain his control. The worst part was that he'd seen the desire in her eyes, known that all it would take was one carefully timed kiss and she would melt into his arms, willing and ready to give in to the passion between them.

'It'll be a story to tell your grandchildren,' Aunt Lucy said, a hint of mischief in her eyes.

'Aunt Lucy…' Alex started, his voice stern.

'Anyone can see the connection you two share.'

Alex sighed, looking down at his hands for a few moments. He loved Aunt Lucy, she'd been wonderful after the death of his parents, ensuring both he and Georgina wanted for nothing whilst they mourned the loss, but sometimes she was a little too free with her opinions.

'I like Lina,' Alex said slowly, choosing his words so she couldn't misinterpret anything. 'I enjoy spending time with her. She's fun and amusing and I find myself happier when I'm in her company.'

'What more could you want from a mate?'

'You know she's a completely unsuitable companion.'

'I can see the spark between you, the desire that is simmering just beneath the surface.'

'That is not enough to base a lifetime together.'

Aunt Lucy shrugged. 'It's a good start. I've been married three times, Alex, and my happiest time was when I followed what my heart was telling me.'

He couldn't believe they were talking about him having a future with Lina. It wasn't even something he had contemplated, not seriously. In the dark hours in the middle of the night he had indulged in a few fantasies, scenarios where he woke up to Lina in his arms every morning and made passionate love to her every night, but he knew they were just that: fantasies.

'She's a gypsy.'

'Why should that matter?'

It was the way of the world. Perhaps people would be much happier if the social order was not such an important consideration, but in today's world it was.

'If I chose to spend my life with Lina, we would be snubbed by society. She'd never fit in.'

'That's only a problem if you care about those things.'

Despite knowing it could never happen, despite

knowing his life and Lina's could never slot together, Alex felt a flicker of hope and anticipation. There would be something wonderful about spending each and every day with Lina, watching her face as he gave her a racehorse to break in and train, persuading her to swim naked again in the lake, indulgently kissing every inch of her body first thing each morning...

'These last few weeks you've come alive again, Alex, after retreating into yourself for so long. If Lina can do that for you, imagine what happiness you could have if you just forget about what society expects of you and focus on what is really important—love.'

Distractedly he shook his head. He didn't love Lina. He liked her, he cared for her, he certainly desired her, but after Victoria had nearly broken him, he'd vowed never to open his heart to love again.

It was true he loved certain things about Lina— her inquisitive nature, her inherent kindness, her ability to shrug off other people's opinions—but that wasn't the same thing as loving her. Or at least...

Alex shook his head, this was not a path he

should go down. If he loved Lina, things would get a lot more complicated, a lot messier.

'All that can be obtained without marriage,' Alex said slowly, an idea forming in his mind. When he'd asked Lina to become his mistress before, he'd tried to persuade her it would just be for a short time, that they could take their pleasure and break away cleanly, both moving on with their lives. Over the past few weeks Alex knew his affections for Lina had grown, he couldn't stand in the same room as her and not want to wrap her in his arms. Perhaps the solution to their difference of opinion when it came to Lina being his mistress could be solved by him admitting he didn't just want a short-term affair.

'She won't have you any other way,' Aunt Lucy said bluntly.

'You don't know that.'

'She's a sensible girl—already she's at a huge social disadvantage being from a gypsy family. All she has is her virtue and her self-respect. If she agrees to be your mistress, she will lose that.'

Alex shook his head, about to protest.

'You know what I'm saying is true. And if she were to become your mistress, everything is taken out of her control. It wouldn't be her deciding on how long to prolong your affair. She would be entirely at your mercy and that is a frightening prospect for a young woman.'

'I'd never hurt her.'

'Yes, you would. In a few years, you will want to marry. The urge for a domestic life will grow and you will want heirs of your own flesh and blood. You are not the sort of man to keep a mistress when a wife warms your marital bed and Lina knows it.'

Alex could hardly deny it. He wasn't sure he ever would want to marry, but if he did, his conscience wouldn't allow him to keep a mistress at the same time.

'I love you very much, Alex. You know I look upon you and Georgina like the children I was never blessed with. I just want you to be happy.'

He *was* happy. The past few weeks he'd felt more content than he had done in years.

'Consider what would truly make you happy, then find a way to ensure it happens and damn the rest of society and what they think.'

Lina sat on the terrace, running a comb through her wet hair, feeling completely rejuvenated and relaxed. All in all, she'd spent over an hour in the bathtub, the maids obligingly bringing her fresh buckets of hot water whenever the chill began to set in. In return, Lina had regaled them with the story of what had happened on the trip home, adding a few embellishments here and there to keep her audience enthralled. By the time her skin was so soft it was beginning to wrinkle, the maids were giggling in delight as Lina described how Alex had saved her life one last time.

Now alone, she allowed her thoughts to turn to Alex—and more specifically the undeniably chaste night they had just spent together. She'd been so close to giving in to her desire, so close to brushing her lips against his whilst urging him to make love to her. The lack of control was frightening and Lina knew she would have to be very careful these next couple of weeks or she would find herself in Alex's bed with no way of protecting her future.

'I'm here to collect,' a low voice growled suddenly in her ear.

Only the hand Lina covered her mouth with stifled the high-pitched scream of shock as her uncle grabbed her wrist. He looked dishevelled, desperate even, and the wild darting of his eyes made Lina pause for a moment. Her uncle had never been a warm or loving relative, more interested in what he could take from people than in building relationships, but never had he been quite so cruel, quite so persistent. Ever since she'd made and lost the wager with Uncle Tom, Lina hadn't stopped to consider why he was quite so desperate for the debt to be paid or the details of how to get his hands on Alex's money.

'You owe someone money,' Lina said, recovering from the initial shock of being pounced on.

'That's none of your concern,' Tom hissed, although by the expression on his face Lina could see she was right. No wonder he'd been so persistent.

'I've got most of what I owe you,' Lina said.

'Most isn't good enough.'

Quickly Lina reached for the stack of notes she'd kept hidden under her skirts throughout the ambush the night before. It was her winnings from the bet on Dawnbreaker at the races. Twelve pounds— more money than she'd ever possessed—but right now she didn't care. All she wanted was for Uncle Tom to leave her alone.

'We agreed on fifteen pounds,' Tom said, counting the notes greedily.

'Take this,' Lina said after a moment's hesitation. It was the silver comb Alex had given her after their first dinner party. She was loath to part with it, but if it meant getting Uncle Tom to leave her alone once and for all it was a small price to pay.

'It's not enough.'

Lina frowned. The hair clip was solid silver and of an intricate and beautiful design. It would certainly cover the outstanding three pounds she owed him.

'I need more, much more.'

There was pure fear in Uncle Tom's eyes now and Lina felt a flicker of sympathy for the man, despite never liking him much.

'What have you got yourself mixed up in?' she asked softly.

'Nothing you need to know about,' Tom said, squeezing her shoulder roughly. 'Just keep your end of the bargain and there will not be a problem.'

'I've paid my debt. We're even.'

'I need more money and you're going to help me get it. Where does your toff keep his stash?'

'I'm not telling you.'

Anger and desperation flared in his eyes and Lina flinched as he raised his hand to hit her. The blow was stinging, delivered with the flat of his hand to her cheek. Lina started to rise, ready to kick, hit and scratch her way out, but before she could start her assault Tom went flying backwards, travelling across the terrace at high speed. He let out a low howl which was cut short as he made impact with the wall of the house.

Before Lina could rise to her feet, Alex was by her side, crouching down next to her and checking she was not too badly injured. His fingers felt cool on the warm, sore patch of cheek where Uncle Tom's palm had connected with her flesh.

'What did he do to you?' Alex asked, his voice low and soft, but with an undertone of repressed anger.

'He just slapped me, truly it wasn't even that hard.'

For a moment Lina wanted Alex to beat Uncle Tom; she wanted him to hurt him, to punish him for the slap and for the threats he'd been making the last few weeks. As her pulse slowed her anger subsided and gently, she laid a hand on Alex's arm.

'It was just a little slap,' she repeated. 'He's a desperate man.'

'That's no excuse.'

Alex kissed her forehead, rose and walked over to where Tom was struggling to get up. There was naked fear in the older man's eyes, as well as a hint of regret. Alex grasped him by the edges of his shirt and dragged him back towards Lina.

'I should beat you to a pulp for what you just did,' Alex said.

'Please,' Uncle Tom whispered, his voice barely audible. 'It was a mistake. I'm sorry.'

For a long moment Alex eyed the man in his grasp, before disgustedly letting go of his shirt and pushing him none too gently into a chair.

'I want to know everything,' Alex said. 'Why you're trespassing on my property, why you hit Lina and why you broke into Lina's room a few weeks ago. I assume that was you?'

Both Lina and Uncle Tom gave small nods and Lina felt her cheeks colouring.

'She owes me money,' Tom said.

'I've paid you.'

'Only just. You're a slippery little fish, I wouldn't have seen a penny if I hadn't chased you.'

'Why did she owe you money?'

'We made a wager, she lost.'

'Is this true?' Alex asked, turning to Lina.

She nodded, unable to meet his eye.

'So all this time you've been following Lina to remind her to pay you?'

'It was my money. She lost the wager, she had to pay.'

'And now she's paid the debt?'

Uncle Tom nodded, his fingers darting to the pocket where he'd stashed the stack of notes Lina had handed over a few minutes before.

'So why hit her?' Alex asked, frowning.

Neither Uncle Tom or Lina spoke, both pressing their lips together, but for different reasons. Lina didn't want Alex to know she'd even contemplated helping her uncle steal from him and Tom was no doubt still sore from when Alex had catapulted him across the terrace not ten minutes earlier.

'Tell me,' Alex said, his voice soft, directing his words to Lina.

'When I couldn't pay Uncle Tom straight away I made a deal,' she said, looking down at her hands as she spoke. 'We agreed I would have four weeks to find the money and instead of the ten pounds that I owed him I would pay fifteen.'

Alex nodded as Tom shifted uncomfortably in his seat.

'The only way Uncle Tom would agree to the extension period was if I agreed to do something else for him…' Lina paused, took a deep breath, then continued, 'He wanted me to find out where you kept your money, so he could sneak into the house and steal it. I was also meant to let him know when the house would be empty so he was less likely to get caught.'

Biting her lip, Lina risked a glance up. Alex's expression was inscrutable, but he didn't look happy.

'You were planning to rob my house?'

'It's not like you'd miss a few pounds here and there,' Uncle Tom said belligerently, although he cowered as Alex leaned in towards him.

'What I don't understand is why you didn't just take a few valuables when you broke into the house a few weeks ago. You'd already risked getting caught by entering, why didn't you steal something then?'

Uncle Tom looked down and refused to speak, pushing his lips together in a manner that suggested he wasn't going to say any more on the matter.

'I think he's been in trouble with the magistrate, caught with stolen goods. He's worried if he gets caught trying to sell anything stolen again in this area, then the punishment would be harsh and swift.'

'But money cannot be traced,' Alex said, nodding his head. 'Right, come with me.'

Alex stood, bodily hauling Uncle Tom to his feet and holding his arms in a way that meant the older man had no hope of escape.

'What will you do to him?' Lina asked. She didn't like her uncle—even less so after the slap that had hurt her cheek so badly—but she didn't want Alex to do anything too drastic. Uncle Tom might be a low-life scoundrel, but he was still family.

'I will send one of the footmen for the magistrate, Sir Peter Lawson. He's a good man, a friend of my father's when the old man was still alive. He can decide what to do with this criminal.'

Within her family, and the larger group they travelled with, all disputes were settled without the outside meddling of the law. Lina felt a little uncomfortable allowing her uncle to be handed over to the magistrate, but she doubted he would suffer more than a firm warning. It wasn't as though Uncle Tom had actually stolen anything, despite his intentions.

'So what was this wager?' Alex asked when he returned a couple of minutes later.

'Promise you won't laugh?'

'I can do no such thing.'

'I bet Uncle Tom ten pounds that I could mount and ride a wild horse the length of a field.'

'You didn't manage it?'

'I was thrown about eight feet from the end.'

'I'm impressed that you managed to mount a wild horse, let alone ride it.'

'Does this mean I'm allowed to ride your Arabian?'

Alex laughed. 'No. Not even if you were the finest wild-horse tamer in England.'

Chapter Twenty-Two

With a theatrical sigh, Lina flopped on to a bench and tugged at the ties of her bonnet. She was just about to lift it from her head to allow some much-needed air to circulate when Georgina gave her a sharp nudge in the ribs. Reluctantly Lina let her hands fall back to her sides, her bonnet still firmly in place covering her hair.

It was hot—far too hot to be wearing as many layers as Lina was dressed in and the cotton chemise and petticoats seemed to be sticking to her body every time she moved. She longed for her loose, cool skirt and blouse, which in the summer months she often wore with nothing else underneath. The people of London were sticklers for being appropriately dressed—that was, if you believed everything Georgina had to say—and everyone was strolling around Hyde Park with far too many layers to be comfortable.

'We've got half an hour before your dress fitting,' Georgina said, fanning herself delicately with a lace handheld fan. 'Would you like to walk further or shall we sit here in the shade for a while?'

'As much as I'm enjoying this heat, I worry for my complexion in the sun,' Lina said, grinning at Georgina's expression.

For the last four days, all the time they'd been in London, Georgina had been suggesting various methods to brighten Lina's skin. Lina had endured hearing about the benefits of milk baths, the juice of lemons, a strange-smelling face cream and only being allowed out of the house with a bonnet and a parasol. She'd gone along with all of it, knowing that years of spending her days outside enjoying the feeling of the sun's rays on her skin were not going to be reversed in a few short weeks. In addition, after Georgina had run halfway down the street after her and Alex when they'd left for a walk one day, Alex had told her he rather liked the freckles that were dotted over her nose and that he thought her skin was the colour of honey. She'd blushed when he'd leaned in and added, 'Good enough to eat,' in a low whisper.

'How are you feeling about the Wilcox ball?' Georgina asked as they sat side by side, watching the children play with their nursemaid in the distance.

'A little nervous.'

In truth, she was petrified. Not of the ball—how bad could one evening be? No, Lina was petrified of the day after, the moment when she would have to bid farewell to Alex for ever. Although she had tried to prepare herself for the inevitable separation, she still knew her heart would break. If she wasn't careful, she might fling herself at his feet and beg him to keep her as his mistress even just for a few weeks, in spite of what she had insisted.

'I think you'll do very well. You've worked so hard these last few weeks, you will fit in with all the other debutantes perfectly.'

Lina nodded absently. She could dance and converse and curtsy in all the right places. Her voice might not be as cultured as the other young women, her knowledge of the opera or Mozart's piano concertos not so in depth, but she wasn't expected to do more than make small talk and dance a few dances in order for Alex to win his wager. The only difficulty would be if anyone enquired as to her background, her family and their home. Alex didn't think it would be a problem; the fact she was being sponsored by both himself and Georgina made up for her lack of pedigree.

'I will miss you,' Georgina said quietly, taking Lina's hand and squeezing it. 'We've had such fun this past month.'

'I'll miss you, too.' It was the truth. Georgina was kind and good fun to be with, just like her brother. 'Although I'm not sure I'll miss all of this.' Lina gestured to the outfit she was wearing and the parasol that laid by her side.

'Nonsense. You'll be wearing a bonnet whilst you tell fortunes at the next country fair.' They both smiled, then sat in silence for a few minutes, before Georgina said softly, 'Are you worried about leaving?'

'I'm worried about going home. I'm not sure how I'll fit in any more. These last few weeks I've seen so much, learnt so much, it'll be difficult to go back to my old life.'

It was the truth, but more than that, Lina didn't know how she would be able to live without seeing Alex every single day.

'You'll be glad to see your family, though?' Georgina asked. 'Your brother and your cousin?'

Unexpected tears filled Lina's eyes. It was nearly

six weeks since she'd last seen Raul and Sabina, and right now she could do with a strong hug from her brother and a long talk with her sensible and loving cousin.

'I can't wait to see them.'

Lina caught sight of Pentworthy strolling towards them, deep in conversation with a smartly dressed young man. It was wonderful to watch Georgina's face light up as she spotted her husband and Lina wondered if she would ever get to experience that same happiness and contentment.

'Miss Lock, may I introduce Mr Braithwaite,' Pentworthy said as they approached the bench. Lina rose and dipped her head, smiling at the earnest young man in front of her. 'Mr Braithwaite runs a large textile company up north. We were introduced by a mutual friend when Mr Braithwaite arrived in London.'

'Miss Lock and I were just on our way to the dressmaker's,' Georgina said, placing her hand in the crook of her husband's arm. 'Perhaps you gentlemen have time to escort us?'

'It would be my pleasure,' Mr Braithwaite said, offering Lina his arm. His voice was low and rich, thick with a northern accent Lina recognised from time spent in Derbyshire a few years ago.

They walked, Lina ensuring her parasol was held high over her head to stop the sun from falling on her cheeks. As they made their way through Hyde Park, they talked about London life, about her stay with the Whitemore family, of the opera Mr Braithwaite had been to see the night before and a dozen other insignificant topics. The earnest young man was a perfectly good companion, perfectly *nice*, but Lina found herself wishing it were someone else leading her through the leafy park. Someone strong and tall, confident and easy in himself. Someone who would be conversing normally one second and leaning down to whisper something wicked in her ear the next second.

'What do you think, Miss Lock?' Mr Braithwaite asked.

Lina felt her eyes widen as she desperately tried to recall what they had been talking about before she'd slipped off into her daydream. They'd spoke a little of how fashions seemed to change so quickly in London, especially compared to the country, but she rather thought Mr Braithwaite might have moved on whilst her mind was elsewhere.

'I completely agree, Mr Braithwaite,' Lina said, trying to sound confident even though she had no idea what she was agreeing to.

Mr Braithwaite beamed and at the same moment a familiar figure came strolling down the path towards them. Before Lina could ascertain what statement she'd just agreed with so exuberantly, Alex was in front of them. Even in public, he stood just a little too close for propriety.

'May I introduce Lord Whitemore, the Marquess of Essex.' Lina paused, turning to Alex and finding herself stumbling over her words as she caught the flash of primal desire in his eyes. 'And this is Mr Braithwaite.'

The two men shook hands, talking easily as they found out common acquaintances and experiences. All the while, Lina felt the heat rising in her body. It was a warm day, but even the heat from the sun couldn't explain the burning sensation deep inside her. This was getting worse. A few weeks ago it had been just a slight tingle, a throb of anticipation every time Alex drew near. Now it was impossible to ignore the sizzle of desire and the need to be close to him. After any spell of time apart Lina felt almost bereaved and their reconciliation was verging on painful as she had to hold herself back from launching herself into his arms.

'Steady,' she whispered to herself. She'd managed to maintain her composure these last few weeks; she wouldn't slip up in the final few days before the wager was over. It was important Alex didn't know quite how much he affected her—although by the amused glint in his eyes she suspected she didn't look quite as composed as she hoped.

'Now you have your escort, I must take my leave,' Mr Braithwaite said as they reached the entrance to Hyde Park.

'Thank you for your company,' Lina managed, smiling at Mr Braithwaite as he bid everyone good-bye.

Georgina and her husband were a few paces ahead as they left the park and Lina felt Alex slow to increase the distance between them.

'Miss me?' he murmured in her ear.

'You've been somewhere?' Lina asked, trying to sound nonchalant.

'Your indifference would wound me,' Alex said, 'if I believed for a second you weren't suffering in my absence.'

'You have a very high opinion of yourself.'

'Maybe you should see if it is justified.'

Alex was still pursuing her, still intent on making her his mistress. Since the ambush and their overnight sojourn in the barn he'd stopped trying to convince her it would only be a short-term affair, instead insisting they would both gain from the liaison.

'Did you achieve all that you wanted to?' Lina asked.

'I did. I have a surprise for you later.'

'What?'

'It won't be a surprise if I tell you.'

He wouldn't budge on the subject, no matter how hard Lina tried, and she was still trying to wheedle information out of him as they entered the dressmaker's.

'This is where I leave you,' Alex said.

'Do you have to go?'

'Why, do you need my help slipping out of that dress?'

'I think the seamstress might protest if you step behind the curtain to do her job.'

'I wasn't thinking of doing her job.'

'Truly, I don't want to know what you've just said to make Lina blush that much,' Georgina said, swooping in and taking Lina firmly by the arm. 'Alex, go away. You're not to see this dress until the night of the ball.'

The chaste kiss he gave her on the back of her hand had Lina's legs feeling all wobbly as she entered the shop and she was grateful when one of the shop girls offered her and Georgina chairs to sit on whilst she fetched the dress.

As they sat and the shop girls flitted around, fetching and carrying all the while chattering away, Lina closed her eyes for a moment and tried to regain some equilibrium. These last few days in London had gone past in an absolute whirl and not an entirely good one. She'd shopped, taken tea, made small talk with women she had nothing in common with. It was only all made bearable by coming home to Alex every evening, joining him in his study before dinner, where they would discuss her day and he would make her laugh and make her blush. It made her realise it certainly wasn't the lifestyle she was in love with. She would be happy if she never had to hold another parasol or spend six hours being measured for a dress again. No, the one thing she liked about her life these last few weeks was Alex.

'Penny for your thoughts,' Georgina said quietly.

'I don't know how you do it,' Lina said. 'The endless polite chit-chat, being perfectly presented all the time, never knowing who is watching you and who is judging you.'

Georgina shrugged in her ladylike manner. 'I

suppose when you've lived like this all your life it comes naturally.'

'Very true.'

Lina knew she didn't fit in in Alex's world, not even as his mistress. She might be able to pull off one evening, one ball, but she couldn't imagine living with this level of scrutiny the whole time.

As one of the shop girls invited her through to try on her dress for the Wilcox ball, Lina realised what she'd just thought. *Not even as his mistress.* It was getting harder and harder to resist Alex, to remember all the reasons why it would be a bad idea to give herself to him. In a way, it was a relief she had less than a week left in his company. When they were hundreds of miles apart, she couldn't very easily succumb to his seduction. The only problem with that was that she wasn't sure how she would survive without seeing his smile, feeling his hands grip hers and hearing his laugh every single day.

'Close your eyes.'

'Promise you won't let me fall.'

'I promise.'

Lina closed her eyes and felt Alex's arms around her. She squealed, but dutifully kept her eyes closed.

'I want you to imagine something. Can you do that for me?'

Lina nodded.

'Imagine we've just been for a stroll in the park, it's a warm day and we've returned here for refreshments and to rest after the exertion in the sunshine.'

'Where is here?'

'Shush. Be patient and let me paint you the picture.'

Lina truly didn't know where they were. Alex had kept her occupied in the carriage ride over here, telling her a little about the guests he knew would be attending the Wilcox ball, and when they briefly stepped out on to the smart street she hadn't recognised it, although that didn't mean much after just a few days in London.

'We have the whole afternoon ahead of us, the whole evening, the whole night to enjoy nothing but one another.'

Lina's eyes shot open as Alex bent towards her and kissed her on the tip of her nose.

'What is it?'

'Rooms I have just acquired,' Alex said, as if that were enough of an explanation.

They were standing in a large, sun-filled room,

replete with splendid furniture and even a grand piano at one end.

'Follow me,' Alex said, taking Lina by the hand and pulling her through the doors into the hallway. Excitedly he flung doors open, announcing the purpose of each room, only stopping when he reached the bedroom.

Lina stepped inside. It was beautiful. A large, four-poster bed filled the centre of the room, but there was plenty of space for two armchairs and an ornate dressing table. Two good-sized windows let the afternoon sun in, which gave the room a warm glow. The view was of the street and beyond that a small park where children were happily playing.

'It's lovely, Alex,' Lina said sadly.

He cupped her chin, gently tilting her head so she had to look up into his eyes.

'It's for us. Just for us.'

'I know.'

The purpose of the rooms was clear. It was somewhere they could be together, somewhere they could fulfil the roles of aristocrat and mistress without society minding. The idea Lina might live in Alex's main residence as his mistress was preposterous—she had to be hidden away somewhere secret and private.

'How long have you rented them for?' she asked, her voice flat.

'Six months initially, but there is the option to extend.'

Six months. She supposed it was as good a length of time as any.

'You don't like it?' Alex said, watching her face carefully.

'There is absolutely nothing wrong with the rooms, Alex,' Lina said, unsure whether she felt more hurt or angry.

'Just imagine us spending lazy Sunday mornings in bed here. It would be sublime.'

'Have you used it before?' Lina asked.

'Used it before?' He looked confused.

'For any of your other mistresses?'

'No. I found it especially for us.'

She turned to the window, not wanting Alex to see the tears in her eyes.

'I'm not going to be your mistress, Alex,' she said, then dashed from the room and towards the stairs.

He caught her before she was halfway there.

'I thought if you could see what our lives would be like—' he started to say.

'I can. It's crystal clear, thank you very much. I

would be shut away as your dirty little secret. My whole life would be waiting for you to call, wondering if you'd grown tired of me yet.'

Alex sighed and ran a hand through his hair. 'It wouldn't be like that, Lina.' He paused. 'I care for you.'

Her heart slammed against her ribs as he said the words. They weren't words of love, but still more than he'd admitted up until now.

'I can't bear the thought of you walking out of my life in a few days.'

'I can't bear it, either,' Lina said softly.

'This is the only way we can be together.'

She shook her head, trying to stop the next words that were already tumbling out of her mouth. 'I love you, Alex. I love you so much my heart sometimes feels like it is going to burst, but I will never be any man's mistress, not even yours.'

He stiffened as if the declaration she'd just made was a physical blow. Lina knew she should just stop now, should back away and nurse her shattered dreams in private, but instead she heard herself carrying on, pushing Alex just that little bit further.

'I love you, Alex,' she repeated quietly. 'I've been

torturing myself these last few weeks. I need to know how you feel about me.'

Lina saw the panic in his eyes, the quickening of his breathing and the slight tremor of his hands.

'Tell me you don't love me,' she said, looking directly into his eyes.

Slowly he shook his head, but seemed unable to speak. Lina felt a flare of hope and stepped towards him, reaching out and taking his hand in hers.

'Do you love me, Alex?' she asked again.

The silence stretched out before them like a gaping chasm and Lina felt her hopes and dreams come tumbling down around her shoulders. He couldn't admit he loved her and couldn't come out and tell her he didn't.

With tears running down her cheeks Lina fled, slipping down the stairs and out of the door, darting through the streets in the late-afternoon sunshine, using every ounce of energy to keep moving, knowing if she stopped she would likely completely fall to pieces.

Chapter Twenty-Three

Alex paced backwards and forward at the bottom of the stairs, every few seconds checking the time on the huge grandfather clock that stood proudly near the front door. It felt as though time was passing excruciatingly slowly, every second stretching out for what felt like an hour. He was nervous, more nervous than he ought to be—and it certainly wasn't nerves over this wager between himself and his sister.

Sometime earlier that afternoon Alex had realised he didn't care in the least if he won or lost the wager tonight. Something much more important was at stake.

Lina loved him. She'd come out and declared the words two days ago, before challenging him to tell her how he felt about her. Alex had been unable to speak, unable to form a single word, still reeling from her declaration. He cared for her, she knew that. It was obvious in everything he did, everything he said, but love was so much more than that. He couldn't deny Lina lit up his world, made each and every day more enjoyable, more worthwhile. He felt bereft without her, but he'd tried being in love before and it had only earned him years of heartbreak. Not that he could try to explain any of this to Lina. She had been working hard to avoid him ever since that disastrous afternoon.

With hindsight it had been a mistake to rent the rooms just off Grosvenor Square. The hurt in Lina's eyes was something he would never forget. He'd felt that pain, felt her unhappiness translate directly into his own unhappiness.

A swish of skirts at the top of the stairs set Alex's heart pounding, but he recognised his sister's slow, elegant gait and returned to his pacing.

'She'll be down in just a minute,' Georgina said, stopping before Alex and giving him a searching look. 'You won't do anything stupid tonight, will you, Alex?'

'Like what?'

Georgina grimaced. 'Anything you might regret.'

'I promise not to do anything I might regret.'

'Remember, focus on winning our wager this

evening, then tomorrow you can sort the rest of your life out.'

He wondered if it might be too late tomorrow, but didn't say anything to Georgina. Even if he'd wanted to confide his plans in his sister he couldn't; as of yet he didn't have the slightest idea what he might do. All he knew was that he couldn't allow Lina to walk from his life after the ball.

'I know you care for her, Alex,' Georgina said, giving him a weak smile. 'But you and Lina are from different worlds. She doesn't belong in ours, even with all the coaching. Ask yourself if you are willing to give up all of your friends, your lifestyle, for the rest of your life for her.'

Alex knew she was just trying to look out for him. Despite being his younger sister she had always wanted to protect him from everything, including himself.

Gently he kissed her on the forehead. 'Thank you, Georgina,' he said.

For a moment she buried her head in his shoulder, before whispering, 'I just want you to be happy, Alex.'

'I know. Trust me?'

She looked up, scrutinised his expression, then after a long few moments nodded her head. Without another word, she walked away, exiting Alex's town house to join her husband in the waiting carriage to take them to the ball.

Before Alex had time to digest his sister's words there was another rustle of material at the top of the stairs. He saw Lina hesitate and then rally, descending the stairs in a faint cloud of sweet-smelling perfume.

This past week he'd been kept strictly out of the dressmaker's, not allowed even a single peep at the dress Lina would be wearing tonight—and now he could appreciate why. It was magnificent. Or more accurately, it made Lina look magnificent. Emerald green in colour, it was cut to show off her curves without doing anything to offend the matrons in the ballroom. The silky material hinted at the body it hid underneath, making Alex want to run his hands all the way from her shoulders down past the swell of her breasts and the line of her waist.

Lina's hair was pinned on top of her head, the decorative silver comb he'd bought to replace the one she'd been forced to give up to her uncle holding some of the strands in place. Her face was fresh, just a hint of colour on her cheeks, and her lips, a luscious and natural red.

Alex was speechless and she'd reached the bottom of the stairs before he recovered. Without thinking he stepped forward and took her in his arms, only coming to his senses when he felt her stiffen under his touch.

'You look beautiful.'

'I hope I look the part of a debutante,' Lina said tightly. 'I wouldn't want you to lose the wager, not now I know how much you despise the idea of love and marriage.'

He wanted to kiss away the frown line between her eyebrows, kiss away the tension in her jaw and make her lips stretch into the smile he loved so much. Instead he offered her his arm.

'I think you'll be the most beautiful debutante in attendance.' It wasn't said to flatter or win favour, it was a simple statement of fact.

Lina glanced up at him, but he couldn't read anything in her eyes. She'd had two days to prepare herself for this moment, two days to shutter her eyes and suppress any hurt or emotion.

Part of him wanted to gather her in his arms, to whisper in her ear that everything would work out perfectly, but he couldn't give her those assurances. Right now he didn't know what to do, didn't know what he wanted, other than knowing he couldn't bear to let Lina leave at the end of the evening. Two days he'd mulled over his options and still he was no closer to knowing how their time together would end.

In silence, they left the town house and Alex helped Lina up into the carriage. With her dress spread around her there was no room for him on the seat next to her, so instead he had to settle for sitting directly opposite. Lina smoothed out the material of her skirts for the third time just as the carriage pulled away, and Alex realised she was nervous—but whether it was about the impending test of her social manners or about spending the time in his company, he could not tell.

It took much longer than Lina expected to travel to the Wilcox ball, given the journey would have only taken twenty minutes by foot, but as they edged closer to the front of the queue of carriages she was thankful for the delay. From what she could see out of the carriage window, the ball was to be a grand affair. Coloured lanterns lit the way to the entrance where liveried footmen stood to attention, welcoming guests into the house and providing liquid refreshments. Through the windows Lina caught sight of a large number of people standing in groups, talking and laughing merrily. Somewhere would be room set aside for dancing and nearby at least a quartet of musicians. All this, Lina had learnt by questioning Alex and his sister about what would happen tonight, but now she saw it with her own eyes it seemed so much grander than they had described.

'Are you nervous?' Alex asked. He was lounging back in his seat, but Lina could tell he was on edge by the way he hadn't teased her throughout the whole carriage ride. The declaration of love that had tumbled from her lips a couple of days ago was no doubt the cause of this change in character.

'I don't want to let you down,' Lina said.

It was the truth. Ever since their afternoon at the rooms in Grosvenor Square, Lina had been wondering whether it would be best for her to just leave, to walk out on Alex and the wager, but she had realised that it was important for her to see this through. She had given her word to Alex that she would do this, and after all the time and effort that had gone into preparing for this evening she wasn't going to walk away just before the final hurdle. Deep down Lina knew she also couldn't bear the thought of leaving Alex, even a day early. Every minute was precious, despite what had occurred between them. He might not have been able to admit his feelings for her, but that didn't lessen how she felt for him.

'Whatever happens tonight I want you to know how grateful I am to you. You've worked so hard to help me. Thank you.'

Grateful. That was his overriding emotion towards her. Not love, not even desire any more, but he was *grateful*.

Resolutely fixing her eyes on a coloured lantern on the Wilcoxes' railings, Lina tried her hardest not to show any emotion. Part of her wanted to grasp Alex by the shoulders and shake him, scream and shout and beg him to recognise what they had between them, but she knew it was in vain. Either he felt the connection, too, or he didn't. She couldn't force it.

Before she was ready, their carriage had pulled to a halt and a footman was opening the door. Alex helped her down, escorting her up the steps towards the door, whilst Lina felt every sense being overwhelmed. The coloured lanterns were complemented by streams of ribbons fluttering in the breeze, all in vibrant blues and reds and yellows. The soft sound of a string quartet floated out through the open doors, an enticing piece of music pulling Lina inside. Infused in the air was the scent of orange blossom, faint but sweet enough to make Lina want to bite into a succulent segment of the exotic fruit.

They hadn't even reached the front door and already it was the grandest party Lina had ever been to. The country dance paled in comparison and suddenly Lina felt awkward and out of place.

They passed the line of footmen and stepped over the threshold, the air inside the house already marginally warmer and stickier than that outside.

'Lord Whitemore, we're so glad you could make it.' An immaculately presented woman in her mid-forties beamed as they approached.

'I wouldn't miss it for the world, Mrs Wilcox, Mr Wilcox. May I introduce Miss Lock.'

Lina and the Wilcoxes greeted each other formally and they were just about to move on when Mrs Wilcox thrust a young, slender woman in their path.

'And this is our daughter, Miss Anne Wilcox.'

The young woman looked decidedly uncomfortable, but bobbed a formal curtsy all the same. Lina supposed she'd been paraded out in front of all the guests so far, and the young Miss Wilcox didn't look too happy about it. As they made their greetings, with Alex dutifully asking their hostess's daughter for a dance later that evening, Lina saw the flare of triumph in Mrs Wilcox's eyes as she secured a dance with a marquess for her daughter.

'The ball is in honour of Miss Wilcox's debut,' Alex murmured as they made their way into the already-crowded ballroom. 'She's making her bow into society tonight.'

'She doesn't look too pleased about it,' Lina observed drily.

'Her parents are ambitious. I think they hope she will ensnare a man with a title.' Alex paused, dropping his voice even lower before continuing, 'They are extraordinarily wealthy with no sons, making Miss Wilcox a very eligible heiress. Of course, in return for all that money, they wish for their new son-in-law to bring a title to the table.'

'How romantic.'

Alex shrugged, as if to say this was just the way of the world he lived in.

The ballroom was even more beautifully decorated than Lina could have ever imagined. Hundreds of candles burned around the peripheries, adding to the light from three glittering chandeliers suspended from the ceiling. The mirrored walls glittered and shone, making the crowded

room seem more spacious and allowing the immaculately presented debutantes to examine their
appearances every few minutes.

There was a jolly atmosphere in the room, much
more so than Lina had anticipated, and she realised
that most of these people must know each other in
some way or another.

'Whitemore! Where have you been hiding yourself away?' A young man with an expressive face
came and clapped Alex on the back.

'Sir Thomas Wainwood, Miss Lina Lock,' Alex
introduced them, leaning in to add to Lina, 'Wainwood is a complete scoundrel. Keep well away.'

'You wound me, Whitemore.'

'It's the truth, no matter how hard he protests.'

'You forget I was witness to all your exploits at
university, Whitemore.' Turning to Lina, he gave
a friendly wink. 'Perhaps you would like to hear
all about it, Miss Lock, if you'd be kind enough to
grant me a dance.'

'I would be delighted to.' Lina handed him her
dance card and he scribbled his name on one of the
lines. Already it was filling up, what with Alex's
two dances pencilled in, and two more with Pentworthy. One half of the wager was almost won. All
she had to do was conduct herself with decorum

for the evening and Alex would have triumphed over his sister and her husband.

They moved on, strolling around the ballroom, having to weave through the crowds now even more guests were arriving. Their progress did not go unmonitored and Lina saw multiple pairs of eyes following them as they walked.

'People are talking about us,' she murmured, glancing at two middle-aged women who were whispering behind raised hands. It was hardly discreet.

Alex shrugged once again. He was much more comfortable with their scrutiny than she was, much more accustomed to it. 'They are curious as to who you are and why Georgina and I have sponsored you.'

'Do you think they'll work out the truth?'

'Never. Most will speculate you're some distant relative or friend of the family.'

Just as they completed a full lap of the ballroom Lina felt Alex stiffen beside her. She glanced up to see Victoria and a tall, slender man walking towards them. As the couple spotted Alex and Lina, they also paused, but after a moment's hesitation Alex gently pulled Lina towards them.

'Lady Winchester... Lord Winchester...' Alex said, inclining his head in greeting.

Lina scrutinised the man standing before her. This was Alex's closest friend—or at least once had been. The man who had eloped with Victoria. He looked nervous, as if worried what might be the result of their meeting, but Lina felt Alex relax beside her and knew nothing scandalous was about to occur.

'It's been too long, Winchester,' Alex said, addressing his old friend as he would have years ago. 'May I introduce Miss Lock, a friend.'

'A pleasure, Miss Lock. You're looking well, Whitemore.'

'The country air agrees with me. I've barely been in town these last couple of years.'

'Whitemore...' Winchester began to say.

Alex shook his head and clapped the other man on the shoulder. 'Life is too short, Winchester. No point in bringing up the past.'

'You always were a good man.'

Whilst the two men talked in half sentences and unspoken understandings, Lina had been watching Victoria out of the corner of her eye. The other woman had pouted as Alex approached, the pout turning to a frown as he cheerfully acknowledged her and then moved on. Now she was biting her lip as if confused about the direction of the conversation.

'We should go hunting together one day soon,' Alex said. 'Remember that time you almost shot a villager?'

Winchester grinned. 'Bloody well thought I'd killed him for a minute.'

Alex turned to Lina. 'He had to pay the man compensation for the shock. The old gent did pop up out of nowhere, though.'

'Whitemore was laughing all the way home, didn't let me forget it the whole week of the hunt.'

'I see Lady Porter,' Victoria said, her voice tight and clipped. 'Come, dear, we must go and enquire as to her health.'

For a moment Lina thought Winchester might protest, but a piercing look from his wife had him saying a reluctant farewell before being dragged away across the ballroom.

'You handled that rather well,' Lina murmured as they continued their stroll, passing by the row of floor-to-ceiling windows that looked out on to a candlelit terrace.

'I did, didn't I?'

'That's the first time you've seen him since he and Victoria eloped, isn't it?'

'It is.'

'Yet you managed to laugh and joke with him. Magnanimously forgive him.'

'I must be over Victoria and what they did to me,' Alex said simply.

'That's amazing, Alex,' Lina said, unsure why he wasn't more excited by this newfound freedom.

'I think I have you to thank.'

'I haven't done anything.'

'You've made me step out into the world again and in doing so I've found the damage Victoria and Winchester did to me wasn't as permanent as I'd thought.'

Although Lina didn't feel as though she'd done anything to help Alex heal, she supposed he had been forced to interact with more people than horses these last few weeks. Soon perhaps he would be able to start thinking of love again. Lina knew it wouldn't be her he declared his love for; over time she would grow to accept her feelings for him were deeper than his for her. Despite that, she wanted him to be happy, wanted him to find love and to settle with a woman who would give him the life he deserved.

Sensing the tears prickling in her eyes, Lina quickly excused herself, keeping her head down and dashing towards the entrance hall. There she followed a flutter of young ladies into the set of rooms that had been made available for the ladies to tend to their intimate needs during the ball. She was grateful to find a small room with a lock on the door and shut herself in before the tears properly began to fall. Tonight she might be on Alex's arm, but before too long it would be another woman in his heart. Somehow she had to accept it, but even here in the privacy of the retiring room, Lina felt her heart squeezing painfully in her chest.

Ten minutes later and Lina knew she would have to return to the ball. Quietly she unlocked the door and poked her head out into the antechamber. When she'd entered, a few young ladies had been positioned in front of the mirrors adjusting various aspects of their appearance as they chattered away. Now the room was thankfully empty and Lina had time to splash a little cold water on her cheeks before the door opened again.

'You need to leave,' a low voice came from behind her.

Lina spun around to see Victoria standing holding the door open, her eyes narrowed and angry.

'I've finished, the room is all yours.'

'No, you need to leave this ball. You're an embarrassment.'

'Pardon me?'

'Don't think I don't know what you are, *Miss Lina Lock*,' Victoria spat. 'Stay and you will make a fool of Alex as well as yourself.'

'I don't know what you're talking about,' Lina said, forcing herself to hold her head up high as she tried to walk out past Victoria. The other woman held out an arm, blocking Lina's way.

'I've checked who you are,' Victoria said, a flash of triumph in her eyes. 'You're nobody. No title, no family, no money.'

'And that is all that matters to you, isn't it?'

'It does matter. It matters to everyone. And having you here is an absolute disgrace. For Alex to bring his mistress to a society event—it's an embarrassment.'

Lina was about to duck under Victoria's outstretched arm, but then she froze.

'Why do you care what he does?' she asked.

'Because it is an affront. I don't wish Alex to be made a fool of.'

'Surely you gave up the right to have an opinion

on what he does or does not do when you ran off with his friend.'

Victoria's pale cheeks became even paler and her lips grew thin and pinched.

'Don't you dare speak to me like that.'

'It is exactly how you are speaking to me.'

'You're a whore, a harlot! I am Lady Winchester, wife of the Duke of Winchester.'

'Actually, I'm not a whore or a harlot,' Lina said, beginning to enjoy herself a little. The other woman was so out of control she was easy to upset. 'I'm a gypsy.'

Victoria's eyes widened at this newest piece of information, but still she refused to back away.

'What I don't understand,' Lina mused, 'is why you are so concerned about what Alex does. You left him, broke his heart and waltzed off with his closest friend without a single thought of how it would affect the man you were supposed to love. And now you're jealous that he's moved on? It doesn't make sense.'

'I'm not jealous of you,' was all Victoria could manage.

'You didn't want him, but you don't want anyone else to have him either, is that it?' Lina asked, leaning in closer and watching as the truth of her words was reflected in Victoria's eyes.

'I certainly don't want him consorting with the likes of you.'

'I suppose there is a power in having a man in love with you. Perhaps you hoped you would hold that power over Alex for ever, despite you moving on.' Lina took a step back. She was thoroughly enjoying herself now. Reading Victoria's reactions was far too easy and she had nothing to fear from the cold woman in front of her. 'I don't understand what Alex ever saw in you.'

On the few occasions Alex had talked about his ex-fiancée, he had mentioned how she was his intellectual equal, how they had enjoyed discussing all manner of topics whilst being able to laugh and relax with one another at the same time. Although Lina had only spent a limited amount of time in Victoria's company, she couldn't reconcile that picture with the woman in front of her, but people could change. Perhaps the old Victoria had been nicer, or perhaps Alex had been blinded by the love he felt for her.

'I take it your marriage is not a happy one,' Lina said as she confidently strode forward and ducked under Victoria's arm, stepping out into the hallway. Before the other woman could answer, Lina had glided away, her head held high, but her heart hammering in her chest. She might have enjoyed getting the better of a woman who'd sought her out to belittle and degrade her, but Lina wasn't so naive to think she could speak to a woman of such a high rank in that manner without their being consequences. She might well have just ruined Alex's chances of winning his wager.

Chapter Twenty-Four

Alex looked at the door for what seemed like the fiftieth time. Lina had been gone far too long. Something untoward must have happened. Despite his initial flash of worry, deep down Alex knew Lina couldn't be in too much trouble; they were in a house full of people and she was perfectly capable of looking after herself. If any gentleman a little the worse for drink cornered her in a secluded spot, he knew it would be the gentleman who came out of the encounter with a sore groin and a bloody nose. Nevertheless, when another five minutes passed without Lina reappearing, he made his excuses to the group of old friends he'd been talking to and stepped into the hallway.

There were fewer people out here compared to the ballroom and the air felt cooler and fresher. Still, he had to weave through the groups to make any progress and before he'd taken more than ten steps he saw a flash of emerald green descending the stairs towards him. Lina's face was flushed as she rushed towards him, her steps measured but hurried, and as she gripped hold of his arm he sensed something had just gone monumentally wrong.

'What's happened?' he asked.

'Can we leave?'

'Of course.'

There would be time to question Lina later, but right now he could see the urgency written all over her face. For whatever reason, they had to leave the Wilcox ball now.

They nearly made it to the door before Alex felt a sharp tug on his arm. Quickly he spun, anticipating danger, but instead came face to face with Victoria.

'We will have to talk some other time, Victoria,' Alex said, conscious of how Lina stiffened beside him as she spotted the other woman.

'You're leaving with *her*?' The question was spat rather than said, her words dripping with disapproval and disdain.

'Let's go,' Lina said quietly. 'I don't want to embarrass you.'

Even though their entire exchange had been conducted in low voices, already people were beginning to stare and a space was clearing around the three of them.

'What's happened?' Alex asked, realising Victoria must be the reason Lina had looked so flustered as she met him in the hallway and requested to leave.

'You can't bring someone like *her* to a society ball, Alex,' Victoria said, shaking her head as if he were a foolish child.

'Miss Lock is a friend of the family. She is being sponsored by both Georgina and myself.' Alex tried to keep the emotion from his voice whilst he figured out what was going on here. The black looks passing between the two women hinted at some harsh words being exchanged before Alex had arrived on the scene, but he couldn't imagine what.

'I should have guessed your sister was in on this,' Victoria said. 'Although I did think she had more morals.'

'What have morals got to do with anything?'

'You don't bring your mistress to a ball with respectable people. Especially one as crude and uncultured as *her*.'

Alex glanced at Lina, expecting to see some sort of reaction on her face, either hurt or anger, but she remained quite majestically neutral, merely raising an eyebrow as Victoria jabbed a finger in her direction.

'Please do not speak about Miss Lock in that manner,' Alex said calmly, despite the explosion of anger he could feel building inside him. Struggling to keep himself under control, he turned again, meaning to make a hasty exit with Lina on his arm before Victoria could cause any more of a scene.

'You used to be better than this, Alex,' Victoria called. 'You used to socialise only with a certain standard of people.'

Unable to stop himself, Alex spun around and took two steps back towards Victoria.

'Lina is ten times the woman you'll ever be,' he said, loud enough for the assembled crowd to hear. 'She's considerate and intelligent and fun to be around, and what's more she's loyal and honest.'

He saw Victoria recoil as if she'd been slapped, saw the tears blossom in her eyes before spilling over on to her cheeks. Anyone else he might feel sorry for, but the remorse for his words just wasn't there. She'd injured Lina, embarrassed her in front of all these people. He couldn't bring himself to regret defending the beautiful woman on his arm.

'Come, my dear,' Winchester said softly, stepping forward and putting an arm around his wife's shoulders. 'Let's get you home.' He flashed a puzzled look at Alex, one infused with a silent apology, and forcibly escorted Victoria through the front door.

'We should leave, too,' Alex said, aware of all the guests trying to pretend they weren't listening intently to every word.

'I'm sorry,' Lina said quietly.

'What for?' As far as he could tell, Lina had been blameless in this situation.

'You've lost your wager.'

'Nothing could be further from my mind.'

'And I've embarrassed you in front of your friends.'

'I think that was entirely Victoria's doing.'

'I've ruined the ball.'

'Far from it.' Alex chuckled. 'Every ball needs a good scandal. The gossips will be talking about this little interlude for years to come.'

They stepped out into the warm evening air and suddenly Alex felt a little reckless. He wasn't sure what had made Victoria act so strangely, why she was so concerned with his life after so long apart, but he found he didn't care. She was part of his past, part of events that had shaped him into the man he was today, and now he was sure he would not see her again for a very long time.

'She still cares for you,' Lina said, as if reading his thoughts.

'Bizarre, when she was the one who decided to leave.'

'I suppose there is a sort of intoxicating power when someone wants you, when they're in love with you. She doesn't like the idea that you might not be under her spell any more.'

'But she's married.'

Lina shrugged. 'She probably always thought you would be there waiting, ready to pick up the pieces if anything did go wrong. When she saw you moving on with your life, it unsettled her.'

Alex nodded, then leaned in closer. 'Or she's just a little crazy.'

'Or that.'

They'd nearly reached the line of carriages when Alex pulled Lina to a stop. He knew he should just carry on walking, take Lina somewhere private where they could work out exactly how they were going to go forward with their lives, but for one

mad moment he just wanted to be reckless, foolish even.

With one arm looped around Lina's waist, he
pulled her in towards him, seeing the shock and
anticipation in her eyes before he covered her lips
with his own. For an instant Lina was completely
still, but then she moaned softly into his lips and
began kissing him back. They were in full view of
the house, in full view of the hundreds of guests,
but right in that moment Alex did not care at all.

She tasted sweet, of lemonade and champagne,
and Alex felt all sense of time slipping away from
him. He could happily have stayed kissing Lina on
that very spot for hours had she not pulled away,
regarded him with heavy eyes and then turned and
walked towards their carriage.

'Even I know you don't kiss a young woman
with that much passion in front of a ballroom full
of people,' Lina said as he caught up with her. She
was up in the carriage before he even had a chance
to offer her his hand, and as he vaulted up, bang-
ing on the roof at the same time to signal to the
driver to start moving, Lina grasped him by the
lapels on his jacket and pulled him on to the bench
beside her.

'I couldn't help myself,' Alex said, as Lina stroked

his cheek with the tips of her fingers. 'You've bewitched me, I don't behave as I should when you're around.'

'You think it's a gypsy enchantment?'

'I'm not sure I care what it is,' Alex said, dropping his head to trail kisses from the corner of her mouth to the line of her jaw. 'All I care is that we're here together, right here, right now.'

Lina allowed her head to fall backwards and Alex took the opportunity to move his lips farther down, kissing her collarbone, the exposed skin of her chest and the swell of her breasts as they peeked above the material of her dress. For a moment he paused, but already Lina was urging him to go lower, so he pushed down the emerald green bodice, pushed down the white cotton chemise and exposed Lina's breasts to the air. He felt her shudder as he captured one of her nipples in his mouth, teasing and biting until he felt her hips start to writhe underneath him.

'Alex,' she whispered, 'please.'

'Please stop?' he asked, pulling away a little, grinning as she gripped his shoulders to stop him withdrawing any further.

'Please don't stop.'

The carriage was moving faster now, speeding

through the empty streets towards home, but still Alex grasped the hem of Lina's skirts and lifted the layers one by one until he could touch the skin of her legs.

Before she had a chance to protest, Alex had dipped on to his knees, his lips trailing kisses up her thighs, his fingers caressing and stroking the skin. At first Lina tensed, but as the seconds passed he felt her relax, overcome by the pleasurable sensations.

As his lips reached the top of one thigh, he paused, but only long enough to appreciate the thrum of anticipation emanating from Lina, then his mouth was covering her most private place and Lina's hips were bucking beneath him.

Slowly he nipped and teased until he felt Lina tense and shudder, letting out a low moan and squeezing his shoulders with a strength he didn't know she had.

'What did you do to me?' she whispered.

Alex simply grinned, joining her on the seat of the carriage just as they began to slow. Quickly he helped Lina rearrange her dress so she looked passably presentable, or at the very least not completely indecent. When the carriage stopped, Alex was outside helping Lina down before any of the footmen could reach them and from there he and Lina dashed hand in hand inside the house.

Chapter Twenty-Five

Lina felt Alex's hand on her waist, guiding her up the stairs and to his bedroom and knew she was powerless to resist him. Ever since he'd stood up to Victoria for her and declared his regard for her in front of the assembled guests at the Wilcox's ball, Lina had known they would end up in his bedroom. All her resistance had been felled in that one instant.

It didn't change what would happen in the future. Tomorrow she would still leave London and return to her old life. Tonight, she would allow herself one night of wonderful passion with the man she loved, but that didn't mean she would become his mistress. One night would be something to cherish, something to hold on to and remember when her heart was breaking.

Alex closed the door behind them and instantly

his lips were on hers. Locked together, they stumbled towards the bed, Alex shrugging off his jacket as they went. Lina untucked his shirt, pulling away just long enough to lift it over his head, revealing the smooth muscle of chest and abdomen underneath. Her fingers found his waistband just as he pushed down the top of her dress for a second time that evening.

Alex groaned, his head falling back as Lina's hand dipped deeper under the waistband of his trousers.

'I want to see you,' he whispered in her ear, as he spun her around and started to tug at the ties that fastened her dress. An excruciating sixty seconds later the dress was pooled around her ankles and Alex was lifting the chemise and petticoats over her head.

For an instant, as she stood there completely naked, Lina felt a little self-conscious, but Alex took her hands when she moved to cover herself.

'You're perfect,' he said, running his fingers reverently over her skin, tracing the curve of her waist, the swell of her breasts and the trail between them, down over her abdomen and into the sensitive area below.

Lina managed to unfasten his trousers before

Alex's fingers found a spot that made her legs weaken and buckle and collapse back on to the bed. Quickly he kicked off his trousers before joining her on the bed, his body covering hers.

With her fingers gripping at Alex's back, Lina felt her hips rise up to meet his as he thrust into her. For a moment there was pain, but then he began to move, slowly at first, but as she moaned underneath him the pace increased and all thoughts of pain were washed away by pleasure. Lina found her body moving instinctively, rising to meet his as a pressure began to build deep inside her. Again and again their bodies met, until Lina felt the pressure release and wave upon wave of pleasure cascade over her body. In the same instant Alex stiffened and let out a primal groan, before collapsing on top of her.

Before Lina even opened her eyes she was aware of Alex's body behind her. His legs and torso were pressed flush against hers and his arm draped possessively over her waist. The dawn light was just starting to filter in through the crack in the curtains and Lina could hear sounds of the household stirring, ready to start their working day.

Carefully, she slipped out of bed, stiffening as

Alex mumbled something and turned over, only moving again when she was sure he was asleep. Leaving now would make things easier. She didn't want a stretched-out goodbye, the inevitable tears and heartbreak. Lina was sure she would cry, but at least she could suffer in private and maintain a little dignity.

Quickly she slipped into her underclothes, picking them up from where they had been discarded on the floor the night before. Thankfully the chemise and petticoats had not been shredded in the heat of passion, although the beautiful silk dress was looking a little crumpled on the floor. With a pang of regret Lina picked it up, straightened it out and laid it on the chair. There was no point in her taking it with her. She would never attend a function where she could wear such a dress again.

Lina stood for a moment, looking down at Alex on the bed. He looked so peaceful when asleep and, before she could stop herself, she reached out and stroked his hair. There was no denying she would miss him, probably every day of her life. She doubted she would ever care for anyone else so strongly again. Surely love like this could only happen once.

Before she could talk herself into staying, she

crouched down and kissed him softly on the lips, forcing herself to pull away before he woke up, then she darted from the room and down the dark corridor.

In her own bedchamber, she dallied only long enough to don her blouse and multicoloured skirt, run her fingers through her hair and gather her few belongings. Most of the gifts Alex had bought her were small in size, although not necessarily in value. In addition to the silver comb he'd surprised her with to replace the one she'd given to Uncle Tom to settle her debt, he'd also given her a beautiful set of pearls with a necklace and bracelet, and a shimmering necklace that looked suspiciously like it contained real diamonds rather than the glass replicas Lina was used to. She also had three dresses, two beautiful illustrated books and a pair of silk gloves.

If she wasn't much mistaken, the value of the gifts was far greater than any amount of money Lina had ever seen, but she knew she would not be parting with them any time soon. They were from the man she loved and if she couldn't have him, she would treasure the gifts he had given her.

Once her belongings were packed into a small case, Lina forced herself to descend the stairs rather than slip back into Alex's bedroom. The front door was locked, but she managed to find the key for the kitchen door without alerting any of the maids and within a few minutes she was standing in the fresh morning air. The streets were quiet— even the maids and footmen of the grand house-holds only just starting to struggle out of bed—but Lina knew as she got to the less salubrious parts of the city there would be more people up and about.

Trying to fight the tears that were already spill-ing on to her cheeks, Lina was just about to step on to the road when she was caught from behind.

'I've been waiting for you,' a slurred voice said.

It was Uncle Tom—although his face was barely recognisable. Both eyes were purple and swollen, the left almost completely shut. A vivid red gash travelled the length of his cheek and his lips were split in multiple places. His entire face had an un-healthy yellow-green hue, as if he was bruised from forehead to chin.

'What happened?' Lina asked in horrified fasci-nation, for a moment forgetting to struggle.

'This is your fault,' Tom spat, pushing Lina up against the railings.

'Hardly.'

'You should have helped me, but instead you put that toff before family.'

Suddenly the pieces all started to fall into place. Lina had been right; when Tom had repeatedly turned up at Alex's country house, he'd been desperate. He must have owed money to some less-than-desirable characters. Normally he would just break into a few houses and steal a few valuables, but with the magistrate ready to swoop in the instant there was any hint of him trying to sell any goods, Tom was clearly in a bind. Hence why he was only interested in the money Alex kept.

'Will they leave you alone now?' Lina asked, genuinely curious. Tom was angry and hurt, but she didn't think he would actually cause her any harm.

'What do you think?'

'Might be best to lie low for a while,' Lina suggested. 'Maybe accosting me in the middle of a London street isn't the best ploy.'

'Shut your mouth. You always did have too high an opinion of yourself.'

Lina wriggled, seeing if she could get free, but Tom's grip on her was surprisingly strong.

'What do you want, Tom?' Lina spat.

'I came to tell you you're not welcome back

home. We don't take kindly to those who betray their families, especially those who whore themselves out to toffs.'

Lina rolled her eyes. 'You travelled all the way here to tell me that?'

'Don't come back home.'

'I doubt you'll be there anyway.'

'I mean it, Lina. You're not welcome.'

With a shove, he sent her careening away, grabbing her small case as he did so.

'Give it back, Tom!' Lina cried, grabbing out with her hand. The case only contained the three dresses and pair of gloves; the jewellery and the small amount of money Lina had was secreted in a small purse underneath her dress, but still she didn't want to lose the clothing.

He pushed her roughly away again and Lina felt her body slam into the iron railings for a second time. She was just about to launch another attack when the front door to the house was flung open and Alex came barrelling down the steps. He threw himself in between Lina and Tom, deflecting the fist of the older man before advancing on him and manoeuvring Tom's arms behind his back to hold him still.

'Are you hurt?' Alex asked, looking back over his shoulder.

Lina shook her head.

'Come inside.' Alex pushed Tom up the steps in front of him and into the house, where she could hear him instructing the footmen to take control of her uncle.

For a second Lina hesitated. It would be all too easy to follow Alex inside, to succumb to his embrace. No doubt in a few months' time she would realise she'd become everything she promised herself she wouldn't ever be.

Quickly she grabbed the handle of her case, and with a final look at the inviting open door, she ran off down the street.

Alex spun around, expecting to see Lina making her way in through the open door, but it remained empty. With a sinking feeling he stepped outside and looked up and down the street. Lina was nowhere to be seen. He cursed loudly and repeatedly, then leaped down the steps in one bound, landing with his knees slightly bent, all the better to push off immediately into a sprint. Without a clue as to Lina's direction or destination, Alex veered left, hoping his superior speed would be on his side. Street after street he crossed, ever vigilant for a flash of multicoloured skirt or her dark, flowing hair.

The streets were more or less empty, with the odd merchant or servant hustling quickly to their daily place of work, but even the few people he stopped to ask if they'd seen Lina shook their heads before continuing on their way.

After thirty minutes of searching Alex had to admit defeat, returning to the house to dress properly before starting the search anew. When he'd been woken by the voices outside his window he'd quickly thrown on a shirt and breeches and pulled on his boots, but if he were to chase Lina farther afield, he would need to be better presented.

'Let me go!' a loud voice shouted as Alex entered through the front door. Making a quick detour into his study, where two footmen were restraining Lina's uncle, Alex glowered at the older man so fiercely he immediately fell silent.

'Where has she gone?' Alex asked.

The man laughed cruelly. 'Not home, that's for sure. I told her she wasn't welcome there.'

'Where else would she go?'

Silence. Alex resisted the urge to punch Lina's uncle squarely on the jaw and instead motioned for the footmen to let him go. He had much more important things to worry about without this scoundrel in his house.

Quickly he ran upstairs, dressed properly and instructed a footman to relay a message to the stables to ready his horse. Within five minutes he was back on the streets, ready to search for Lina until nightfall if that was what it took.

As he rode, Alex cursed his stupidity. Last night he had decided he couldn't live without Lina—that he didn't want her as his mistress, but as his wife, his lifelong companion. Stupid fool that he was, he hadn't told her, somehow expecting her to know his change of heart without him ever uttering the words. When she'd given herself to him willingly, he'd thought she had understood. Then he'd even allowed them to fall asleep with the words unspoken, thinking that there was plenty of time today to declare his love and plan their future.

Love. Even just the word made him nervous, but that was the only way to describe the deep-seated feelings that had developed these last few weeks.

'I won't lose her,' Alex vowed, knowing he would not stop searching until she was safely back in his arms.

He rode through all the major London streets that

morning, visiting various coach stops and inns. As he ventured towards the less salubrious parts of London, he felt thankful for Lina's worldly knowledge—she would know how to look after herself in a place like this.

As each hour passed with no one admitting to seeing Lina, Alex felt increasingly despondent. Perhaps she'd left London already, caught an early coach. By now she could be well on her way to any part of the country. He wished he'd paid more attention when Lina had talked about where her family would travel to next. Despite her uncle's insistence that she wasn't welcome at home Alex felt sure she would return to her brother and cousin. It was six weeks since the Pottersdown Fair, so they would surely have moved on, but even with the stakes this high Alex couldn't think of where Lina could have gone.

Chapter Twenty-Six

Lina attempted to summon a smile, but failed quite spectacularly, unable to shift the deep frown from her face. She must have looked frightful, as the young woman next in line to have her fortune told recoiled and then stepped out of the line, glancing behind her as she retreated to a safer part of the fair.

'You're scaring away my customers,' Sabina said, giving Lina's hand a quick squeeze.

'Sorry.'

'Take a break. The dancing will be starting soon.'

Lina nodded, slipping away from the queue of eager young girls ready to have their fortune told and trying to lose herself in the crowds of the fair. She couldn't believe it was only two months ago she'd first met Alex at a fair very much like this one. Even now she could remember every detail so vividly—his confident smile as he'd outlined the wager, the way he'd convinced Raul to let her go, how he'd taken her in his arms on the dance floor and made her fall a little in love with him even then.

When she'd left London just over a week ago, she'd thought she was doing the right thing. Time and distance were meant to help a broken heart, but it seemed like every day her pain got worse. She just wanted to see Alex one more time, look upon his face, perhaps even kiss his lips once more. It seemed so cruel that after so long in close company they would never be in the same room again.

As she neared the grassy space near the musicians that was to be used as the dance floor, John came striding over.

'Ready to start the dancing?' he asked.

Apart from Raul and Sabina, no one else knew the extent of Lina's heartbreak, although everyone had been careful around her for the first few days after she'd returned. Uncle Tom had not reappeared, no doubt hiding from his creditors, and his threats that Lina was not welcome back home had been completely unfounded.

'Shall we do the double spin at the end of the first round?' Lina asked.

John grinned. 'Sounds good, girl. The audience always loves that one.'

As the pace of the music began to increase, Lina felt a little of the gloom lift from her heart. Dancing at least provided a momentary respite from her heartbreak.

'May I have this dance?' a low voice asked just as they were about to step out in front of the audience.

Lina turned around slowly, barely able to believe it could be Alex standing behind her.

'Alex! Wh-what are you doing here?'

'You ran off without saying goodbye.'

Lina swallowed. It had been cowardly, but she hadn't been able to face a long goodbye.

'Are you dancing, Lina?' John asked.

'Find one of the village girls, John. We'll start together.'

Alex led her out in front of the assembled crowd, placed a hand in the small of her back and pulled her towards him. Even through the material of her dress Lina's skin sizzled at his touch and momentarily she forgot the steps that she'd been dancing for years.

Thankfully Alex improvised, whirling her round in great circles but always managing to keep her body close to his. Every so often his thigh would brush against hers, reminding Lina of that wonderful night they'd spent exploring each other's bodies.

'I didn't think I'd ever see you again,' Lina said as the music slowed and John started encouraging more of the villagers on to the dance floor.

'Come with me,' Alex said. He gripped her hand and pulled her through the crowds, only stopping when they were at the edge of the fair. It was quiet here, away from the hustle and bustle, but the sounds of merriment drifted over on the warm autumn breeze.

'I missed you,' Lina said before she could stop herself.

'I missed you, too.'

His lips were on hers before Lina knew what was happening and she felt her legs go weak and buckle at the knees as he kissed her deeper and more passionately than ever before.

'I'm sorry, Lina,' Alex said, breaking away after a few moments. 'I wronged you so completely. Can you forgive me?'

She frowned, unsure what he was asking forgiveness for.

'I should never have asked you to be my mistress. I see now it was demeaning and stupid.'

'You wanted me, I wanted you. It was the only way it could have happened,' Lina said quietly.

'No, it wasn't.'

'What do you mean?'

'At the Wilcox ball I realised something—something I'd felt for a long time, but I hadn't been able to admit to myself.'

Lina felt a fizz of anticipation. She wasn't entirely sure why Alex had sought her out, why he'd brought her to this remote corner of the fair and kissed her, but already her heart was soaring. She just hoped it wouldn't crash back down and break with his next words.

'I love you, Lina, and I can't bear to spend one more day without you.'

'You love me?'

'I love you.'

She swayed slightly on her feet, unable to fully comprehend his words, and immediately Alex's arms were around her waist, holding her up.

'You love me?'

'I love you,' he repeated for a third time.

'I love you, too, Alex.'

'I know,' he said with a mischievous grin.

'So arrogant.'

He shrugged. 'Can you bear to spend your life with such an arrogant man?'

'You mean…?'

'Marry me, Lina.'

'Surely it wouldn't work? We're from different worlds.'

'I don't care.'

'You'll be shunned from society.'

'I don't care.'

'No one will ever accept us.'

'I don't care. The people who matter will come around when they see how much we love each other. The rest can gossip and whisper about us for years to come. All I want is you. Will you marry me?' he asked for a second time.

'Yes.'

He kissed her then, and time slowed so she felt every caress, every nip, until he reluctantly pulled away.

'On one condition,' Lina said, barely able to conceal her smile.

'What's that?'

'You let me ride your Arabian.'

'You drive a hard bargain, Lady Whitemore.'

Epilogue

'Shush, he's coming,' Lina said, trying to stop her cousin from squealing with excitement.

They were tucked away in a quiet corner at the Pottersdown County Fair and like the previous year the weather was glorious and the day already hot despite it still being an hour until noon.

'I thought I'd find you here,' Alex grumbled good-naturedly. 'Although I was half suspecting you to be dressed in your old clothes and telling fortunes.'

'Lina never was very good at telling fortunes,' Sabina said with a grin. 'She didn't have the patience, although she can read people well…'

Alex took Lina by the hand, pulled her towards him and kissed her.

'Lord Whitemore, behave yourself. We're in public.'

'I apologise, Lady Whitemore, I don't know what came over me.'

'There's a queue building, Sabina,' one of the men shouted over the noise of the fair.

'I'll be two minutes, Peter,' Sabina yelled back. 'Don't leave without saying goodbye,' she said, pulling Lina in close for a hug.

It was a few months since Lina had seen her cousin and Raul last. She made sure she visited every time they stopped somewhere close to Whitemore House and Sabina had been to stay on a couple of occasions, too. She missed them and missed the closeness of their family group, but never once had she regretted leaving to become Lady Whitemore, Alex's wife.

'This brings back good memories,' Alex said as they strolled arm in arm around the fair. 'Over there is where your brother punched me for the first time. And over here is where I made that awful wager with Georgina and Pentworthy.'

'You're still sore about losing that?'

'Not at all. Who wants a perfect debutante anyway?'

Not surprisingly they had not received an invite to the Wilcox ball this year. In fact, their social calendar for the coming Season was looking rather bare. A few people had extended invitations to Lord Whitemore and his gypsy wife out of curiosity, but in the main they had been snubbed. Not that either Alex or Lina minded; much more fun could be had by staying at home anyway.

'I thought I might find you two here,' Georgina said as she came bustling over, herding her excited children in front of her. Georgina kissed them both warmly on the cheeks. 'Revisiting where the romance started?' she asked with a wicked glint in her eyes.

'We have you to thank, dear sister. Without your wager Lina and I would never have been thrown together.'

'Don't tell the society ladies that,' Georgina whispered. 'Then I'll be shunned, too.'

Despite her reservations about a marriage between two people of such different stations, Georgina had come around to the idea of a union between her brother and Lina surprisingly quickly. She was their staunch defender and even the most formidable society matron didn't dare disparage Lina when Georgina was in earshot.

Whilst Georgina was distracted by her daughter asking if she could ride one of the ponies plodding around the fair, Lina tugged at Alex's hand.

'Come over here,' she said, leading him to a quiet spot. 'Care to know your fortune, good sir?'

'You're going to tell me my fortune?'

'Cross my palm with silver and the secrets of the future will be revealed.'

Alex raised an eyebrow, but handed over a shiny coin all the same. A little distance away, Lina could see Sabina watching intently. She'd confided the details of her plan to her cousin and now Sabina was almost as excited as she was.

'What a lucky man you are,' Lina said, tracing her fingers over her palm. 'A beautiful wife, kind and generous, skilled on horseback, the best companion a man could ask for.'

'Are we talking about the same person?' Alex asked, dodging as Lina tried to thump him on the shoulder.

'You're happy, that I can tell. You have a *wonderful* wife, a champion horse…and another little surprise on the way.'

'Another surprise?'

Lina took Alex's hand and turned the palm over so it was facing her and placed it on her abdomen.

'Another surprise,' she confirmed.

'We're going to have a baby?'

Lina nodded, squealing in surprise as Alex lifted her and spun her round again and again.

'You're sure?'

'I'm sure.'

They'd been married for nine months, eager for a new addition to the family for the entirety of that time, and each month when Lina got her monthly courses she'd felt a little more worried, a little more unsure if it would ever happen. Of course, looking back, nine months was no time at all when trying for a baby, but whilst they were living through the experience of trying to conceive, it had felt like an eternity.

'I'm going to be a father?'

'You are. Soon there will be another little White-more to join our family.'

He kissed her then, wrapping his arms around her protectively and placing one hand on her stomach as if letting his son or daughter know he was right there.

'You know what this means,' Alex said, his voice serious. 'No more horse riding.'

'But we've got the new thoroughbred arriving next week.'

'And you'll be keeping well clear.'

Lina pulled a face, but nodded in agreement; she would do nothing to put their child at risk, even if it did mean leaving all the training of the new horse to Alex and the trainers he employed. It was a small price to pay.

As the music started somewhere towards the middle of the fair, Alex pulled Lina in close once again.

'From now on I'm going to make sure you rest,' Alex said, shaking his head as Lina pulled a face.

'Perhaps one last dance, before I'm confined to gentle strolls and drinking tea?'

'One last dance.'

Arm in arm, they walked towards the green space reserved for dancers, stepping out whilst it was still empty. Raul saw them coming and, just as Alex took Lina in his arms he whispered instructions to his fellow musicians, who instantly changed the tempo and timing.

'They're playing a waltz.'

It sounded odd played with fiddles, violins and the variety of other string instruments that made up their band, but it was a waltz all the same. Lina leaned back in Alex's arms and soon they were twirling across the grass, the perfect combination of gypsy and gentleman.

* * * * *

LET'S TALK

Romance

For exclusive extracts, competitions
and special offers, find us online:

f facebook.com/millsandboon

⊚ @millsandboonuk

🐦 @millsandboon

Or get in touch on 0844 844 1351*

For all the latest titles coming soon,
visit millsandboon.co.uk/nextmonth